A NOVEL

The Cromwell Rules

ANIA RAY

For those who show up

The Cromwell Rules

No One Night Stands Allowed

The packaging had warned "DO NOT IRON," but there Lily Cromwell stood, ironing curtains in the middle of her living room. She double-checked the fabric to make sure it wasn't smoking. Unfortunately, it remained its neutral beige. The pleated fabric folded back to where it had been before she ran the hot iron over the material. Useless. Why hadn't she dropped these curtains off at the cleaner's earlier?

The sounds of traffic outside the third-floor apartment made her want to throw the iron across the room. It was another day on the corner of 5th and 97th Avenues. Ambulance sirens blared beneath her window and a baby's cries joined in the cacophony. The drivers were mad at the pedestrians, the pedestrians were angry with the faceless humans driving two-ton vehicles and she was upset that her mother's impending visit drove her to *ironing curtains* on a Friday afternoon. Lily *should* have been working on the presentation she was assigned to give for the new product launch on Monday morning, but her boss was way more lenient than her mother, so she ran the iron over the pleats one more time.

The fabric sizzled. There had been way more fun fabrics that she'd have preferred, but Anne would approve the modern crème of these curtains. Lily lifted the fabric against the bright grey of her living room wall. She had made the right choice for the situation. The pop of red-orange she wanted would have reflected the kernel of spunk within her, but these had a gentle grace about them that garnered attention and demanded respect—qualities that were instilled in Lily since she was a teenager. *How else will anyone take you seriously?* Anne Cromwell would ask. *Surprises make people nervous. Be consistent.*

Yeah, Lily thought. *Consistently boring.*

Lily rested the iron, ran her fingers along the seams, and frowned. It was futile. Lily didn't care if the damn curtains were wrinkled—she just didn't want to give her mother another reason to be disappointed. She rubbed her eyes with stiff fingers. Despite years of her best efforts at defiance, she was becoming everything she told her mother not to fret over.

As much as she complained about them most of her life, Lily had to admit the Rules had guided her well. After Lily's father died when she was four—no wonder Anne claimed people didn't like surprises—, Anne had always made it clear who Lily was to become: someone who could get anything she wanted with education, charm, and beauty, and have the upper hand in every relationship, so her heart would never be broken like Anne's was when her husband died. *That's what happens when you let someone have too much of you, Lily Pad. It's not worth it.*

It wasn't that Lily didn't want a second toothbrush in the holder next to hers; it's just that the type of man Lily was taught to intrigue was hopelessly boring or infuriatingly condescending. And Anne seemed to know many of these types. With every invitation from her mother for dinner, Lily knew there would be another eligible, yet inadequate, bachelor waiting to charm her around the maple table. Anne was always so hopeful that *this* one would work out, but it always ended with Lily leaving early or with the poor man feeling so overwhelmed by the two women that he excused himself from the ménage.

Lily unplugged the iron and swiped her phone to reveal the message. The latest fiasco was probably the reason Anne was coming over now. In fact, Zach had just texted her asking if she'd like to try again some time. Poor Zach. His enthusiasm about competitive fly-fishing didn't have a chance of baiting her. She swiped back a "Sorry, good luck!" and dropped the phone on the dark blue couch cushions. She shuddered thinking about how much other women worried about hurting men's feelings instead of asserting their own. Her best friend Marley would have jumped up at the opportunity to try this fly fishing stuff—"It's not about the fishing, it's about being with that person and sharing in *their* interests," she'd say. Lily rolled her eyes. Sounded like a waste of time and life. Anne's advice was helpful here; for instance, the Rules told her to protect her own heart and not worry about breaking others'. While most females were uncertain and insecure when it came to relationships and dating, Lily genuinely enjoyed the dating game. She knew how to avoid appearing flustered or weak. Other women spoke too much, or too little. They rambled when they should give an air of intrigue, or were aloof to the point of freezing. This, and her ten years of dating practice, made Lily's seduction efforts effortless.

Lily was glad she was working on IceStorm's RACE project. She couldn't think of anything more useful than artificial intelligence that would lead humans to safety in an emergency. Now *that* was worth her time and energy. But here she was, making sure the curtains were as straight as she could make them, so Anne Cromwell couldn't feel compelled to call Lily's training a waste of time. Again.

Lily sipped her lukewarm coffee and smiled smugly. No... A waste of time they certainly were not. Zach hadn't worked out, but after that dinner fiasco, a quick stop at a bar on Columbus was effective. She lured Paolo in with a wink and a laugh. He turned out to be a magnificent palette cleanser in more ways than one. His empty cocktail glass sat on the end table like a trophy. No, there was no denying the continued success of the Rules.

She walked over to the bay window bordered by stark white trim. The first snowfall of the season was trying to blanket Central Park West, dodging between tourists and residents. Not even snow could find a place to rest in this city. Gusts of wind threatened to push through her windows. Lily swallowed the rest of her coffee and grabbed the curtain rod. When she was done pushing the rod through the top of the curtains, she climbed onto the couch, bright pink socks shuffling to and fro against the plush cotton. Though she was a dignified 5'8", she couldn't reach the end of the window sill from her couch. Lily jumped down, ran to her coat closet and reached below for her highest platform boots. Now tall enough to reach, she easily clasped the rod against the holders and rubbed her hands in satisfaction. She was a problem solver, alright. This was what she was paid the big bucks for.

The knocker fell heavy on her door and draped her in unease. *Shit.* She didn't even have a chance to see whether her efforts at ironing had made a difference. Eyes wide, she grabbed the ironing board, iron, and Paolo's cocktail glass, cursing the boots that were making it difficult to hide the evidence in time. Opposite the entry door was a closet where Lily irreverently threw the ironing board behind her faux fur coats, the iron on the top shelf, and her boots against the wall. The boot's cuff folded over like a dog's ear and she winced like Marley would have if someone had bent the pages of her books. Leaning her back against the door, Lily let out a composing breath.

Mommy had arrived.

* * *

The door swung open and the cold rushed in with Anne Cromwell. Lily reached around her, protecting her warmth.

"Darling, hello!" Anne Cromwell said. She was smiling, but the grin didn't quite reach her eyes. She opened her arms and brought Lily to herself, but the hug felt artificial, like they were only playing roles written in a script—and they had acted out this scene so many times before.

"Hello, Mother," Lily muffled against her mother's strong perfume. Lily drew a breath as her mother detached and marched down the hallway like a soldier looking for evidence of treason. Her mother's shoes resounded

through the hallway. Why she was wearing stilettos when they were not practical for walking on icy sidewalks should have been more of a mystery, but she
was sure that her mother's chauffeur, Trevor, had been directed to accompany
her. Lily rolled her eyes. If it were socially acceptable, Trevor would carry her
mother everywhere. Just like Paolo carried her in last night. Lily groaned as
she heard her mother's footsteps heading towards her bedroom. She started
to follow her so she could quickly explain away any incriminating evidence,
but stopped short and pivoted to the bar instead.

What would Anne find? The bed was made and last night's clothes were
in the hamper. There should be no lingering sign of Paolo. But even if there
were, why should Lily have to hide it? She was a grown woman! But Anne
had always had this notion that she needed to play the father role, too, so
Lily let her play it. Lily always told herself—and Marley— that she was free
to live her own life, but truly free people didn't have to hide their lives from
the eyes of others, did they? Panic shot through her veins. Did she forget to
throw the second towel into the hamper? Hopefully Paolo didn't leave any
ridiculous "I'll miss you" notes under her pillow. Lily didn't want to hear
that she had disrespected the family name. Again.

Lily frowned, gaze turning to the closet. The glass was the only sign of a
visitor, and even that could be explained. She prepared the defense anyway:
*of course she had female friends other than Marley and what do you mean
there's a glass in the closet?* As if Anne Cromwell were Nancy Drew. And if
she was, what did that make Lily? The criminal? Anne wanted her daughter
to find the most eligible bachelor, but Anne also believed that legs should
be crossed until the Wedding Day, as she had often told her and Marley,
warning them not to be loose with their morals. Anne must suspect she
had a hidden boyfriend on the side. Lily laughed, imagining Anne as the
suspicious husband who was determined not to be blindsided.

A quarter-full bottle of Ruby Port caught her attention. Anne and Lily
didn't have much in common, but a sultry red wine was ground on which

they could both firmly stand. Lily swished the bottle; it was enough for a quick evening visit. She poured two glasses to the rhythm of her mother's shoe staccato. For real? Such high heels in a snow storm? Anne really did think she was above the elements. Or was she just a strong woman and Lily was still learning how to be one? For a mother who expected her daughter to be fiercely independent *and* a master in finding the perfect man to marry and act submissive to, Anne Cromwell's seemingly conflicting requirements made it difficult for Lily to satisfy any expectations her mother had of her.

"Did you get your maintenance staff to look at the heat yet, dear?"

Lily didn't bother responding; she knew her mother didn't really care for the response. Of *course* Lily had talked to someone; it was in her nature to cover all her bases, and both she and her mother knew it.

Lily heard drawers opening and shutting. She was certain no other women her age were under such strong investigation from their mothers. She sipped more wine to discover there was none left and emptied the rest of the bottle in her glass. What was Anne looking for, really? Maybe she should start digging for a stronger relationship with her daughter because that was as far away as the bachelor who could satisfy both Anne's requests *and* Lily's desire for love.

The freezer door was open now. "So much ice cream, Lily? Really?"

Lily wanted to respond, but her voice caught as she broke out into a grin. Marley had called earlier to schedule a long-distance movie night for later this evening. They'd sit in comfy pajamas, watching a chick flick that would span thousands of miles—Lily in New York, and Marley in Madrid—feeling all the best parts of being seventeen. She couldn't wait to be in the company of someone who really *knew* her. And besides, ice cream solidified *any* relationship. Nostalgia and longing for Marley threatened to derail Lily's composure. She drank the rest of the rich red wine.

Anne sashayed back to the living room and towards the bar. "Alright, Lily Pad," her mother directed, wine sloshing against the side of the wide brimmed glass. She sat on the edge of the couch. "Tell me all about the dates you have lined up for this week."

Lily rolled her eyes.

"Don't tell me you canceled on that handsome banker I found for you!"

"No, Mother, I didn't cancel. Well. Not quite. I just didn't accept the invitation. Bankers are like ants—they climb all over each other. I don't need that kind of ego in my life. I've got enough of it in you. Don't need more of it."

Lily gulped. *Too far?* Anne shook her head slowly, sliding palms from her waist to her knees, making a show of fixing her skirt.

"Do you know how many strings I had to pull to get his number?"

Lily willed her mother to take a sip of the wine.

"Is men all we ever talk about?" Lily asked. "Anything else, and it seems I wouldn't know what to say to my own mother." Lily didn't want to lose another parent, but years of the same conversation over and over again were exhausting.

"Well, do you not want a good man? Like your father?"

Lily narrowed her eyes.

That much was true. But what a "good" man looked like for Anne and what it looked like for Lily were different.

"Did *you* meet Dad following 'The Cromwell Rules', mother?"

Anne laughed. "No. I didn't have to. It came naturally... Like honey from a bee."

Lily didn't want to mention that it took an entire hive to make honey. Anne's Southern Carolina drawl had revealed itself for a moment and Lily let herself sit in it. She always loved the sound of it, imagining her mother in a different world than the one Lily grew up in. With it, Lily could easily imagine her father being smitten by her mother.

Anne continued. "And isn't a mother supposed to teach her young all she knows? Besides, I'm fairly certain it's *because* you know what type of man I expect for you that you aren't cooperative. At least this one seems to have some style."

She lifted an embroidered handkerchief with the monogram PW. *Crap. Paolo left his stupid napkin. What was he, a Victorian lady?*

"Men who leave behind clothes after a one-night stand are *not* what I expect for my daughter. Will you bring *him* to dinner?"

Lily slumped deeper into the couch, feeling like a scolded puppy. Her colleagues would stare wide-eyed if they saw this submissive Lily.

"Well, maybe I could bring him to dinner." It was a lie, of course. But it got Anne to sit straighter, which was typically a sign of approval.

"What day would work best?"

"I don't know. Last night was a fluke appearance. He's a banker. He works all the time." She didn't wait to see Anne's reaction. Lily knew speaking quickly was a sign of her nerves, but she had to keep going.

"I'm up for a promotion. You remember me mentioning that I'm lead architect for the IceStorm system that directs people in any natural disasters. With climate change dominating human tragedy…"

She could see Anne's eyes glossing over. Lily spoke louder. "The point is, IceStorm connects emergency response operators *with those in danger*. If there's a fire in a condominium building, for example, the operators guide people to safety, telling them which stairwells to avoid and which rooms have been compromised. 'RACE to Exit': Remote Assist Coordination and Evacuation. Wyndham has already agreed to implement RACE. We're working on a government contract next. This is huge, Mom. If we close on these deals, I'll have so many options. I can become Director of Engineering."

Lily waited. Anne's blank gaze stared back at her.

"Does that make sense?" Lily stammered. *Why is this so hard?*

"A promotion!" Anne exclaimed. "And then what?"

"At 27, I'd be way ahead of the game."

"This would give you many options to socialize, yes?"

"I'm sure. There will be a party celebrating IceStorm and the partnership in one of the hotels."

"Maybe you could take Zach."

Lily groaned. They were back to this again? "We'll see. I hardly know the guy."

"But that's in your favor! Remember the ground rules?" Anne waited for Lily to answer, like a tutor checking for comprehension. Lily rolled her eyes, but recited from memory like a robot, "Be bold. Be mysterious. Be just enough, but leave them wanting more."

"Well you certainly weren't mysterious with this PW fellow. Let me know how the preparations for the IceStorm party go. I'd love to be in on the details." Anne glanced at her watch. "Does a week from today work for you? We can find a gown. Don't let your figure change in these winter months. So many of these female engineers don't know how to use their assets to their advantage in such a male-dominated field. Or how to stop eating Christmas cookies in February." She kept talking, but Lily had stopped listening.

"Yes, Mother," Lily said absentmindedly. "I'll see you then." This woman needed to leave.

"Wonderful." Anne stood, straightening her skirt, hugging her coat closer. Lily made a mental note to ensure that the heat would be fixed by Saturday, too. Lily opened the door and Anne stood in the doorway, pushing her hands into black leather gloves. "Oh, and Lily Pad?"

Lily crossed her arms. "Yes?"

"Make sure you iron your curtains before you invite anybody else over."

Lily nodded in faux agreement. She could feel heavy smoke gathering in her green eyes. Anne's "*Tootles!*" bounded down the hall after her, and Lily slowly shut the door, as much as she wanted to slam it.

Lily picked up a pillow from her couch, thought about hugging it, and then threw it across the room, hitting the fire place screen. No ironed curtains, no approval, and no prepared presentation. She didn't know which was worse.

Be the Glamorous Socialite

Others had to walk to their kitchen for coffee; Lily did not. The coffee pot sputtered on the nightstand directly to her right and released a steaming cup of coffee. She had been laughed at for the set-up in college, but within the year, she'd overheard a group of sleep-deprived grad students claiming that whoever thought of putting the coffee machine right next to the bed was a genius.

Lily stuck her feet into the fuzzy bunny slippers, careful to avoid the bowl with sorbet swirls, the only evidence of last night's video call with Marley.

The path to her ensuite bathroom was clear. The cool water on her face was as refreshing as it was a reminder that, though she had spent much of the night with Marley, she had to be alert not just for work in a couple hours, but for Genny.

Lily wiped her face with the lavender scented towel and sashayed to the sliding doors, hoping to catch a ray or two from the 7:00 a.m. sun. It was a rare sight these days and she missed the warmth. Unfortunately, heavy clouds stretched around the Central Park trees directly across from her building and hid the sunrise. At least the wintry morning was not as harsh as normal. She carried her mug from the top with spread fingertips. A steady step later, she was on her balcony. Even though snow weighed down the branches, Lily's thick cotton pajamas were just enough to protect her from the chill.

Lily loved being able to see the persevering runners and laugh at the tourists who got in the way. Leaning on the railing, she smiled in spite of herself to see an older man in a jogging suit encourage his shoe-wearing beagle to run alongside him. On the man's way out of her field of vision, a group of retired women walked with speed, their breath one collective exhaust. Lily was grateful for the inherited real estate that allowed her to disappear into nature when the noise of the city became too much on the other side of the house. Even though it was a highly appraised home, she would have gladly traded the luxury view for a childhood spent with her father. Lily dug her phone out of her pajama pocket and pressed its side to check the time: 7:06. She stepped back to sink into her padded seat, sipped her steaming coffee, and waited.

From around the trees, a woman her age held a little girl's mittened hand. Lily cupped the warm mug in her left hand to free her right, raising it to a wave. The little girl's bright face broke into a grin. She ran to the edge of the sidewalk.

"Hi, Miss Lily!" Genny called to the third-floor balcony, tugging her mother's hand forward. Lily nodded to Genny's mother Vanessa in her usual way and Vanessa returned a smile. Lily gave Genny her brightest smile.

"Hello, Ms. Genny! How are you this morning?"

"I have to play with the snow before it all melts!" Genny said.

"Don't you worry, pretty thing. It'll still be snowing well into April," Lily said. The tenderness in her voice was a surprise even to her. She had to calm down on the nights spent with Marley; too many and Lily would turn into a softie.

Vanessa smiled and patted Genny's braids. Genny turned around and pressed a snowball against against her mother's cheek.

Vanessa jumped back. "Genevieve!" Lily's mouth fell open, wondering if she should run down to protect her little friend from her angry mother.

Genny giggled and ran towards the tree at the intersection of the park and the street. Vanessa crept around, over-exaggerating her legs to appear as a robber on a cartoon would. Lily watched, breathing out in relief, soaking in the pure, unscripted, silly love between them. She faintly remembered playing like this with her father, but never with Anne. Realizing that made her sadder than she wanted to be right now, so as she watched the pair play, Lily recalled instead the morning she had met the mother-daughter duo before winter had settled in the city. Un n CC.

It had been the morning after she'd woken up with Jack. Jeremy? He had gone to shower and Lily told him she'd meet him after he was done. Once Lily had settled in to her balcony seat, satisfied that the night had gone well enough to bring him to dinner with Anne later that week, a bright yellow jacket and boots amidst black umbrellas and heavy autumn leaves had caught Lily's attention. She couldn't help herself when she called out.

"I love your rain boots!"

The little girl would have kept hopping from puddle to puddle, but it was the woman with her who had looked around to find who had called down to them.

Lily had gestured toward the puddles. "It's so cool that you let her jump around. My mother would have never allowed it."

The woman had frowned in sympathy. "But isn't that why the holes aren't filled in?" She turned and her long black hair flowed along. "We support childhoods here in New York."

Lily remembered the real laugh that escaped her lips. "I'm glad somebody does." Lily stopped short of sharing what her mom would say: *Mary Jane's today and stilettos tomorrow; if you can't see through it, you can't trust it.*

"What grade is this little girl in?" Lily still thought this woman was too fit and good looking to be her mother.

"I homeschool her, so 2nd grade according to New York Public Schools, but we're already working on third grade multiplication." The pride in her voice was obvious. Lily found it endearing.

"That's awesome! When I was in second grade, my big lesson was that my mother did not, in fact, carry a spare pair of socks with her if I hopped in the puddles. There was one day my feet couldn't carry me home fast enough." Lily laughed nervously. Why had she felt so comfortable unloading her problems onto this stranger? She shrugged. "But those were the older, stricter days, I suppose."

"Yeah, I much prefer these more compassionate new days myself. Makes it easier to raise a daughter - hopefully she resents me less in her later years." Though the woman had flinched—probably worried that she'd said the wrong thing—Lily was grateful she had found a woman who spoke her mind.

It didn't take long after that to realize that Lily wanted to see more of them. Somehow - miraculously - even though one was eight and the other was four times older, they appeared untouched by the skepticism and ugliness of the world. Because Lily didn't have the words to explain exactly how they were making her feel, she just kept grinning and laughing every time the girl jumped into a puddle.

Now, three months later, Lily's joy came from snowballs flying into the air and landing on a runner. Genny and Vanessa's eyes' magnetized to each other, jaws open in surprise. It was Lily's laugh that sounded loudest of all. There was something about this little girl that made Lily feel little again, too. Vanessa lifted her daughter like a potato sack over her shoulder. Lily laughed along with Genny's squeal, until she saw Genny frown as if someone had just stolen a cookie off her plate. She lifted her head, furrowed her eyebrows, and yelled. "Miss Lily, have you figured out what your favorite flower is?"

Lily's cheeks warmed. Genny had grown accustomed to asking this question, but Lily still hadn't granted the time to think about it. Lily's favorite flower was always the kind her date brought to her doorstep, or presented to her at the restaurant when she arrived. In fact, whatever the flower, she would always exclaim, "Wow! How did you know *these* were my favorite?" Her date's chest would puff up in pride and the flowers would stay on her dining room table until the next bouquet arrived, prefaced by the same reaction.

Vanessa must have noticed Lily was having a hard time answering—again. "Let's give Miss Lily a chance to enjoy her morning coffee, love."

Lily gripped the railing but smiled, shoulders easing. Genny waved and was already scooping more snow. Lily exhaled. She was off the hook this time.

Three months ago, Lily couldn't put into words why she loved Vanessa and Genny so much. But now she knew: the girls challenged her to find the good, rather than the lacking—and that was something Anne couldn't comprehend. Anne couldn't enter a room without finding something that was wrong or missing. She managed to find fault with curtains, for goodness sake. Had she always been like this? If so, how could her father have been happy with Anne? If it were Anne and Lily below the balcony, Lily wouldn't have giggled post-snowball: she'd be crying, listening to the reasons little ladies didn't act like she just did—like a *kid*. It was always about the most shallow, most "appropriate" topics with her mother, and the more Lily pushed to swim beneath what their relationship *appeared* to be in order to fix all that was broken, the more her mother drowned them in nonsense. Was she the only daughter that had such difficulty pleasing her mother? So much *had* to change. By the time of the IceStorm party, Lily resolved, she'd have the man, she'd know her favorite flower, and she'd finally feel her mother's pride.

* * *

Hours before anyone would arrive, Lily was as put together as ever: crisp khaki colored pants, flowy white blouse, and hair that was pushed back in a loose bun. As the elevator doors opened, Lily straightened her shoulders. She was ready to put the finishing touches on her code so it could be ready for review the moment her colleagues arrived. There was nobody between her and the glass doors at the end of the short hallway. She paused to admire the new logo decal affixed to the door: blinding light preventing shards of ice from crashing down to Earth. If all went well, this logo would be recognized by hospital, hotel, and restaurant patrons all around the world. With this RACE party coming up, her job was to get an "in" with the Wyndham. *Everyone would follow,* she had promised her company. *And I will get us there.*

Steven and his buddies liked to find flaws in Lily's ideas: "Why *not* the Ritz?" Steven would challenge.

"Because the Ritz is one, but the Wyndham has many. RACE won't— should not—discriminate which lives it saves. *Right,* Steven?"

She tried to forgive them. The poor boys didn't realize Anne Cromwell had raised her. There was nothing they could do or say to intimidate her.

The key card was recognized and accepted with a beep. The doors swung open to reveal rows of desks that filled the space between the windows and the receptionist's desk. All chairs were currently unoccupied. The only noise was the hum of servers tucked in the corner rooms. Lily could have purred herself, grateful to have the chance to be done with the heart of her work by the time people started to walk in, wiping sleep from their eyes.

Where her home was evidence of her mother's taste, Lily's desk was her own. Battery-operated mini-lights hung wrapped around her space. A picture of her and Marley hugging in front of the Alhambra Palace was to the right of her stationary monitor and a small photo of her father kissing her outrageously happy mother rested in a wooden frame to her left. A mini-volleyball stress ball was where she placed her laptop. She scoffed and reached over her monitor to place it at her colleague's side of the table. He was always saying she needed to let off some steam and play with his recreational volleyball league.

"A bunch of women who'll automatically assume I'm a bitch? No, thanks."

"What?" Jeremiah had said. "Because you're tall and blonde? Please come play some time. You never know whether you'll find Mr. Right there."

"I'll think about it," Lily had said. But judging from the look on Jeremiah's face, they both knew she was lying.

Lily lay her Saint Laurent bag next to her chair and rolled back and forth until she felt comfortable enough to flip open her computer. The screen revealed lines of code, and Lily relaxed into her seat, focusing in on the changes her colleague had written and sent to her for review.

She felt powerful knowing that *her* ideas were building a program that'd reach across the globe and save people she'd never know in terrifying crises. As Lily read, a rush of pride surged within her. Just like someone had to blaze a trail for women's suffrage, so too had Lily ignored the "boys only" stigma when she'd studied the simplest commands in software programming classes for young girls and later in male-dominated classes at MIT.

It was also one of the only endeavors her mother had not pushed her into. Lily's code was her escape into another world, where her only expectation was improving the inner-workings of a system. It didn't matter if her code was ironed, though she certainly wanted it to be clear enough for anyone to read. All that mattered was that it *functioned*. Engineering could be a quick-paced, high-pressure field, but it was one of the only places in Lily's life where she felt totally in charge. The repetitive clacking of the keyboard mesmerized her into meditation and the lines of the code were like lines of music that played melodies in her mind.

Lily was putting the finishing touches on a feature that'd tell users where exactly in their home they needed to hide to avoid the worst of an oncoming tornado when Jeremiah came into view.

"Lilian!" Jeremiah hissed dramatically.

"Jeremiah, whoa! Back off!" Lily said, narrowing her eyes. "You know I hate that name. Also, if you see I'm in the zone…"

"…leave a message after the tone," Jeremiah said. "I know, I know. But this is an *e-mer-gen-cy*."

"That's what you said last week about Mario's absent wedding ring," Lily said, more gently this time. "I'm serious, J. There is some serious coding going on for RACE here. You know we're going live with it soon and need to make sure it's perfect."

Jeremiah steam-rolled her concerns. "It *was* an emergency and you *know* it! That ring was the *only* indication he gave me that he was off-limits. Not. Fair." Jeremiah pursed his lips in a pout.

"He didn't even know you were interested!"

As outgoing as Jeremiah was in Lily's company, it pained Lily to see Jeremiah choose to fade into the background when others were in the room. She didn't know if it was Jeremiah's relatively average height and unobtrusive clothing choices, but people looked right through him. Jeremiah claimed he liked it that way, but it drove Lily crazy. She could see that, if Jeremiah embraced his full potential, he'd be wearing hot pink pants and rocking a faux-hawk to accentuate his five o'clock shadow. Jeremiah's Dominican roots made his turquoise eyes pop, but no one else seemed to appreciate them except Lily. They were enough, however, for Lily's attention now.

"What's today's fire?" Lily asked.

"Well, if you weren't all focused, you'd have heard that there's a stand-up meeting. Right now. About a certain *par-ty!*"

Lily cursed under her breath and stood, shutting her laptop. In the time she'd been focused, hundreds of bags, jackets, and mugs had appeared. She jumped over messenger bags and shimmied past slow walkers to the edge of the office with Jeremiah right behind her. After a few lefts, rights, and steps down, she saw the auditorium of benches, perfect for all-hands meetings like this one. Surrounding the deep center stage were hundreds of employees scattered throughout. Lily hustled down the stairs as quickly as she could in her nude pumps. When she arrived, she mouthed "Sorry!" to Greg Henderson's side-eye and motioned for him to continue.

"You have made me proud to be IceStorm's CEO. I have witnessed our incredible growth from a small app that warns users about dangerous weather conditions to a future partner of major hotel chains, universities, and hospitals that will help guide millions of people to safety. Together, we have created incredible products. Head architect Lily Cromwell has seen to it. She's going to tell us where we are now and what to expect for launch." Greg smirked in Lily's direction as the audience broke into applause. She noticed a group of four men in the second row who crossed their arms instead. Steven was one of them.

Lily stepped forward.

"As you know," Lily began. She scanned the room, landing her gaze on the four men who were whispering among themselves, jabbing each other with elbows and laughing. She knew how to project her voice since she had rehearsed with Jeremiah the afternoon before, but this time it felt weaker. "As you know, securing a partnership with Wyndham is critical to our future success." Steven rolled his eyes. Just behind him, Jeremiah winked at her and flexed his muscles. She injected more conviction into her voice, explaining what was left to do and how important it would be to work together, quickly, and with confidence. "If we get a major chain on board, then everyone else is more likely to follow suit. This party will be our way of telling the world, 'Here's IceStorm. We built RACE: the only reliable system to keep you safe when it matters most.'"

The audience clapped again and Lily stepped back, refusing to look at the second row and smiled at everyone else instead. Greg had asked her to vouch for this event since the majority of their employees would rather stay home and play board games than socialize with potential investors and clients. Not everyone knew Lily's fine dining, wining, and socializing after-work life, and she was happier that way. Engineering really was an escape from her mother's world in more ways than one, but to see her strengths come together for something so important was an exception she was willing to make.

Greg had seen Lily in her element, once, when she was with an investment mogul at a charity event where Greg happened to be a guest. He'd cornered Lily later and said in awe that he couldn't believe his head architect was also a glamorous socialite. Lily had blamed his adoration on the liquor, but she'd accepted the compliment nonetheless. When Greg approached her last week, she'd told Greg adamantly that she would *not* be training her staff in manipulation tactics, no matter how badly IceStorm needed the funding. But she knew Greg counted on her to schmooze most of the guests at the RACE event and, to be honest, she found she didn't mind. It was like a passenger coming to the rescue when someone called for a doctor; Lily Cromwell could triage all social catastrophes. Or cause them, if you asked Anne Cromwell.

Greg's voice boomed around them, a commander telling his army the mission. "Lily and a team will investigate the hotel to check for its compatibility with RACE. The rest of you: run those tests, catch all bugs, and for the love of all things righteous," Lily grinned on her way up the stairs, "wear something besides plaid."

Be Mysterious

Lily looked at the white glove on her left hand and shuddered. It was covered in the grime of a New York City bus. She couldn't stop the heavy sigh from escaping her lips and glanced up to find Jeremiah staring at her in amusement. She just about leapt off the bus, so careful was she to avoid touching anything else.

After visiting the Wyndham, they needed to keep discussing how RACE could demo in that hotel in the most successful way. The bus was the only option.

"I don't usually ride the bus, okay?" Lily said, taking the gloves off and chucking them into the nearest garbage bin. "It's a new thing. Now you know how much I wanted to spend time with you today. And after work, no less." The wind lifted her hair and hit her face with such force it felt like it was cutting her cheek. She stuffed her hands in her pockets.

"It's alright, Princess," Jeremiah said. He unwrapped the bright blue scarf from around his neck and tucked it around Lily. "There. Makes your eyes look even more stunning."

Jeremiah pulled her into a hug. "Random love: thanks for taking a chance on me, Lil. You were right. The work isn't easy, but I've learned so much with you. RACE is going to change lives. I think you try to hide it, but I can see the compassion behind your drive to make RACE a success. If you let other women know, they might not assume you're a bitch so often. And then you could play volleyball with me! I don't care what anyone else says - you're a real pal. You should let more people see it."

Lily's laugh came out vibrating from chattering teeth. "You're being a little too sentimental, Jer. The cold is getting to you. Time to go home and sleep off your fatigue."

Jeremiah winked, blew her a kiss, and skipped the curb to head home.

She really liked him. Jeremiah was the closest Lily had to having a guy who saw beyond her long hair, manicured nails, and toned muscles. He was right that she didn't show others her "weird" side: the Lily who wondered what it'd be like to go paint-balling or show up at Dungeons and Dragons meetups (how else would she ever reconcile with Steven from marketing?). She was always on the lookout for more adventure, but never had the courage to try. If anyone from Anne's circle ever found her outside of the acceptable social arenas… it'd not only be social suicide, but also anti-strategic to having a good relationship with her mother.

Lily looked around her. Good old Brooklyn. She hadn't been here in a while. She scowled at the deserted city street full of graffiti and cars driving way too fast for roads so slick. Had she known she'd be out in the freezing temperatures, she'd have at least packed extra hand and feet warmers. Just a shake and she'd be fine for eight hours. It was only for Jeremiah and IceStorm that she'd choose to weather both public transit *and* dirty snow.

The wind gusts threatened to numb Lily's fingers and she tried to hide deeper into the bus shelter, hugging the waist of her white wool coat tighter around her, hands bunched up like a worried mother. She wished the next bus would hurry. Her phone had died while they were looking up how to legally pull off a mass fire drill, so her option for ride sharing was null. Jeremiah had explained how to make it home from here and slipped a piece of paper with his address written on it into her pocket, just in case she wanted to stay the night. She considered it for a second, then shook her head. She never stayed over a man's house, even though Jeremiah was as safe as they came.

Rule number two was right on this one: *Never stay overnight at his house.* It was a natural follow-up to rule number one to leave the man wanting more. *He'll think he won, like you're some sort of conquest. You are not to be conquered, my love. You* are *the conquistadora.*

The next bus was her only way back to Manhattan. Jeremiah had been adamant that she couldn't miss this one, as it was the last bus of the night. She rubbed the piece of paper between her thumb and fingers. It was nice to know she had a Plan B just in case.

Her stomach rumbled.

As if on cue, the scent of sugar and donuts pulled Lily's attention to her right. A bakery was softly lit in its final hours of the evening. Two men stood outside, sipping their coffees, engaged in conversation. Peeking under the brim of her hat, Lily's gaze rested on the taller of the men. He was the type of tall that was Cromwell-approved: her head would rest at his chest in a hug and her five foot eight figure could still wear three inch heels if the event called for it. She caught him squinting in her direction and smiled. This hat had a way of inspiring intrigue and she knew the blue scarf did flatter her. Her blonde hair was styled in flowing ringlets today, so she let them speak for her as she pivoted, suddenly curious about the neighborhood that welcomed such a handsome gentleman. This was part of the first rule, after all: to be mysterious. But any thought of playing the game tonight disappeared when she saw a flower shop directly in front of her. The frosted windows were something out of a Christmas movie and it made Lily wish she had the coffee currently in Tall Man's hands to complete the scene. She looked down the street to see it still deserted and resolved that she'd be able to look around the shop and still spot the bus in enough time to board and make her way home.

Bells jangled as she pushed open the door and stepped into the shop. It felt like she had stepped into a sauna, so warm and humid compared to the icy tundra outside.

"Welcome!" called a friendly voice from the back.

The scent of Sarah Jessica Parker's *Lovely* embraced her, hints of Southern peaches making Lily want to wrap her arms around her and keep it all in. She had never been in a flower shop before, as she —and her mother— always ordered flowers online, or asked one of the house staff to take care of it. Lily noticed a path of painted-on cobblestones from the doorway to the checkout counter and tiptoed from one fake stone to the other, wondering which flower would give her something to report to Genny the next morning. Lily recognized colors and flowers given to her over the years, but found she couldn't begin to name a quarter of them. The bright reds attracted Lily like the leather straps of a strong stiletto, but the gentle white buds -*Baby's Breath?*- reminded her of simpler days on the boutonnières and corsages of high school dances. She scanned the colorful jungle, until she found flowers that rose tallest of all. The flowers looked like little tufts of red tissue paper climbing up the stalk. The plant's structure reminded Lily of a first-grade project her teacher had made her create for Mother's Day. There was something about *this* flower: some stalks were completely filled, but others were still growing. A few buds were open at the bottom, but those at the top were still closed, hiding magic.

"Lovely hat, darling." Lily turned to see a portly woman, clad in a black apron, cradling long stemmed roses in her arms. Lily watched her place each rose gently in a glass vase. When they were all in place, she opened a large glass door and placed the vase on a shelf. "I should just save th'money and put them out the doors until the morning, eh? But I don't wan' the lovelies catchin' cold." The Scottish accent was a welcome surprise and it made Lily grin. Lily didn't want to speak, but drink this woman's character in.

The woman walked over to Lily and put her hands on the sides of Lily's arms as if they'd known each other forever. "I just love that these hats are comin' back in style. They mus' be, anyway, if they're on such a pretty girl as you." She winked, and Lily's heart swelled with affection for this woman she had just met. "They never left Edinburgh, but America's got 'er own idee of style, I s'pose." She turned, busying herself with the flowers standing around Lily.

"Which ones d'ye like best?" she asked.

Lily pointed at the red tufts.

"Ah, the gladiolus. They're a real treat to look 'at since they won't be in season until the mid-summer an' these are the only ones we'll have for a while." Her freckled dimples and deep green eyes crinkled in a smile. "Y'know, not everyone gives 'em the attention they deserve. They're some of my favorites. My name is Janie, by d'way." She wiped her hands and extended the right one. "I'm the proud owner of this establishment. Is there anything I can help ye with, sweet 'art?" Lily loved the way Janie's *r*'s rolled and her *t*'s came down with certainty.

"I'm just browsing, actually. I've actually never been in a shop like this before." She didn't want to admit that she'd *never* been in a physical flower shop. "I don't even have a favorite flower." For a reason unbeknownst to Lily, some shame threatened to crawl up from behind her ribs, around her heart, and into her cheeks. Why was she admitting this to a perfect stranger?

Lily thought she saw Janie's eyes soften at the corners. She straightened her shoulders and took out scissors from one of the four pockets at her waist. "Lemme get one of these for ye. Y'know, my granddaddy founded a shop 'like this' back in Scotland and m'uncle took over after that. I din't know my favorite flower for a while, either. There were so many to choose from. When I met m'husband at the time and 'e told me 'h 'ad this idea to move to New York for 'is business, I thought why the 'ell not? Poor ol' William is gone now, but I still feel 'im 'round." Lily watched the nostalgia pass over Janie's face. Lily had seen that look on her mother's widowed face many times before. Janie must feel his loss over and over again.

The cloud evaporated as quickly as it had appeared, however, and Janie's smile was as broad as ever. "And 'e's surely 'ere now, smilin' that your favorite flower is still waitin' for ye to notice it."

"I bet he is incredibly proud of you. I know I would be. Heck, I barely know you and I think you're amazing."

Janie beamed. "Why, thank ye, lovely girl." She paused. "Wait a wee second." She turned back to the gladiolus and cut the half-bloomed, half-growing stalk. "Why don't y'take this one?"

"Why, I couldn't—" Lily said.

"Nonsense. Take it. It's already cut. Please. I insist. For listenin' to m'story." She pushed the flower stalk into Lily's hand and wrapped her fingers around it like a grandmother would, making sure her granddaughter would keep the five dollars. "You can come back in the future and choose another from *Janie's Flowers* for a special occasion." The woman winked and Lily beamed.

Suddenly, from the corner of her eye, Lily saw a blue bus slow down right in front of the shop. A sound between an "ugh" and "no!" slipped from between Lily's lips.

Lily wished she could properly thank the woman, but there was no time to waste. The bus was already lifting its steps once the elderly man stepped off.

"I'm so sorry I have to run!" Lily yelled over her shoulder and shoved the door open. The bells jingled like singers tired of being in the same choir.

She sprinted from the shop straight to a bus driver not interested in delaying his route.

"Oh, come on! I know you saw me!" she called, tucking the flower into her pocket. She stepped around sheets of ice and piles of snow. She would have to run. To her great relief, the men at the bakery were no longer there. Her hopscotch was as uncoordinated as it could be and it wouldn't do to have Tall Man see her flustered. It'd throw the whole game off. *I thought we weren't playing tonight, Lily.*

A response from deep within confirmed. *We're always playing.*

She was just about to cross the street when a strong gust of wind sent her hat into the middle of it.

Her height would usually help her retrieve it in mid-air, but Lily slipped in the tall snow bank. "No!" she cried, not knowing which was worse: dirty snow on her white coat or the prospect of having her hat run over by a car. She saw a quarter-block down that the stop lights changed, signaling traffic onward. She looked for other avenues to reach the hat and scowled. Janie had shared so much of herself simply because a hat had reminded her of home, and now that was gone.

She picked herself up with a sigh, brushed off marks of ice and dirt, and hooked her finger into her pocket to make sure the gladiolus was intact. Though a bud had fallen off, it was still mostly whole. At least she still had this souvenir to show Genny the next morning.

Thinking it'd be smart to avoid frostbite while she figured out what to do from here, Lily decided to return to *Janie's*. She would apologize for the hurried exit, ask to borrow Janie's phone, and call for her mother's driver to bring her home. She was inches away from the doorknob when loud honking caused her to stop and turn towards the street.

A man in the middle of the road was illuminated by oncoming headlights. His hands up, a brown felt hat rested in his left hand. Tall Man! A shout caught in her throat. All she could do was watch, helpless in stopping the skidding car. She hid her eyes inside her arm and wished she could block her ears from the hit she knew would be fatal. The screech of tires came to a halt without the sound of a ricocheted body, so she dared to peek. The car had pulled to the right and was driving away, the driver with a finger up, muttering muted curses.

The man turned to face Lily and she inhaled sharply. Under the streetlights, his eyes shone a cerulean shade that reminded her of a Grecian sea.

His jaw looked like it'd been cut with chisels, but what sharpness was along his face was softened with parted lips, a sideways grin, and lifted eyebrow.

Someone who had almost become roadkill shouldn't be so happy. "Are you ready to stop playing in traffic now?" Lily called from the sidewalk.

Instead of nodding and walking towards her like a normal person would, he laughed heartily and placed the hat on his head, dancing away from the center of the road like a regular Gene Kelly. He stepped on the curb and back onto the street numerous times to a song only he could hear. He spun twice, added what she remembered from beginner dance classes as a kick-ball-change. A leap later, he was within steps of her.

Hand in her pocket, she rubbed the stalk of the gladiolus, willing its beauty to empower her. Men often approached her, but under circumstances that were under *her* control—not this, where she was standing in disbelief that he was still alive. Was it the wind or her hand that was making the petals shiver?

More importantly, was it her mother's advising voice, or her own, that shot through her like a flare gun in the night? *Use this. Now's your chance. Game on.*

Pulling her hand out of her pocket, she made a show of crossing her arms and pushing her weight onto her right hip, letting the tight jeans accentuate her left calf muscles.

Lily waited. Tall Man lifted the hat in a formal bow, twirling the brim in his fingertips. Though her hands were exposed and it was getting colder by the minute, she felt clammy sweat in her palms. She balled them up tighter inside the crooks of her folded arms.

"You know, Anybody else might say, 'Excuse me, ma'am, I believe you lost your hat' instead of almost getting run over by a car."

When he smiled, it reached his eyes. "Too bad I'm not like everybody else."

Lily un-balled her fists. *Clearly.*

He leaned against the streetlight pole, placing her hat on his head once more. The shadow of her hat showed fine hairs along his jaw and Lily felt the urge to press her hands against his cheeks just to feel his warmth.

At the same time, she wanted to slap that smirk off his face. A proper gentleman would have retrieved the hat, to be sure, but have mercy, Cupid. No one has to die for love.

"You dropped your contraband," he said.

Lily looked to where he was pointing. Tall Man reached down, picked up the gladiolus that had fallen out of her pocket and offered it to her.

"It was a gift, thank you," Lily said, receiving it. "And certainly not as much of a crime as you failing to follow simple courtesy."

"Oh? And what's that?"

"Not getting run over by a car, for one," Lily muttered.

"My manners are just fine, I promise." He winked, sweeping open his arm dramatically to demonstrate, bowing as he rested the hat in his palm towards Lily. She rolled her eyes and reached for it. He straightened his back too soon and she missed the brim by inches. "On second thought. Because I did risk my life in this chivalrous act, I think I deserve a little something in return."

Here we go. She had known it was coming. He was playing hard to get just enough to make her wanting more; it worked on other women all the time. Standard move. She had moves of her own, but she'd play. What else did she have to do? Get home to an empty apartment?

"I won't return it until you agree to thaw with me sometime this week," he said.

"'Thaw' with you?" Lily couldn't suppress the guffaw. "You're right, I'm not in the mood to 'chill' any more than I already am." Her voice sounded harder than she intended, but he took it in stride.

"'Atta, girl. I knew the cold must have frozen your sanity when I saw you walk away from the bus stop when there's only one bus left. Looks like you're stuck with me."

That's fine. Your eyes are perfect, Lily thought before she could stop it, then swallowed the butterflies. Smooth and sterile, girl. *Don't let him think he won too early. You are* not *easy.*

"Where did you come from anyway?" Lily asked.

"I noticed you when I was outside the coffee shop. Don't try to change the subject." He wrapped his hand around the pole and twirled around it, resting his other shoulder against the bus shelter. "In fact, if those shoulders don't loosen up by the time you're done with Logan West, you never have to see me ever again."

She mirrored Logan's lean against the shelter's glass and pretended to think about it. She hugged her arms tighter around her.

Logan frowned. He took off his gloves and handed them to her. She shook her head, but then reconsidered. It *was* cold. She uncrossed her arms to slide her thin fingers into the warm wool. "But only because I want my hat back," Lily said. "It would impossible to find one just like it."

Logan whistled. "And what is the name of my gloved and graceful girl?"

She lifted her eyebrow. "'My'? Someone's a little sure of himself."

"You're wearing my gloves, aren't you?"

That made Lily laugh.

"Clever. I'm Lily Cromwell." She didn't offer the back of her hand like she usually did. He still wasn't relinquishing her hat. But more than that, she didn't feel like these rules were working with Logan, dancing fool of confidence. He wasn't exactly playing along. In fact, it seemed he had a game all his own—and she was intrigued by it.

"So what do you say, Ms. Cromwell? Would you join me for dinner tomorrow night?"

Aim.

She smiled.

Hold.

Lily started to strip his gloves unceremoniously and tried not to wince at the biting cold clasping around her instead.

Fire. "Someone who's already claiming me as 'his' girl is too cocky for me. I'm almost ready to let the hat go in the name of self-respect."

Logan almost looked hurt. *Almost.* He said in a convincing Southern accent, "Now I may tease you, girl, but I'd never disrespect a woman."

Anne would have loved such a gallant response. This gave Lily pause. She slipped the gloves back on. "No," she considered. She had no reason to believe otherwise, but she felt she could trust this man. Maybe it was the confidence with which he carried himself, chest out —but not puffed out like someone trying too hard— and head back. Maybe it was the way he frowned when he noticed she was cold. Or how he reacted when she almost turned him down.

"No. I don't suppose you would. Not on purpose anyway." She winked. Man, it was cold.

She looked him up and down again, reappraising the man in front of her. Attractive, silver-tongued. He had a touch of silly that made Lily excited to hear what he'd say next. The perfect combination. She'd say that he was too good to be true, but more time in conversation would reveal interesting flaws. He was still a perfect stranger, but she could feel he was honest, and that was more than she could say about most of the men she dated. The pinched skin by his eyes and the slight frown in his lips made her smile. "You *did* almost die in the name of fashion. That must count for something."

"Now you're getting it," Logan said, and she noticed he eased back into his heels and relaxed his grip on her hat. He rested the brown felt on Lily's head, tucking her hair behind her ear as if he'd done it a million times. She looked into his eyes, mentally sending Jeremiah a million thanks for living in Brooklyn. She shivered.

"The bakery is still open." Logan nodded towards the opposite side of the street. "Are you up for some coffee? Hot chocolate? The last bus has left for the evening and you're not going to walk home in this cold. I'll call you a Lyft from my phone if yours is dead."

Lily started to decline, but looked over Logan once more. His eyes were earnest. And it wasn't like Paolo was waiting for her at home.

"All right, Sir Logan." She made a triangle with her arm, resting her hand on her hip. "Help warm this girl and get her home."

"Aren't you supposed to make me wait?" he asked. There was that stupid smirk again, but her heart fluttered knowing she put it there. He smiled wide.

"Apparently, tonight is an exception to the Rules."

Sentimentality Weakens Stability

L ily tiptoed in the footprints Logan left behind. She was pleased to see the smooth soles of Allen Edmonds; the man was of ideal height with blue eyes that stunned her *and* he owned a pair of respectable shoes. This evening's spontaneous date was becoming more and more promising.

Lily was having so much fun following in Logan's footsteps, she didn't stop in time when he spun. She ran right into his chest and his arms shot out to steady her.

"Whoa, girl, slow your roll." She looked up, blinking fast to keep her eyelashes from sticking together from the cold.

"Well you're not walking fast *enough*. To warmth, please." Lily pointed to the bakery door with *Frankie's* painted on it, then thrust her hands back into her pockets.

"Good thing you pointed to the door; I'd have never found it."

Lily made a show of rolling her eyes. "Yeah, you may have run out to play traffic again."

Logan ignored her, which both annoyed and thrilled her because he was such a gentleman about it. And he wasn't playing, was he? So many years of manipulating the male made her wary of anyone trying to fool her in return.

Logan's arm gestured to the door. God he was taking forever. "Welcome to *Frankie's*, one of my favorite places."

Her teeth chattered. "So you come here often?" *Obviously, Lily. Obviously he does if he said it's one of his favorites.* She resisted the urge to slap her forehead with an open, frigid palm. The cold must have frozen her brain.

"Not as often as I'd like, actually." He pulled the door open and waited for Lily to enter. She stepped in eagerly.

The warmth of the bakery made Lily's face feel like it was on fire. While she shook her coat of icy snow, Logan pushed passed her to the counter. The cashier's counter looked like it was guarding a library tucked within cave walls. Lily removed Logan's gloves and inhaled a deep breath of Danish pastries, fresh coffee, and powdered sugar. Heat wrapped around her cold fingers like an eager friend pulling her forward to see more.

As Logan ordered their drinks, Lily explored the rest of the combination bakery- cafe-and faux library. She heard laughter and turned the round cavernous corner to see a group of friends holding their breaths over a redheaded woman's hesitant move with a Jenga block. More games were crammed together on the oak bookshelf featuring more than ten decks of cards, a beaten-up box of Twister—who'd play Twister *here*?—and another Jenga game. She walked over and claimed the latter. Maybe Logan liked this cafe because he and his friends spent time laughing over a board game every Saturday night. Maybe he enjoyed the fact that it smelled like fresh pastries at 9pm just like it did at the crack of dawn? She didn't even judge him for choosing the opposite of where Rule Number Six usually required she be—in a charity event or art gallery following a ballet. *How else will you ensure his wealth?* Sitting here with the only expectation being a laugh with pals sounded like a dream. Who would *she* invite in the same scenario? Jeremiah and Marley were the only ones to come to mind. Nobody else was a permanent fixture.

Though she had initially gotten excited by his looks and knew Anne would approve, being here with him planted a seed that Anne would *not* find him worthy. Not really. If he liked a place like this, he already seemed too sentimental and, according to Anne, sentimentality wasn't stable. Feelings didn't keep the roof over one's head. Lily forced herself to ignore her mother for a moment and focus on the present surroundings instead.

Pressed against one wall was a classic tufted linen Victorian sofa, something ready for a princess to perch herself upon. The sofa looked out of place when compared to the beat-up, bright red leather chair next to it, sporting cuts and stains. She thought of the gladiolus in her pocket; it, too, was red and beat-up, but still beautiful. She thought of Genny. Forget what Logan liked about this place—what did *Lily* like? Nobody asked her that very often, so maybe it was time she asked herself.

She wondered how far she could sink into the leather chair directly in front of her, let the material accidentally swallow her hand on the way down, kick her legs up and have Logan find her there, already making herself at home. Maybe that's what she liked about this bakery herself: that she didn't feel like she had to pretend.

But there couldn't be too many changes at once; she passed the leather couch and sat at the edge of the Victorian.

It was a shame that there wasn't a more inconspicuous location to warm her feet. A place like this would have a blanket, wouldn't it? She thought about how many strangers would have touched it, however, and reconsidered. She smiled at an approaching Logan, who handed her a steaming mug.

"Straight black with a dollop of sugar," Logan said.

"I'll take it, thank you." Lily preferred tons of cream, but she wouldn't bite the hand that brought her coffee. She lifted the Jenga box. His grin would have melted the last snowflake on her.

"Am I close to why this place is so high on the Logan List?"

"Great name. You're close."

Lily patted the space next to her. "Maybe you need to get closer so I have a stronger vibe of what it is you like."

Lily needed to know that she made him as uneasy as he made her. He was so destabilizing, in the most invigorating way. She felt her ears burn red when he kept standing there, only tilting his head like a dog that didn't understand.

"I don't think I've ever seen anyone sit on this couch before," he said. "Maybe when every other seat was taken? People sit on the rigid benches before coming here. Come over to the comfy chairs at the tables instead."

Lily shrugged and followed Logan. Before they crossed in front of the counter, Logan pointed over his shoulder and said, "I asked Katie if you could charge your phone while we wait and she said she'd be happy to watch it for you." He stood with an open palm, waiting for Lily to hand over her phone.

"This isn't some complicated robbery scheme, is it?"

"Did I command the wind to take your hat? Surely I don't appear that godlike." Logan motioned with his fingertips again, feigning impatience.

She handed it over. This was so different than any date she'd ever been on. In other circumstances, she'd let her bare shoulders do the talking, waiting for one bachelor or another to approach her and try to schmooze his way into her heart. When the conversation would inevitably grow dull, she'd pirouette to find another man waiting for her. But here, Lily only wanted the attention of *this* man. And he was giving it to her. No challenge whatsoever.

Logan thanked Katie, who shared a warm smile that seemed comfortable and knowing—something Lily usually earned before any other woman did. Lily felt her stomach knot. Did this bus to Brooklyn drop her off in some alternate reality? As if this stranger's smiles would only be reserved for her from here on out since, what, half an hour ago? She usually created the envy instead of feeling it herself and now this *barista* was humbling Lily Cromwell?

She shook her head as if doing so would shake out the thought. Logan led them to a table in the corner. While Lily sipped her coffee, she watched Logan flip over the box and lift it like a magician to reveal their game board. Lily set her coffee down and was relieved the feeling in her fingers had returned.

In an impressive tenor, Logan sang, "*Uptown girl… I bet she's never had a backstreet guy.*" He gestured to Lily.

"Not exactly Billy Joel, but not bad."

He frowned, but the scowl didn't reach his eyes and he continued to hum. He pointed at the stack of rectangular prisms. She suddenly wished she'd played Jenga more as a kid. Or any game, really. She nudged the middle block on the lowest row. It wouldn't budge. She looked for an opening in rows and columns above, but found Logan had packed them, making it difficult to find an easy way to move a single block, let alone have a chance to win the game. She grabbed a block on the right side of the tower and placed it gingerly on top. Logan nodded approvingly and a surge of pride bolted through her. She picked up her coffee and lifted an eyebrow with bravado.

"Can you best that?" It was much too early for Lily to be feigning confidence. But it was almost 10pm in Brooklyn in a bakery with a man she'd just met, so why the hell not?

Logan found a loose block quickly and set it on top. "Can't I?"

Lily smirked. "You like this place because there's no one here, so you can win against the same people over and over again."

"Alright, alright. You caught me."

"Did I?"

"Oh, honey, you know I can't say, 'Yes.' The moment you think you've won is the moment I'll have lost you."

He stared at her like he couldn't wait to watch her reaction. She remained stoic, refusing to reveal what she was really feeling. Caught. Naked. Nervous. He was right, of course. She used that rule all the time: keep him chasing. No one should have the time to look closely at broken pieces lest they find somebody more put together. Lily had written that one by herself.

The tower from the other group's game fell in a loud crash.

Over the clatter, Logan said, "Now play, so I can say I beat Lily Cromwell at something other than good looks."

Lily laughed. Her shoulders eased. Feeling returning to her fingers and toes. She could stay here for a while.

She lifted a block and set hers perpendicular to his. She knew it shouldn't be so easy—that they should be sabotaging each other's future moves—but she didn't want the game to end so soon. On the other hand, she never wanted a Jenga tower to fall so badly. The quiet was almost deafening, and she wanted to know more about him, but she didn't want to give herself away as someone who only asked the shallow questions—the custom for most of her dates with Wall Street bankers and Manhattan lawyers. As Logan lifted another block, she studied his profile. His strong jaw housed the pink lips that needed a bit more Chapstick… she could help moisten them, if he'd let her.

She smiled into her cup and took another sip.

Logan said, "You'll have to come back here Sunday when we break out the Twister. I hear yoga pants is the garb of victors."

Lily didn't have a chance to answer. The blonde barista—*Katie?*—was standing over their table.

"Logan, you've got to stop letting your friends win all the time!"

Friend zoned already? Lily thought.

Logan shared a wide grin with the barista and winked. "Don't call Lily my friend just yet. Don't wanna jinx it."

Katie shrugged, and Lily couldn't help seeing that Logan locked eyes with Katie. In warning? In jest? Was *Lily* the pawn to make this girl jealous? Because nobody used Lily like that.

"More coffee?" Katie asked Lily a little too curtly.

Lily shook her head. "No, thanks. I don't want to be up all night." Lily couldn't help the glare she hoped was piercing into this lady's forehead.

Lily placed another block on top. It quivered for a moment, but settled. She asked as casually as she could, "So the way you danced for me—is that how you dance for all the ladies?"

Both Logan and Katie looked over at her like Lily couldn't have realized that she'd just said those words out loud.

"Does he dance? Of c—." She was cut off by Logan's hand. Katie pursed her lips and pivoted back towards the counter. *Weird.*

"I dance all the time," Logan said, "but only almost die for the ones who can't resist a gander into a flower shop. You know Janie closes way earlier than when you walked in tonight? She must have been feeling particularly nostalgic today."

That surprised Lily. "You know about William?"

"Of course. Who doesn't? They've got the best love story I've ever heard." Logan took a block from the third row from the bottom, so most of the tower was counting on the one remaining block in that row. He rested it on top like it was a cement addition on the strongest foundation.

She pointed to the block. "That's impressive." Then, she pointed in the direction of Janie's. "But there are lots of love stories out there. What makes theirs so special?"

"Janie and Will were a forever kind of love, and they should have had more than the twenty-something years they got."

Lily looked up, the words knocking the wind knocked out of her. They reached deep within her to a place she thought had been closed and buried a long time ago. Her mom should have gotten more years with her dad, too. *Lily* should have gotten more years with her *dad*. She grabbed a block underneath the row Logan had just weakened. She placed it on top. The tower was no longer strong enough and fell over itself. She tried to catch all the blocks, but she missed and hit her elbow on the table. Some coffee spilled over, but she pretended not to notice.

Logan stood immediately. "Let me get that for you," Logan said. Lily lifted her mug to her nose, looking over the brim of the cup to catch any more clues from the interaction between Katie and Logan. Katie only handed Logan a few napkins, and he mouthed "Thanks" in return. Lily rolled her eyes and sipped the coffee with greater gusto. It was time to go. She was cool with someone taking care of her, but not if it meant losing hold of her emotions. *Sentimentality weakens stability.* The best way to avoid losing someone twenty years too soon was to not get started at all.

When Logan sat down and eased into the back of his chair, Lily said, "You know, Logan, it was really sweet of you to get my hat and do all of—" she gestured around her "*this* to get me warm and charge my phone, but I should really be heading home."

"Not much of a night owl on a Monday night, huh?"

That gave Lily pause. This guy really was getting a totally different version of Lily Cromwell. Monday nights usually ended with a man leaving her room on a Tuesday morning.

"No, I guess not," Lily forced a smile. Then, she lied. "I'll call you about a night that's good for our dinner date." She added for the semblance of truth, "Do you have a business card or something?"

Logan showed his stupid beautiful smile. "Just come back here Sunday afternoon. Don't forget the yoga pants." Lily couldn't believe this man's confidence that Lily would return. Such a forward comment was from the type of man she was used to, but for some reason, it didn't fit the picture she had of Logan. So she called him out on it.

"Really? You're that type of guy, huh?"

He looked wounded. "Too desperate? Too soon? Alright," he said. "Then I'll tone it down." He handed her a business card. "Travis Investments, Logan West. You'll get my secretary, but give your name and I'll make sure she knows to get you through right away."

She stood and waited for him to stand. When he didn't, she nodded. "It was a pleasure meeting you." *For real*, she wanted to add. *You've been such a breath of fresh air. Thank you for being here.* Instead, she wished Logan West a nice night and turned her back on him. Twenty years too short would end tonight.

After retrieving her phone from a nosy-looking Katie, Lily pushed open the door and stepped into the bitter cold. She closed her eyes and breathed in the icy air. Each strike away from the bakery was deliberate, but uncertain. When she was satisfied with the distance she had placed between herself and Logan, she turned on her phone and watched ice crystals dance into the mist as she exhaled. Two minutes later, she hopped into a Lyft and sped down Atlantic Avenue toward the bridge that'd take her out of Brooklyn. Her heart raced as quickly as she hoped the driver would. No matter how quickly he drove, however, Lily already knew she wouldn't be able to escape the feeling that she was running away from the very thing she'd always wanted.

Only Count on Yourself

Anne had startled her awake ten minutes prior with a phone call. She had to be in the car in one hour. *No* excuses.

Lily stumbled over the coat and boots that she had left lying on the floor last night. A stranger would have noticed the trail of clothes leading to the bedroom, but Lily knew the only clear trail in her home was to the gladiolus tucked in the black glass vase no taller than a bird. Though she had large vases to choose from—vessels for the many bouquets from too many bachelors—this vase with ornate designs was the only one that would fit the only flower she had ever brought home for herself.

She let her gaze fall from the flower to a floor-length dress. In the bright sunshine of morning, the deep purple sequins shimmered as Lily held it over her body. *Too much.* Logan would think it was ridiculous. He seemed like the type of guy who didn't care what his date was wearing as long as she was wearing a smile. Lily rolled her eyes at the cliché. Of course he cared. But it didn't matter what Logan thought, Lily assured herself. He was one man, one random night almost a week ago. She'd never see him again. She rolled up the dress and threw it down. Some less wealthy women would have dropped their jaws at her irreverence, she knew, but she wished she could tell those women that sequins wouldn't bring them satisfaction. Having the upper hand in every situation would.

Lily walked back into her closet and withdrew another five dresses in plastic wrap. Anne had sent these earlier in the week, but Lily had not remembered what the event was for. *Some fundraiser? Another brunch at mother's to meet some expectant bachelor?* She discounted the first two dresses immediately and dropped the others on the bed: silk was out, and the other was an abhorrent yellow. What had her mother been thinking?

A pink gown was hugging the largest throw pillow and though a younger Lily would have liked it, it wouldn't suit on-the-brink-of-a-promotion Lily.

The long-sleeve of a grey cotton sweater dress touched the gown as if it wanted to switch roles. Lily shook her head. *Too conservative.* The crimson Jill Jill Stuart shoulder dress with puffy elbow sleeves stood alone, unintimidated by the competition, so Lily gave it a promising glance-over. The length was right, at just above the knee, but it would still draw too much unwanted attention. She didn't want to be noticed by anyone today, but it did have to be just right for a quick stop in a bakery, in case she needed a coffee on the way home.

Lily dug both hands into her messy hair. If Logan had been able to flirt with the blonde barista right in front of her, maybe it was time to invest in a new coat, or scarf, or shoes because clearly this style wasn't cutting it anymore. She wondered what it would be like if she were one of those women who could run into Target and buy a basket full of products. She had heard rumors of women bragging about how much they purchased after time there. Who were these women and how could she switch lives with them for a day?

Lily's phone rang.

Something between a huff and a growl came out of her mouth on the way to the phone buried beneath the dresses. When she saw that Marley was calling, Lily swiped right and let out a relieved breath. Her best friend's brown eyes and mischievous smile lit up the screen.

"Hey, Lilo!" Marley said. Lily grinned at Marley's nickname for her. "I missed you already and decided to see what you were up to this fine Sunday morning. Relaxing, I hope?"

"I wish," Lily said. "Anne reminded me of some event she supposedly RSVP-ed for a while back."

"She's always reserving you for something. And on a Sunday? Ugh. When are you going to learn to say, 'No, I'm staying in bed all day'?"

"Maybe when there's someone in bed with me," Lily said.

"But then she'll wonder if something's wrong with either of you if there's no grandchild by the first wedding anniversary."

"What if I *want* a child by the first wedding anniversary?"

Marley's shoulders went up in a shrug. "Has Anne ever wanted what you've wanted?"

"You're making my future look so glamorous. Thank you." The bitterness in her own voice surprised Lily, but Marley only shrugged again.

"Do you disagree? Let's say you find this guy Anne has imagined up for you since our sophomore year. You'll essentially be buying into her whole plan for the rest of your life, right? You know that. You've always known that."

"Aren't you just jumping right into the facts this morning," Lily said. The red mini-skirt peeking out of her closet suddenly caught Lily's attention and she lunged for it, dropping the phone. "Oops, sorry!" She picked up the phone gingerly, cradling Marley's face in her palm. She rested the phone against the coffee machine, slipping on the mini-skirt, not caring that Marley had visual access to the mess.

"Spring cleaning a bit early, no? For a girl who sets everything out neatly the night before..." Marley said.

"Ha, I know. I totally forgot about the thing today until Anne called."

"It's not Ashley's wedding shower, is it?"

A stone dropped from the top of Lily's esophagus, lodging itself in the bottom of her stomach. She swore.

"You're right. I think I'd forced myself to forget." Lily started to unzip the skirt, but something kept her fingers at the zipper. She pivoted to her closet, straight to a black long-sleeve top with thicker knit material stretching like sun rays from her neck, but everything else was see-through. If her mother said anything about this being inappropriate, she'd simply state she was still single and looking, wasn't she? And a bakery in Brooklyn welcomed any dress, so it'd be perfect when she took a detour back home later. She tuned back to Marley, who was nodding approvingly at Lily's choice of dress.

"Ooh, I like that. And I don't blame you for forgetting. Ashley is one of the daughters in Anne Cromwell's circle to have recently gotten engaged, right? I think I read something about it in the Spanish tabloids. They're so obsessed with New Yorkers. I read she found a real winner. Robert—"

"Fitzgerald," Lily finished. "He owns a few bull ranches. Big deal. I don't know what Ashley sees in him."

"Maybe it's not so much what Ashley sees but what her mother does."

"Please. Ashley's too hard-headed to submit to her mother's wish list."

"Still. It's gotta burn that Anne is going to be goo-goo-ga-ga over Ashley's wedding plans while you're—"

"Gimme more credit," Lily said. She sat at the edge of the bed and pulled on black Blondie stiletto boots. They were the only thing she retrieved right before bed, taking them out of the cramped closet and letting gravity do the work of straightening them out in her boot rack for the night. "In fact, you'll be happy to know I just met a potential keeper of a guy last night."

"Oh? And which mother does this one belong to? It must be a big circle if you haven't exhausted all the single sons yet."

"Hey! You'll be surprised to know that this one isn't known by any Cromwell compatriots. As far as I know, anyway. I guess there's always a chance." Lily pulled again at her skirt. It *was* short. But Lily's butt was also always one of Ashley's Achilles' heels. One look at Lily and Ashley would be less likely to point out that Lily didn't yet have a rock on her finger in front of all the mothers—especially her own.

"So what's his name?"

"Logan."

"And what's this Logan do?"

Lily rearranged herself, unable to find a comfortable position.

"I'm actually not sure. He works for Travis Investments and apparently has an assistant, which means he's a big dog," Lily said. She lifted the crumpled business card that had been resting next to the phone.

Lily thought she saw Marley sit up a little straighter.

"And how did you meet this Logan with a secretary?"

Lily swallowed. "At a bus stop."

Marley laughed. "No. Really. Stop playing." She paused. "Wait. For real? You, at a bus stop?"

Lily made a face, trying to play a pout. Then, Marley whooped in exuberant victory. "What happened? All the cabbies went on strike?"

"I was at the bus stop because I wanted to accompany a friend from work a little bit longer, and he takes the bus home."

"A male friend... a bus... What would Anne Cromwell say?" Marley meant it as a joke, but Lily answered seriously.

"She'd be positively aghast, then congratulate me for entering a new pool of men to find the man who's a millionaire in disguise."

Marley nodded as she considered this. Lily knew she was right.

Lily pushed the clothes off the left side of her bed and laid down, lifting the phone above her face.

"So are you gonna tell me or what?" Her friend's encouraging eyes were a green light for Lily, and Lily didn't hold back. She told Marley the whole story, from walking into the bakery, to getting jealous of the barista, to the hope that they'd set up a dinner date soon, to him being so different from the "others."

Marley paused, then asked, "But even if he didn't satisfy your mother's... conditions... would you still choose him?"

Lily pretended to think about it, then shook her head. "I honestly can't imagine going against my mother. You know her. Plus, she's already lost so much. I wouldn't want to add to her list of grievances." As she said the words, she felt they were true. To defy Anne would be to stop being her daughter.

Even after Lily and Marley exchanged their pleasantries and promised to talk again soon, Lily couldn't shake the feeling that there was something Marley wasn't saying. Marley usually expressed how much Anne wasn't in the right.

Was this the first time Lily had ever vocally *agreed* with Anne's vision for Lily's life? Wasn't becoming "like your mother" what everyone resisted, but everyone eventually became anyway? What was the big deal? Maybe it was Lily's turn to let go of this notion that she was somehow going to end up differently than her mother.

As Lily waited for her mother's driver to receive her, she reflected on her friendship with Marley. It was Marley's relationship with her mom Peggy that had revealed just how calculating Anne Cromwell was.

Peggy had always scooped Lily into a big hug the moment she walked into the Harrow household. It's like she had some sixth-sense telling her that Lily didn't receive enough hugs, so she had offered her warm embrace to Lily's usually stiff reception. Then, they'd go to the second-floor bedroom-library that Marley slept, read, and dreamt in. The books surrounding Marley's small queendom stunned Lily's curiosity, but it was Marley's reaction to her mother's gentle knock at the door that had surprised Lily the most. Lily would wait for Marley's quick "Not now, Mom!" but it never came. Instead, Marley welcomed her, and Peggy would set a plate of sliced apples and oranges on the floor next to her crossed leg, where Marley and Lily would describe their day, wrapping Peggy in a tapestry of teenage worries. Instead of showing condescension or boredom, Peggy would crunch thoughtfully on apples while she listened to the current events of their sophomore year. The ease with which Peggy conversed with her teenage daughter befuddled Lily. They spoke of just narrowly avoiding detentions, or saying the wrong thing that had earned a scolding from a respected teacher. It made her question what happened to her own mother: why was Marley forgiven for her teenage blunders, but Lily, never at all?

She didn't want to think about what Anne would say if Lily told her that Logan had made her *feel*. That wasn't *wrong*, was it? It was just different from what she was used to. Knowing she owed Logan an explanation of her quick escape, she unlocked her phone. Having looked at his number so many times deciding whether to call him the night before meant that she had accidentally memorized it, an impressive feat in the 21st century. Her finger pressed the telephone icon and typed *312-872-8474*. Her finger hovered over *Call* when her mother's photograph appeared with a message that Lily was to *hurry!!!*

She'd call him later. For now, it was time to avoid any Anne Cromwell land mines, especially those laid by bride-to-be, Ashley Proctor.

* * *

Anne's scowl made Lily want to return to her room and burrow back under her covers. Instead, she lifted her chin higher and settled instead into the leather seat of her mother's Cadillac Escalade.

"What took you so long?" Anne demanded.

"Marley called me. It would have been rude to hang up," Lily said.

Anne lifted an eyebrow. "That's a lie and you know it. You look flustered. Did you have that monogrammed napkin over again? Did you even shower?"

Lily drew in a breath.

"Good morning to you, too, Mother."

Anne waved the nicety aside like a fruit fly in her face. "It'll be social suicide if we walk in late, Lily. I promised Claire I'd help monitor her drinks so she would be just—" Anne held up her thumb and pointer finger "—buzzed enough to deliver a charming speech but not sloshed enough to be the talk of Manhattan. Now I won't know how many martinis she's in." Lily normally would felt bad for causing a kink in her mother's plans. Instead, heat prickled up her neck.

"There are worse problems in life, Mother. Ashley's mother will be fine." But Lily knew Anne was right. Claire's drinking problem was infamous. It was typical of Claire to make this request of Anne, who also enjoyed her alcohol but never let it have the reigns.

The honking horns of Fifth Avenue were alive with tourist traffic. The entire rush of the morning made Lily miss the quiet of last night's bakery, tucked within the city but relatively untouched. As she watched the city streets pass her, she leaned her head back and wished she could vacation to where there were no work expectations, daughterly duties to perform, or men who flirted with other women right in front of her. The car came to a sudden stop and Lily closed her eyes as if it would stop the wave of nausea. When was the last time she had skipped town for a while?

A sharp fingernail dug into Lily's left shoulder. "Let's *go*, Lily Anne. Are you on another planet? Ashley is one of your closest childhood friends. The least you can do is act like you're excited for her. Marriage has not eluded her like it has you, so maybe you can learn something today."

Fantastic. Land mine number one: the reminder that Lily wasn't married or even engaged yet. She was actually grateful Anne had revealed it so early on.

"At least pretend to be happy for them."

Lily followed Anne through the revolving door and took her gloves off, stuffing her phone into the clutch purse that was a darker shade of red than her skirt. Hopefully no one would notice the discrepancy. Rookie mistake. A distracted mistake, like not telling Logan how grateful she was for the hat save, or that she was so glad that he used it as leverage to spend more time with her. Instead, she ran out like he was venom. Maybe it was better that he didn't know that she was the poisonous one.

Once they were out of the door and in the lobby, both women appraised the room. Staircases curved up to higher landings and mirrors on either side showed Anne's body relaxing into her demeanor as a would-be hostess and less as the disgruntled mother of a 27 year-old teenager. Her mother greeted woman after woman with a radiant smile, though Lily had previously heard Anne say something negative about each one. Though Lily offered crooked smiles to their daughters, she kept her eyes above their heads. She didn't want them to have any reason to pull her back into their drama, their cattiness, their gossip. Lily grew up with these girls, making fun of the entire establishment of proper attire and behavior, but she still couldn't shake the desire to show off and prove why she looked better than they did. Why she was more successful as an engineer than as a charity poster. Her height was always in her favor, so she used it to survey the hall.

Chandeliers were "out" this season, so instead, lit candles brought the focus onto circular tables covered in silver cloths. Lily had to admit that it was well done, like a castle's mead hall glowing in the evening hours.

The moment she saw the color scheme of the room, however, she chewed her favorite curse word. The chairs were covered in deep red, and so was Lily.

She shut her eyes as Anne sidled up beside her and hissed, "Rule number five. You didn't even look at the invitation, did you? Are you new at this? You really felt like being fifteen again, didn't you? Single, late, and underdressed."

If the room had been kindling, Anne's burn could have lit Lily on fire. She would have been willing to throw the skirt in as kindling.

One of the Rules was to be prepared fully for an event. To other women, this might mean a nice mani-pedi, or blow-out, or new dress. But to Anne, preparation meant taking notes on the details of an invitation to get the vibe of an event *just right*. The only way to stand out is to fit in, Anne would always say.

Lily wanted to scream. *Why does this even matter?*

Interrupting her anger was an eager, sing-songy "An-n-ne!"

Lily made a note to book a massage right after this was over; she could feel the tension headache making its way through her corpus callosum. How would Logan act if he were here? What would he think about all of this? She imagined him laughing at the absurdity of the entire situation and dropped her shoulders.

But really - how could she have messed up so royally? Though her choice of a mini-skirt had emboldened her, the choice of red had really backfired. She felt the stares of women around her and looked around the room for an escape. Lily suddenly wished that she were in a room full of men, where they didn't care about whether the color of her dress clashed with the room, just whether she'd clash with one of them later. If she knew this crowd well, then she knew they were now discussing her. It was much safer than discussing real matters like how to save a failing marriage or coping with loneliness in a house-full of people.

Because she was usually best dressed, it was hard to be on the losing side of the "Who Wore it Best?" column.

"Anne and Lily Cromwell! He—l—l—o!" A drawling voice that was louder than it should have been resounded in Lily's ear. Lily felt Anne's glare burning through her, but Lily refused to meet her eyes.

Ah, shit. Claire is already drunk. Ashley Proctor's mother, Claire, was short in stature, so Lily and Anne both had to lean down for a small embrace and cheek kisses that were more like hen pecks than tender salutations. She reassured herself that all she really had to do today was give Ashley a quick "Congratulations" and then smile and nod at others' comments. She wasn't going to give these women any ammunition. *Silence only bothers the self-conscious.*

A shrill voice called behind her. "Lily Cromwell, is that you!?" She'd recognize that voice anywhere, the brassy off-tune notes of a trumpet that should have been retired years ago.

Lily spun around to face Ashley. Ashley was wearing a cocktail length dress that looked as if one of Genny's rainbow glitter glue pens had exploded all over it. Lily wished she could say it clashed with her red hair, but damn it, she looked good. Personal trainers were a hot commodity before a wedding and it looked like Ashley had paid big bucks for hers. Ashley grinned widely, reached to grab Lily's hands and placed her left on top, the shine of her ring too inviting to resist catching a glimpse of. Ashley must have noticed the intrigue because she lifted their hands to examine the rock more closely.

"Isn't it gorgeous? Robert sold one of his *best* bulls for this stone."

The rectangular ruby stretched from knuckle to knuckle, diamonds hugging it on all sides. She imagined a child might think it was a Ring Pop, in which case it should come with a choking hazard on Ashley's small hands. Lily wondered if she needed to take it off after a long day. She'd certainly be too weighed down by it if she had to write code with it on.

"Wow. It's really something." It came out flatter than she had intended.

"Isn't it?" She squeezed Lily's hands, making it very obvious that Lily did *not* have a large rock in the way and released. Ashley turned to Anne. "Thank you *so* much for being here for me and my mom." As Claire sipped a Manhattan, Ashley subtly showed three fingers to Anne, who immediately took the glass from Claire.

"Thank you so much, dear. I'm sure Lily would love to try this one." She pushed the glass into Lily's hands, and the liquor sloshed over the brim. The skin around Lily's eyes tightened, but Claire's smile widened at Lily in gratitude. Her mother forced Claire to chug the glass of water that had seemed to magically appear out of nowhere. *Classy.* Lily cringed.

When Claire had swallowed the last of the water, she called out to the room. "Ladies, please make your way to your seats!"

Though Lily was upset with the scolding she had received from Anne for her color faux pas, Lily did feel bad about being a contributing factor for Claire's inebriation. She wondered if Logan drank a lot of alcohol. She hoped not. He'd definitely not pass the Anne test if he did; a man who spent the majority of his time drinking just wasn't attractive to the Cromwell girls. Logan had flirted just fine without it, so maybe he was safe.

She arrived to table *31,* joining the usual suspects of her childhood.

Across from her was Rose, the first to cut ties. It still made her nostalgic to see Rose's kind eyes watching Laura as they were deep in conversation. Lily used to be as close to that pair as she was now to Marley.

Laura's palm was resting on a healthy baby bump. Lily waited for the heart squeeze she knew most women around her age claimed to feel, but she noted a blissful nothing. No babies wanted here. *Yet.* How would she get into this skirt otherwise?

As Lily and Anne sat down, Claire smiled broadly at the room of hushing women, rushing waitstaff, and clinking glasses. Claire began her welcome speech, mentioning how lucky she was to have such a great community of women. *Ha!* Lily wanted to laugh. *Liar. We're all cut-throat manipulators.* Lily sipped her drink and let the bitters of the Manhattan soothe the fire in her throat.

"Now, as you all know, Robert has already shown himself to be a worthy son-in-law to our Ashley. He's proven he values a woman more than a bull—"She waited for laughs and Lily rolled her eyes when everyone giggled on command. "But, more importantly, he has vowed to make Ashley the center of his world. And isn't that what every mother wishes for her child?"

Lily snuck a glance at Anne to catch any reaction from her mother. Anne played with her bracelet, rotating the pearls over and over and over again. Like the cycle of Lily's lack of nuptial promise. Lily stared at the top edge of her metallic charger plate as Claire's voice became stronger.

The headache was going to get worse if she didn't take a painkiller soon. She clutched her purse, as if having her hand around her phone would summon Marley and Ibuprofen. Ashley's mother kept speaking, but Lily zoned her out. Where was this woman's Oscar?

Lily bore her gaze into the centerpiece and memories flooded back from when they were all sixteen. They had given Ashley plenty of warning: Brian hadn't been the first guy to get with Ashley and then make up some lame excuse to leave her once he was satisfied. When Ashley ignored Lily and Marley's ultimatums after being dumped by Dan, and Luke, *and* Johann— and then got hurt anyway—she and Marley decided to drop the drama and let Ashley learn the hard way that real love didn't come or go so easily. Granted, what did they know at sixteen? Anne had been repeating over and over that it was easy to get the guy and leave the guy—but even Anne had taught them that *real* love was hard. And it could end with the death of the one you vowed to love for life. Who would ever want to run *that* risk?

Claire's voice was right next to Lily's now. "But because of the choice to choose love—despite all the tears and heartbreak—Ashley is going to be the prized darling of the Fitzgerald family, and I couldn't be more proud! Theirs is a *true* love story!"

The room erupted in applause, yet Lily could have sworn she heard her mother mutter, "Oh, bullshit."

Without missing a beat, Anne stood, lifting her glass. Her face broke into a wide grin and her voice commanded the room. "To our girls - may they show their husbands who the boss really is." The women laughed and nodded approvingly. Leave it to Anne Cromwell to capture everyone's attention.

When Anne sat down, Lily couldn't resist asking, "But what of us who have no husbands, Mother?"

"Why, it's rude to remind a woman of what she's lost." Anne unfolded the napkin and laid it across her lap. "Being a widow at a bridal shower has its own challenges. You would know if you weren't so self-centered. I take blame for that. I shouldn't have mistaken your youthful bratty-ness for grief. You got away with entirely too much as a child. It's showing now, darling."

The headache climbed. The throb was an ax being lodged into her skull. Lily started to apologize, but Anne lifted a hand.

"I know what you meant." Anne sighed. "Don't worry. I have no concerns about your future ability to demonstrate control over a spouse." Lily couldn't tell if her mother was complimenting her or not.

A waiter set a salad of Romaine leaves, slices of thick red onion, and the typical tomato and cucumber on the silver charger plate. She would have loved the Ranch dressing the waiter offered, but declined. She didn't need Anne reminding her of empty calories.

But apparently Anne wasn't done. Lily was grateful that Rose and Laura were wrapped up in their own conversation to hear.

"I am so glad I've taught you how to be one step ahead of any 'tears and heart-break.' Remember: if a man ever brings on unnecessary emotion, steer clear. You make *him* feel. He gives you what you need - money, sex, and children if you want. You'll do plenty by letting him call you his wife. Never let yourself fully *fall*. Life isn't a Disney movie."

Lily speared her fork into a cucumber slice and bit into the crispness, allowing the cool to soothe her tongue. There was nothing Lily could say to argue with her. Her mother was right. Healing heartache took too long, and for some reason, women seemed to spend their lives looking for It—*The One*— and were surprised when Love didn't work out the way they wanted it to. Lily crunched, wincing at the onion that'd make her breath stink. *Great. Another thing to worry about.*

Lily lifted her fingertips to her mouth and breathed out, waiting for the putrid smell. It was faint, but nothing Anne would notice. Lily turned to face her mom. "You're right. You know, thanks to you, I haven't cried over a guy since high school."

"Of course I'm right, dear. But it's kind of you to say so. Letting yourself get too close to a man is a recipe for disaster. Like this salad. The least they could do is place an apple slice on the side so we won't all end up smelling like onion rings. The only person you can count on is yourself." Anne reached into her purse and placed a small plastic container of Tic-Tacs next to Lily's plate and patted Lily's hand. "Make sure you take one before you speak to anyone else."

Lily pressed her back against the chair, shaking her head. She couldn't help but smile. Her mother was something else. She shut her eyes, fluttering them open to a movement at her right side. On her bread plate lay a small croissant wrapped in pink ribbon, with Frankie's written in small letters along the edge. For a moment, her fingers clasped around the edge of the table and her eyes scanned the area for Logan as if he had sent her a message right then, like little kids passing notes.

While Lily halfway listened to something about baby beds and nannies, she took a closer look at Rose, whose ring was a simple gold band and looked so humble compared to Ashley's. There were bags under her heavily-powdered eyes and a crooked smile was on her lips. And Laura was clutching that baby bump like the child was going to be her savior. The women, though married, weren't safe from life's harsh realities. Emotions weighed heavily on their shoulders, and the realization made Lily breathe easier for once. She wasn't missing out. In fact, the fact that she hadn't found someone to call her 'wife' yet was only because she hadn't settled yet — something of which her mother was certainly proud. Logan seemed promising, but she needed to get to know him better. She had planned on the typical 'Wait to call and schedule a date' but she was afraid that if he had too much time, he'd have too much of an upper hand. She needed to catch him off-guard — find him in his element and then interrupt his normally-scheduled programming. The interruption would be enough to keep him wondering how he could get her attention again, and again, and again. Then, she'd have the man, and he'd know that to take his eyes off Lily Cromwell for even one second would be the biggest mistake of his life. She *had* to go to that bakery today. There's no way he expected her to show up, so being there would definitely fall under the "be bold, be mysterious, leave him wanting more" part of the Rules.

She cut the croissant and peeled the ribbon from Frankie's, setting it to the side delicately. The ribbon bent up, like it wasn't satisfied to be free and would have much rather preferred being tied down, setting up a roll or pastry for a quick sale. She smiled at the memory of Logan dancing in the middle of the street and wondered where they would go on their first official date. She cut into the softened butter and spread a thin layer across the top of both sides. She imagined he wouldn't be rigid and uptight, but ready to move the conversation where she did, nudging her into nooks and crannies she didn't even know were there. He did tell her to loosen up, after all. She bit into the roll and let the soft crust melt. He was a Californian stuck in a New Yorker's suit. Being around him was what she needed after twenty seven years with Anne Cromwell. Maybe losing the stress might help in securing her IceStorm promotion.

Against the stiff conversation around her, she suddenly yearned to discuss things that mattered with Logan. People spent way too much time on scripted conversation. *She* spent too much time entertaining shallow topics. Maybe he'd like to hear about her project - how out of all the engineers at her start-up, her architectural plan was the one that gained most traction, beating out even the CTO's ideas. She shook her head, recalibrating. She didn't want to *bore* the man. Did men really appreciate a smart woman? The good ones did, right? If they existed?

Anne excused herself and Rose turned to Lily like she had been winding up to do so all afternoon.

"—no perfect man for Lily Cromwell?"

"I'm sorry?" Lily asked.

Rose rested her arms on the table and leaned forward. "The ever-elusive Perfect Man. You kept telling me to wait. You could be with that one guy from high school right now. You two really liked each other. He was so into you." She looked over at Laura. "What was his name again?" Laura mumbled something and Rose spoke louder. "That's right! Roger. Poor guy.

You really stomped all over him. He was so nice. You should stop being so picky. Seriously. The Perfect Man doesn't exist. I thought Henry was close, but even he has his flaws."

"Uhh, thanks." Lily felt around her plate for the Frankie's ribbon. What did she want Lily to say? Sorry? Of course Henry had flaws. She had seen him at one too many charity events getting cozy with someone else; she was pretty sure he had tried hitting on *her* when he was too drunk to realize who Lily was.

Laura's laugh was heavy and inauthentic compared to the lightness of Logan's laughter last night.

Laura said, "You're so beautiful, especially in all this red." Her voice dripped in sarcasm. "Goodness, Lil, if you wait too long, all the eligible bachelors will think something is wrong with you, when you're perfectly fine." She paused. "I think."

Lily's hand stilled. Rose reached over Laura's arm and rested her fingertips on Laura's inner arm. Rose whispered something to Laura, but Laura's voice only increased in volume, turning both shoulders towards Lily. "I know, I know, it's none of my business, but Lily always had a way with the boys in high school. I just thought she would have secured one by now. It must get lonely in that Central Park apartment."

There was so much Lily could have said, but she thought of Logan waiting at Frankie's and stood up instead. "I understand if you feel like you have the richer deal in life right now—"

Rose mumbled something and her timidity emboldened Lily.

"But I assure you that you have it no better than I do. In fact, while you're losing sleep worrying about whether Henry really is working late, I know that I'm the type of girl he's staying up late for."

Lily turned away as her mother sat down.

"It's so nice to see you girls catching up." She stared at Lily a second longer to suggest it was anything but nice. "How long has it been?"

"Not long enough," Lily muttered.

She felt around for the Frankie's ribbon but couldn't find it. She lifted her plate and checked underneath, but it was gone. The waiter must have taken it, confusing it for trash. This made her even more furious. Lily clutched her purse, apologized to no one in particular and left. She was sure Frankie's would have better coffee, anyway.

Surprise Him

Thirty degrees of wind pushed hard against Lily's body as she exited the revolving doors. She charged against the cold anyway, the grey skies matching the storm she knew was brewing in her eyes. Boots resounded with each stride as Lily made forceful contact with the ground. She imagined breaking through layers of black ice, no longer caring which accidental mines she might step on. She didn't need the approval of women who surrendered their freedom and sanity in the name of *love*.

Despite oncoming traffic, she entered the crosswalk. A car came to a screeching halt, the front bumper a few feet from Lily's knee. In the Midwest, that'd have appeared suicidal; in New York, it was efficiency. She glared in the driver's direction and marched across the crosswalk, trying to ignore the crass honking. She'd show them. The party of the year was on its way, and their husbands would all be looking at *her*, buying into IceStorm and Lily would have the promotion and…

A stride before she stepped onto the curb, her heel slid, forcing her left knee and open palms onto the sidewalk. It felt like an icicle plunged into her knee cap. She bit her bottom lip to prevent from yelling out. Pedestrians walked around her like she was an inconvenient traffic cone in the way. She tried to extend her knee, but doing so made tears spring to her eyes. She pushed herself off the ground and limped to the sidewalk. She leaned against the marble building of Hostiel's Manor. Exiting patrons didn't notice her, and if they did, they never let on. Lily supposed this crash to the ground was her comeuppance for reminding Rose of her cheating husband. Marley always said people were eventually humbled by life. Lily wouldn't apologize for it, though: it was better to be honest than pretend that everything was perfect. She had learned that best from Anne. Then again, it was also what cost her so many friendships—*including Ashley's,* Lily thought.

Lily rubbed her knee with one hand and pulled out her phone with the other. She pressed the side and watched the digital 13 turn to 14. One of the best decisions she made was to switch clock settings to show military time; it made it easier to count six hours ahead to know if she could call Marley. She unlocked her phone and smiled at the photo of her and Marley making faces with the Don Quixote statue in Sevilla. Lily chose the speed-dial option and waited for the phone to ring. It was the heart of the evening there. Marley would be on the couch, watching a movie alone, like she preferred. The wind clasped itself around Lily's hand, but Lily ignored it, ready to vent to her most loyal friend.

Marley answered on the second ring.

"Back so soon?"

"What a fucking disaster."

"Ouch. Tell me about it." The phone crackled. Lily imagined Marley settling into her seat, opening a chocolate candy, ready to listen to Lily.

"Of all people, Rose got under my skin. And Claire. And Ashley. The whole damn lot."

"And that surprises you?"

"Kind of." Lily switched the phone to her other hand, stuffing the numb one into her pocket.

"Well, what'd they say?"

"Something like all my eggs will dry before anyone has a chance to see what beautiful babies I could make."

"What?!"

"Okay, maybe not those words exactly."

Marley laughed. It eased the squeezing around Lily's heart enough for her to slow down. "But it was close enough to it that I left before they served the main course."

"Dang, girl. You're just all in a jumble lately, aren't you?"

Lily sighed, suddenly very tired. It was true; it didn't seem to matter how confident she felt lately; she was slipping in far too many situations where she used to feel solid—literally and metaphorically.

"I just want to focus on my project at work and maybe enjoy a date with Logan. I've never really gone on a date with someone who my mother didn't choose for me, or in some way approve of. Logan is still fresh. New. Unknown. I want to explore him on my own before getting my mother involved."

"You're a grown woman. Of course you're allowed to choose the man you want to spend time with."

"I *know* that." But did the Rules allow her to believe it?

The phone beeped in her ear to indicate an incoming call. She shifted the phone to see a photo of Anne with her lips pursed. No way was she going to speak with her mother now. Lily rested the phone back on her shoulder, cool cheek pressing against the screen.

"So now what?" Marley asked.

"I think I'm gonna go home, change into something more comfortable and then find my way back to that bakery." Yoga pants, he said. She had the perfect pair.

"Since when is it allowed to pursue the bachelor? Isn't that, like, Anne's cardinal rule? In fact, the whole rule stuff started *because* you were sad that James wasn't noticing you." Lily grimaced. James Kullner—heartthrob of the 12th grade and shoe-in for Prom King— was Lily's first heart ache. How anticlimactic it had been when Lily was finally crowned, slow dancing with James instead of Roger, her lab partner, who she *should* have been pursuing the whole time. Rose had been right about that one. That's probably what had stung so much.

"James was gorgeous and every girl would have just died to be his prom date," Lily said. "It was natural that I wanted to be noticed."

"Yeah, but when you came home that day, Anne called your emotions 'messy.'"

Lily remembered it clearly.

That next morning, clothes she had never seen before were lying on her bed. When she'd walked into Biology first period in a mini skirt and a hot pink streak in her hair, she'd done the ignoring. It had been the first day of her practical training, her mother had said. Her main goal was to keep her eyes far away from any potential connection with James. Start talking to other guys more frequently.

"And that's when I started talking to Roger," Lily said.

"We don't have to go there," Marley said gently.

"Well. Maybe we should. You'd think I wouldn't be regretting what I did to him all this time, but Roger hadn't deserved that game-playing. That wasn't me." He had been too good for her from the start. Marley had seen it all and knew how much Lily still blamed herself for ruining the end of Roger's senior year. She was sure that they'd still be good friends if it had ended differently — maybe she'd have avoided this single-but-dominating life entirely.

Lily swiped to the right and opened the rideshare app.

Marley sighed, like it was too much work to keep up with Lily's musings. "Okay, well. If you think this game-playing Lily isn't 'you', it's time to change up the rules, isn't it? Anne Cromwell identified James as your first 'prey', training you for months. He was the guy your mom chose for you to try and 'catch.' You spend most of your time attracting guys who never initially show interest. And if they do, you're aloof. *All the time. Even when they finally show interest!* I am ready to fully support you if you're ready to change it up, but just be careful. Make sure you're doing this for *you* and not just to get back at your mom and her cronies."

Lily nodded, even though Marley wasn't able to see it. Lily's voice hushed, like they were in a huddle about to score a game-winner. "I'm going to get in with the barista. See what's going on. Then I'll have a better idea of what to do with this Logan guy."

Marley didn't need to know that Lily wasn't planning on talking to the blondie at all. Hopefully, there'd be a cute hipster behind the counter and Logan would walk in on them mid-laugh...

"All right," Marley's voice lowered. "But keep me updated."

"I will!" Lily said it with as much cheerfulness as she could muster.

The phone call ended and Lily waited for the Lyft, stretching her knee and wincing each time she tried straightening it. It was swelling, fast. The pain dug itself into Lily and pulled out more thoughts of Logan, along with the realization that there was no way she could hobble into the bakery. She couldn't draw him in with pity or play a damsel in distress. She needed to know he would stay for when she was strong and intelligent and witty and *messy*—and choose her for her anyway.

She *would* call him. And Marley was right: that'd be as against the Rules as she could get. Maybe it was time to revise them a little.

It was so liberating to choose to let go of the chase. She was already wrapped up, ready to send herself into arms that she knew would be strong. With such an earnest invitation, Logan had already put a priority stamp on her, didn't he? She was just going to expedite the process.

\<del> Never Be the First to Call \</del>

The warmth was a welcome comfort, but it was the teal wall in front of her that finally made her relax. *Home.* She pressed her forehead against the plaster and allowed it's coolness to soothe her like a cold rag easing a fever. She pushed herself off with stiff finger tips and reached into her pocket. It wasn't the worst thing ever that her knee prevented her from stopping in on Logan at *Frankie's*. She hadn't asked someone out on a date since… well, ever. She needed time to devise a plan. Besides—Sunday nights meant quiet, uninterrupted Lily time anyway.

She fumbled with the phone until she found the appropriate button and held it down. As the phone turned off, Lily set it on the top of the couch, which was sticking its arm into the hallway like a butler ready to serve his lady. She shrugged off her coat and hung it in the closet. It slipped off its hanger, and Lily pretended she hadn't noticed.

Lily sat on the edge of her grey cotton couch, removing her boots one at a time, careful not to aggravate her knee. It reminded her of all the times she had scraped her knee as a child. Her dad was the one who'd settle her down when the alcohol stung. He was the one who'd blow on it, anoint it with Neosporin and remind her that all the best warriors got back up after a fall. Lily blew up into her bangs. Positioning herself at the edge of her couch with most of her weight resting on her right heel, Lily cupped her palms under her left knee, lifting her leg so it'd lie on the same level as her hip. The idea of calling her mother dashed into her thoughts and Lily dismissed it as quickly as it had come. It's not like Anne would know how to take care of her like she wanted—and Lily certainly didn't need a reminder of why having a partner would be really useful for a time like this. *Obviously* it would be way better. *Right?*

She wondered what type of Sunday-evening guy Logan was. Or maybe he preferred relaxing on Friday evenings when the working week was done. *Maybe he'd like to come over?* Lily laid her head back and closed her eyes, willing the squeeze of her abdomen to go away and shrugged Logan out of mind. A night on the couch was hardly the most inconvenient event, and she couldn't imagine trading her solitary Sundays under any circumstances. She wouldn't let them go until the company she spent with someone else really was better than the time she enjoyed alone.

She reached for the lighter on the console table over the back of the couch. With a nudge of her thumb and a trigger of the finger, she lit her favorite candle, a turquoise pillar that accented her walls. Then, twisting to the other direction, she lifted the remote and flipped on the TV. Holding the arrow, Lily watched the stations scroll one at a time past R&B. Hip hop. Not in the mood for classical. Ah. *Classic country.* Not the typical choice of "her type" of woman, but what Anne didn't know wouldn't kill her. Conway Twitty crooned that he didn't *know a thing about love* and Lily released the last bit of strength she had and sunk into the cushions, waiting for sleep to take her. She hadn't felt this relaxed all day, but still she stirred. Maybe the adrenaline from her fall was making her anxious. *Or maybe.* She muted the TV.

She switched her phone *on* and punched in the numbers she had memorized from the night before. Lily cleared her throat.

She practiced a sultry "Hello?"

Ridiculous. But she touched the call button anyway.

She felt like she was sixteen again, and it didn't feel good. Messy emotions were a recipe for disaster, Anne said. But what if they were the only thing that also made life exciting and worthwhile? The phone began to ring. She was about to try out another greeting when Logan answered.

"Hello? Logan speaking."

Lily grinned. She couldn't help it. Was he hoping she'd call? His voice sounded hopeful, like a child asking "Really?" after being told they really were going to the waterpark.

Lily crooned. "I thought you said I'd get your assistant."

"Why, hello to you too, Lily Cromwell. I was wondering if you'd make me wait or not."

"I really couldn't, believe it or not." What? The truth? Lily widened her eyes at her own audacity.

"It was Frankie's coffee; I should have warned you. That caffeine will keep you wired for days. I'm sorry I misled you. Would you like to call back and I'll have it go to voicemail, so you can leave the voicemail you've been practicing in your head all day?"

Smooth—and so sure of himself.

"Well, the voicemail was for your assistant, so I'm not sure it was the type of seduction you were hoping to get."

"Just hearing your voice would have done me in, sweetheart."

But oh, his voice sounded so *comfortable*. Like when she didn't mind the cold air sneaking in through the cracked windows because all it took to be okay again was to wrap the plush blanket tighter around her. She wished she could reach in the phone and wrap herself in him.

"Well, thanks for making it so easy. I'm here, and ready to go wherever a crazy dancing man goes. But I draw the line at WWE matches."

"Way to just Swanton Bomb my childhood. And since you probably don't know Jeff Hardy and his signature move, I think we should just call this thing quits before it gets too serious."

Lily laughed. It felt like crystal after seeing melting plastic all day. She wanted to hold on to it, put in on the highest shelf, and keep it as a reminder that her giggle wasn't gone—just not available to those who didn't earn it.

"I mean," Lily said. "If that's really what you want, I can go as quickly as I stumbled."

"Your stumbles are pretty cute."

"I had one today. That's why I won't be making it to Frankie's today."

"Bummer!" Logan said. He sounded genuinely disappointed.

"If I'm already letting you down, maybe we *should* call it quits. It's going to happen fairly often."

Logan laughed, but it was softer at the suggestion of disappointments in the *future.* "I was never one to back down from a challenge."

Right answer, Lily thought, but she responded in jest. "Are you calling me a 'challenge'?"

"So is Mount Everest, but people want to climb it all the—"

"Whoa! Aren't you supposed to wait until I'm good and drunk to reveal your true intentions?"

"You didn't wait to call, so I thought we'd go ahead and—. Ah, hell. I'll stop there. My mom would have smacked me a long time ago." Something in his voice changed. "I didn't mean to suggest anything. It just sounded—"

"—fun. No, it's okay. You are. It is." Lily sat up on the couch.

"You'll just have to come on a different day. My sister, Katie, is the barista there, so I thought I'd be a good brother and keep her company on this lovely Sunday."

Ohhh. "That was your sister!"

"Yes."

She didn't have to be in front of him to know there was a smile on Logan's lips.

Logan said, "You have to know that there's no other barista in my life. If you have a side-gig at Starbucks, you have to come clean now, because I *will* find out."

"Man, you have a lot of non-negotiables," Lily said.

"I figured if I had more than you, then you'd stick around long enough to give me a real chance. I have a feeling I'm more like the schmucks you normally pass by, but I don't want to be."

"You're quick to judge."

"You were quick to call. Which is more surprising?"

"Touché," Lily said. "It does bother me that you think you have me all figured out. I don't know why that makes me want to prove you wrong."

"Exactly. Game on, Miss Cromwell."

"Where shall we commence this contest?"

"At Burkette's. I want to watch you decide between salad and steak. Prove you really are different than the girl who just wants to please."

"Ha! You have so much to learn. I'll meet you there. Grand entrance and all, you know."

"I'd expect nothing less. Let's give you until Tuesday evening to prepare. I'll call for 7:30 reservations. Good night, fancy hat."

Never Surrender

S he placed her phone on the edge of the sink and bit her bottom lip. Where Frankie's was a family room with well-worn couches, Burkette's was that princess plush that wouldn't give when she sat. She remembered she'd been to the fine dining establishment once before on a date with a... dentist? Surgical resident? She squinted into the brightly lit mirror. Somebody in the medical field. Thanks to him, she had fixed one of the main constraints in RACE. Also thanks to him, she realized she wanted someone who was going to be more available for her. Call her selfish, but when she wanted to eat, she needed to eat, and Lily Cromwell didn't eat alone. Imagine the gossip columns—*Lily Cromwell, finally surrenders.*

She pressed dark green eyeshadow at the edge of her lids and began to blend. What had the restaurant looked like? Had the food even been good? The only thing she knew for sure was that she had never called him back. Anne had been upset with her after finding out about that one. Lily had admittedly been a little sad, too.

Who had told Anne about that anyway?

Rose.

Ugh.

Lily had mentioned something at somebody else's wedding shower. *A real winner you could have had, Lily. Imagine: a doctor as a son-in-law.*

At the memory, Lily pressed too hard and the eyeshadow smeared. The make-up remover would erase too many layers of foundation, so she made the arc wider instead. The smokey shades were much more severe than what she had originally planned. Was this too much for a Tuesday night? Logan danced in the middle of the street. Of course it was too much for a guy like him. But sometimes one had to go to extremes to be memorable.

* * *

If buildings could go to a plastic surgeon, Burkette's had received a facelift, tummy tuck, and fatter lips. The last time Lily was here, the restaurant's Moroccan accoutrements hadn't fit the steak cuisine or the American fare, but Burkette's *had* been pretty. In the few months she hadn't been a guest, however, Burkette's must have been told to remember it was on American soil and should behave as such. Beautiful ceramic tile had curved into mirrored walls, but now the tiles were painted in black and white checkered patterns. Red flowed through the room in accents on light fixtures, chairs, and cloths on deep black tables.

Burkette's was the total opposite of Frankie's, and it made Lily nervous. Logan didn't care about impressing her the first night they met, so Lily was worried that he'd be too much of a pretender and not enough of who she had been so initially intrigued by. Logan was rolling out the red carpet treatment for her. Literally. The clay floors that had caused many a lady in stilettos to slip was now a smooth carpet. Where was the challenge in that? To master the catwalk was to master the audience after all. Lily had executed that saunter like a pro with Mr. Doctor watching. That's what helped her bring him home with her—too bad he had been called away that night. But she supposed she should be happy he may have been helping somebody else's dad.

Lily needed a way to impress Logan, especially with a lined red carpet weaving its way through the restaurant.

She was sure he had already been seated. The gold watch hanging loosely around her left wrist revealed it was now twenty minutes past their scheduled time. Though Anne thought it too long to keep a "man of high-standing" waiting, Lily had devised this rule herself when she was a sophomore in college. The unwritten rule was that if a professor didn't show up within fifteen minutes of class time, students were allowed to leave. But there was one professor—Dr. Natasha Sterling—who was so captivating, so engaging, and so... entertaining... that everyone waited for her, every time. So now she Dr. Sterling-ed all her suitors. Marley was a fan of this method and it hadn't failed Lily yet.

Lily scanned the restaurant for a hint of blonde hair. For a Tuesday night, the dining room was busy. Couples were walking hand in hand to their tables. An older man was pulling a seat out for his much younger date. From behind a group of smartly dressed interns, Lily finally saw him. He was rearranging his silverware, tapping the knife against the table. She watched him lift his hand to run it through his hair but stopped to check his watch.

When the group moved out of the way and Lily knew Logan would be able to see her, she made sure to give the maître d' her biggest smile. In what she hoped looked like a movie scene, she descended down the few steps while holding onto the railing with one hand and lifting her gown in the other.

She didn't get very far when a short brunette cut in front of her.

"Fancy seeing you here on a Tuesday evening!" Rose said with forced excitement and a grin that Lily knew hid all the nights Rose spent alone. Rose's hands clasped in front of her as her husband slipped a thick white coat over her shoulders, fur causing gold earrings to dance. He did so hurriedly, returning his attention to his phone. Rose waved him off like he was a child still learning better.

Lily raised an eyebrow. "Is there a rule now that fine-dining is only reserved for weekends? Otherwise, you're quite the rebel, too."

Rose laughed too loudly and wrapped her hands around her husband's arm. He looked up, surprised to see her there. Rose hugged her husband closer. "Why not act like we're still young and in love?"

Lily nodded seriously. "Yes—and it's good acting indeed."

Rose's smile was still broad, but something in her eyes darkened. She lowered her voice—as if her husband cared what she was saying. "You are no better than you were in high school, Lily Cromwell. Let's see what prize-winner you have tonight." Rose craned her neck, and her gaze led her to the back of the restaurant where Logan was seated, nose in a menu. As if he could feel them looking, Logan set the menu down and scanned the restaurant instead. His eyebrows shot up when he found her. Lily loosened her grip on the pole, grinned and waved. He fanned a couple fingers in response, then dug his hand into his pocket.

Lily stepped around Rose and her husband. Her husband kept an eye on Lily longer than he should have, and Rose noticed. Lily saw Rose's hand tighten around his arm.

Lily sauntered towards Logan, who looked up right on time. With Logan in front and Rose's stare blazoning into her back, Lily felt like she was being held in balance.

Logan pushed his chair back and stood, eyes widening. He took a step forward, then brought his foot back to stance. He swung his arms, as if he were cracking his back. Then, he stood at ease.

She smiled and looked up at him in faux-innocence. He rotated his watch once, twice. It felt good to make him nervous.

Logan went to step around to the side, probably so he'd be ready to pull the chair out for her, but rammed into the edge of the table and the glass of water tipped over, hitting the edge of the candle. The water and wax ran together like a bad science experiment and the spell was broken. After a stunned silence, the guests' voices increased in volume and he looked grateful for their cooperation. The busboys ran to the table to assess the situation and Logan seemed relieved to see that nothing had caught fire. No one was hurrying to re-seat them, but Lily didn't blame them. All the tables were occupied.

Logan said, "I should have called ahead to ensure Burkette's is large enough for spontaneous dance parties and accidental twerking. Apparently, it is not."

She was about to giggle when she clamped her mouth shut, fingers hiding her red lips. *Get it together, Lily Anne. You're in your element. Use this.* "It certainly is not, but I don't think you're in the business of following standard etiquette."

Now that she had pushed the challenge in front of him, she waited for his hand to rest on her back and guide her to her seat. Or to reach for her hand and kiss it. But neither came. He pulled out his chair and sat down, grin sprawled across his face like a little boy who placed his drawing on the fridge and was waiting for his mom to notice. Lily scrunched her eyebrows together in confusion. He just let his blue eyes shine.

Busboys passed by, but one paused to watch. Though heat crawled up Lily's neck, she strode towards her chair. She gripped the top of it, but her sweaty hand slipped.

"Is everything to your liking, ma'am?" the older of the busboys asked.

She wanted to shout, "No! Of course not! The man I was putting all my bets on won't get off his a—!"

Instead, Lily nodded curtly, and turned her full attention to Logan. "Aren't you going to..." Her voice increased in pitch.

He shook his head, grin getting bigger.

He said, "You expect me to pull out your chair. If I'm going to stand out in your mind, I need to make sure I do the opposite. Besides, if I pull out your chair now, you'll expect me to do it all the time, and what if I end up in a wheelchair when I'm 80 and I physically cannot do it for you anymore? Then you'll just find the next guy whose muscles can handle dinner etiquette and I'll be left all alone."

"You'll force me to leave you all alone if you ever behave like this in front of my mother," Lily said.

"Ah, so Mother is the mastermind behind all of this, is she?"

"*'This'*?"

"Yeah. Acting like you can't pull out your chair just so—"

"It's basic principle to stand for a lady and pull out her chair. I shouldn't have to explain this to you."

"Whose basic principle?"

"The Cromwell Rules."

"The *what*?!" Logan's eyebrows shot up his forehead.

"You know what?" Lily said, annoyed and regretting the decision to go out with someone with such ill-bred manners.

"What?" Logan said, not asking at all.

She dragged her chair along the carpet, but it snagged the material and the metal top of the chair ricocheted off her wrist bone.

Lily gasped at the sudden sharp pain that dug into her bone and through her nerve endings. She wrapped her left fingers around her right wrist to soothe the sudden throb. How many times was Logan going to have a front row seat to her clumsiness?

Lily swore she could hear a loud cackle came from the front of the restaurant and Lily's ears felt like they were on fire. Rose was a reminder of the world she came from, and it was only a matter of time before word got back to Anne that Lily's choices in men were severely decreasing.

She waited for him to apologize, realize the error of his ways, get up in apologetic murmurings and pull out her chair *this* time. But he still sat, resting his chin on folded hands. She sat down, rubbing the wrist bone. She wondered if it'd swell into an orange like her knee had.

"See? You figured out how to do it all by yourself."

He's close enough to slap, isn't he? It was only a matter of time until Lily would offer her standard faux apology—"It's not you, it's me"—and leave.

As a waiter came to ask Logan what he'd like to order to drink, Lily scanned the contents of the table. A black lacquered wicker basket boasted a cacophony of seven seed bread, French rolls, and sourdough slices. Lily rolled her eyes as she could hear Anne now: *A place that tries to please everyone doesn't actually take a stand.* Lily unrolled the silverware from a thick black napkin that she lay over her lap. Burkette's must have downgraded; they used to have the silverware set up like a Victorian manor welcoming its evening guests. Soon, the waiter would ask if she wanted cheese grated on top of her Ceasar salad.

I don't have to put up with this. In a voice that came out strangled, she said, "Did you just get some bad news or something?"

Logan shook his head once, but kept staring.

Okay...

How did this man close any business deals? Logan was still watching her over praying hands. What was he waiting for? If he thought the stillness would make her uncomfortable enough to get the conversation going, he had another thing coming. The man should always take the lead in dinner conversation; to do otherwise would suggest an aggression that scares off even the best suitor. He lost his privilege to a happy-go-lucky Lily when he didn't greet her as a proper gentleman does. She scooted to the edge of her seat and rested her hands on the bare space in front of her, thumb rubbing the bottom of her palm. It was better to get this over with sooner rather than later.

"Listen." Lily folded and unfolded the napkin in her lap. "Obviously whatever led us here is no longer a factor. We're not in the middle of a street in Brooklyn. We're in a world that will tear you apart if you don't... if you won't subscribe to..." *Why is this so hard?* "We do not have to continue this if..."

The table rocked gently and she saw from the corner of her eye that Logan was standing now. Lily kept her stare fixed at the center of the table. The pain wasn't enough to push tears to her eyes, but she didn't want him to see her all the same. The hot disappointment was a surprise even to her. Of course a crazy dancing man wouldn't have the manners of an Anne

Cromwell-approved suitor. How sad that she couldn't have both in one person. All she had to do was open her eyes, lift her head, and tell him *he seemed nice, but she just realized she had to go attend to something at home.*

A gentle nudge—then gripping cold—of ice froze her fingers. Like a rod lodged itself against her spine, Lily straightened her back. "Oh!"

"'Scuse the cold fingers. Here. This might help." Ice cubes were in Logan's black napkin. Others had already cascaded onto her hands or the table. He was wrapping the caught ones into a makeshift ice pack and tied the ends together.

She opened her mouth to thank him when he said, "I've never had the pleasure of having the most beautiful woman in the room walking towards me. You shocked me. I'm usually better at closing deals because I'm more attractive and charming than the person I'm talking to. But not you." Logan's hand slipped under her upturned palm and rested the flatter edge of the ice pack against her wrist. He moved the napkin pack and Lily winced. Logan grimaced apologetically.

"Now you're hurting because of my own ego. I really am so sorry." The gesture was enough to melt some of the ice around her cool demeanor. "I feel like a fool for making you pull out your own chair." He hesitated, and Lily finally looked up into his eyes. Crystal blue. Genuine. He smiled.

"I tried to think of something witty to say, but all it ended up doing was making me sound like an ass. Seriously, though, you look… Well, you know it already." He bit his bottom lip, then smiled. He steadied the napkin and pulled his hands away, sitting back in his seat. "I almost wish we were back at the bus stop. You were way less intimidating after losing your hat than you are with this whole leather-jacket and gold earrings deal you got going."

"Well, bus stop Lily is as frequent as a solar eclipse, so if you can't handle the outside, then the inside is going to be way too much for you." Lily's wall was erecting faster than she could tell it to *Stop! Wait! He's different than the others!* but the stones were being laid again. Each time he acted contrary to the way she had been taught, it seemed to throw her into a state of bewilderment and mistrust. She wished she could shake him and say, *"Yes! Break the rules! All of them! But just one at a time. Gently. And make it feel like I'm the one ripping them to shreds."*

"It's the inside I saw on Saturday night. Your makeup had been almost non-existent after a presumably long day. You had been cold, and sad-looking…"

"So you only liked me because I looked miserable and needy?"

"It's way easier to feel like I'm in control when you're in that general state, yes."

"Logan, what are you saying?"

"I'm saying you have to suspend everything you thought you knew about dating in order to 'get' me."

"But why?"

"Because everyone does the same thing, and everyone is still miserable. What if the key to all of this is doing the opposite? Instead of playing it cool, we jump in hot. Rather than wait for the right moment, what if we *created* the perfect moments?"

Their waiter asked them to follow him, muttering something about the ice being a mess and moving them to another table.

This time, Logan's movements were graceful. Easy. Like they had done this a thousand times before. Logan thread Lily's hand through the open window he made with his left arm. *Where was Rose now?* He rested his hand on top of Lily's careful bones and carried the full ice pack gingerly against her skin. When he bent down to get a better look, his hair fell out of its mold. She decided it made him look sexier than if he had kept every hair in place. She could hear Anne now: *street rats had hair that danced when they did; only princes kept their hair still, every piece a commanded tether. Wouldn't you prefer a Prince Charming, darling?*

No, mother. Didn't you see how Jasmin lit up when Aladdin danced?

With each step toward a new table, Lily walked straighter, renewed confidence emboldening her, but filling her in different ways than normal. *This* was the Logan she had hoped would be present. Somebody else would have his palm against her back, fingertips sliding along her waistline to signal an early conquest. The numb pain in her knee caused Lily to lean against Logan as they walked. She wasn't demanding the attention of everyone in the room; it was enough that Logan's hand was cupped around her fingertips. How the ice hadn't melted already was a mystery.

Lily pressed his palm. "So tell me something about yourself."

"How deep do you want me to go?"

Lily raised an eyebrow. "You're asking me that on a first date?"

Logan threw his head back and laughed. She grinned. The waiter led them back, back, back into the rear of the restaurant. She didn't even know this part existed.

Lily said, "What a cool space." Then, "Tell me about the home you grew up in."

He squinted as if something had just gotten into his eye and smiled. "We were the house that all the neighborhood kids hung out in. We used to play video games *all the time*. We didn't grow up in the best neighborhood, so my mom didn't want us playing outside. Instead, we spent all our time in the living room. My mom loved it, though, and all my friends loved her back."

"It was actually pretty cool having all my friends in my room almost every day after school. We'd do our homework together and then play until their moms called them home. Anyway. I'm telling you this because although life doesn't often hand-out second chances, video games always have a restart button. And I'm pressing this one."

With a flourish, Logan pulled out the chair of the new table, bowing down and indicating her seat with an open hand. When he bent down, more strands of hair escaped their mold. Something in Lily stirred. Logan had seen a disheveled Lily, yet he was still here. She was seeing his hair out of his hard gel, but it made her want to bring him home. Maybe not tonight. She didn't want to rush a good thing. *Who* am *I?* Even if he just ended up sleeping on the couch, she would have been satisfied just to feel him near.

Lily sat down and said, "I wasn't allowed to play video games. My mother had this rule that if I was going to be around video games, I had to learn how to create them instead."

He pushed her chair in. "But how did you know what to create if you had never played them?"

"Just because my mom had the rule doesn't mean I followed it. My best friend Marley had the best games; I think the one where you had to crash the cars for the most damage was my favorite."

Logan laughed. "Well, I suppose it's better I know now that you have a secret desire to be so destructive."

"What can I say? I'm in the business of wreaking havoc in order to get the benefits." She lifted her hand and the ice tumbled out of the tied napkin. Logan frowned.

"Too soon?" Lily asked.

"No, no, I deserve it."

She leaned forward on her elbows. "Wait. So how did someone from a bad neighborhood end up in I-have-an-assistant Manhattan?"

Logan took a deep breath. "Maybe I misspoke when I said it was a rough neighborhood. All I meant was that, compared to your life, Summit is a working-class village where so many of the residents stay put, working in the corn starch plant, Frito-Lay processing center, or a gas station. If you're lucky, you have a gig at Portillo's. Sure it has some graffiti and theft, but otherwise it's a quiet town where the trees and children still grow."

"So poetic," Lily said.

The waiter poured red wine into their glasses.

"I hope you don't mind Malbec," Logan said.

"Not at all."

Lily lifted her hand to her earring, rubbing it like it'd give her ideas to help carry the conversation from here. Her upbringing had been completely opposite: the competition for advancement started the moment a woman found out she was pregnant. The men Anne wanted Lily to date *could* boast diplomas from those coveted schools. What would Lily say to Anne, or to women like Rose? *This is Logan. He's from Summit.* They'd ask what kind of mountain that is. Only Marley wouldn't care. And, as it turned out, neither did Lily.

"So is Summit, like, a mountain town?" She pictured candle-lit cabins and cozy lifts they could ride up the mountains.

Logan guffawed. "Absolutely not. It's as flat as you can get. Right on the edge of Chicago. That's why New York feels enough like home sometimes." Lily ignored the slight deflation and made sure she kept her face straight. She knew Logan was being vulnerable by showing his humbler background this early in the game.

"How long *has* New York been home?"

"About six years. I was in my first years of culinary school and studying in Milan when my mom called, saying my dad had suddenly fallen ill. She didn't need to ask me to come home. I spent the trip home hoping I'd make it in time to say goodbye. Right after the funeral, I knew I needed to find a way to secure my family's future. I took business classes at the local community college and transferred to NYU for a finance degree. I found the firm I'm at now and the rest is history."

"That's amazing," Lily said, her admiration genuine. Anne *would* appreciate Logan's story; Lily just had to present it in the right way. This man's tenacity and loyalty was worth so much more than a man "with high social standing and an investor's checkbook."

Lily reached for the seven-seed slice and spread butter on it. Logan took the French roll.

Logan said, "I'm glad you're not one of those girls who only wants to order salad when she goes out."

"My mother's jaw would drop if she saw me carbing it up before dinner." Lily bit into the bread and tore it with her teeth.

Logan's eyes softened when he smiled; that is, his normally alert furrowed brows rested, like leaning elbows on a Southern porch rail. "Boy, you're a rebel. Playing video games *and* eating bread?" He leaned forward. "How do you manage to keep your figure?"

Lily lifted a mini imaginary barbell with her pinky once, then twice, and then pushed the rest of the slice into her mouth.

"What an effective work-out strategy. You could sell that for millions."

Lily chewed and swallowed. "Summit could be my first market."

Logan lifted his wine glass. "I'll be your first customer."

Lily hadn't expected the rush of tenderness that came from looking into Logan's eyes. She loved the way he looked at her, like she didn't need to be the one who turned the head of everyone she passed— it was enough to turn the head of *this* one. Maybe her mother was wrong. Though Logan as a boy wasn't raised in perfection, he was certainly close to it as a man. Which one of her past dates would have made an ice pack out of a cloth napkin at an upscale restaurant? Lily hadn't realized how much she had missed the lightness in her chest and she wanted to keep feeling it. Though she constantly worried about pleasing her mother, Lily didn't feel the need to justify everything to Logan. He was easy-going and she wanted that going into this IceStorm party. She wouldn't have to schmooze anyone at that party with Logan on her arm; they'd all be coming to her to convince her that they were worthy of her product. She lifted her glass to his and said, "If you're the first customer, you have to leave a good review. I'd hate to settle for mediocrity."

He raised an eyebrow. "I doubt you'd settle down for anything less than success. The leather jacket itself says, 'Catch me if you can.'"

"You've really got to cool it on all the jokes you have in your arsenal about running and catching and falling and hats and buses."

"But why? The fates graced us with such a memorable origin story; we have to milk it for all its worth."

Lily gripped the table and leaned forward in her seat. "You think of origin stories, too?" she whispered.

"Some guy named Ovid came up with a collection of them, I hear. Or read. Ms. Johnson and that English class…"

"You do know the big names. Not bad for a Summit boy."

"Hey." Logan furrowed his brows in faux-objection. "Don't get too excited. I only have enough names to make it sound like I know what I'm doing when I'm in those network-cocktail 'party' meetings."

It took all of Lily's effort not to drop her jaw. She didn't know whether to scold him for mocking the environments she was a dominating force in, or hug him and welcome him to the club. Instead, she fixed the napkin on her lap and smiled up at him.

"I take it you don't want to discuss work then, since that'd sound too 'network-cocktail party' for you."

Logan winked at her, tendril falling across his forehead. "I knew I liked you for some reason."

"Well. Since we're being so honest. I'm still trying to figure out the reasons I like you, too. You've got so much unfounded confidence."

He erupted in such laughter that those seated around them looked up. Some scowled. Some smiled with him. Lily froze, unaware of how to react.

"You are so much fun, Lily Cromwell. How do I get to keep you for longer?"

"Just keep up the confidence, and you'll keep fooling me. It makes you incredibly attractive."

"I'll take what I can get."

His mannerisms were considered so uncouth and so akin to all she'd been taught to *avoid* that, though she knew Anne would be disappointed to find her still sitting here being teased by a near-stranger, she refused to leave. She wanted to know how Logan was able to roll the stares of others so smoothly off his shoulders. If she was the stiff tree in the orchard, she wanted to learn how to be the hammock calmly swinging in the breeze. Nothing bad ever happened on days with a breeze like that.

* * *

They tumbled out from the revolving doors. Logan held out his arm and Lily reached around it and shifted the weight of her body to lean against him. She'd blame her own unbalance on her knee, but she couldn't feel that too much anymore, what with the lightness of the conversation and the steadiness of her man. She loved that he adjusted their bodies enough to hand the valet ticket to the attendant, but her never let go of Lily. In fact, the rising wind made him hold her tighter.

"So what other rules did your mother create for you?"

Lily threw back her head. "Ha! You don't want to know. But somewhere between dinner and dessert, I was probably breaking all three just by being around you. You're quite disarming." Logan beamed.

"But seriously. *Should* I be practicing these rules for when I meet your mother?"

Lily shrugged. "Shoulds are for suckers." She was surprised by her own reaction.

"Let me know, though. I don't think I've followed one and things are still flowing fine. I'm starting to think they don't really exist."

Lily turned to shoot a laser gaze into Logan's blues. "Excuse me, but you should always stand for a lady at a table, whether she's being seated or excusing herself."

"If it were so important, then why didn't you just turn and walk out?"

Lily hesitated, straightening the cuff of leather jacket. This is exactly what happened when she didn't create consequences for crossing boundaries. "I really should have, you know," she snapped. Especially with Rose watching them like that. Somehow, her mother would end up finding out...

Lily sighed. "I honestly don't know. It doesn't make sense to me. There's something about you." She considered it for a second. "Maybe I like I don't have to act around you."

Lily shuddered from the cold and Logan pulled her closer against him. His hand was bigger than it looked. His palm covered her hip.

She looked at him. "You broke the game when you started dancing with my hat on. A gentleman shouldn't be so... open, you know? Ya have to be a bit more Victorian England before you meet *the* Anne Cromwell."

"Victor— what? You're using your big words again."

Lily scoffed and playfully hit Logan's shoulder.

"You say I 'broke the game.' That presumes it wasn't already a broken—"

Lily stopped listening as a black Maserati pulled up in front of the restaurant and Lily's heart quickened. With a car like that, Anne might excuse everything.

Lily began pulling forward. "If it were broken, marriages wouldn't come out of it, right? Dating just happens to be full of stupid rules that everyone agrees upon. Whether you make it to date two depends upon if you follow, alter, or break one."

Logan whistled. "Love really did die a while ago, didn't it?"

"Even before the time of Victorian England courting, yes. It didn't matter that you were involved with the footman; there were rules of etiquette an ambitious woman would never break. Marrying someone of greater breeding was the only way a woman could ever advance in society."

Logan made a show of digging into his pockets. "So you want my wallet, is that it? Because those student loans are not going away any time soon. You might be disappointed."

"Of course not!"

A Maserati with student loans still over his head? That was a little risky. Unless this investments career of his was really that secure...

It was like he could see the thoughts swirling in her mind. "Forgive me if I don't believe you," Logan said.

She smiled, but it felt forced. She didn't know what to say and she didn't want to lie to him. While she waited for the valet man to exit the driver's seat and open the door on her side, she thought. It'd be hard to deny the truth: cars, money, real estate were all things Anne, and the company they kept, cared about. Anne always reminded Lily that not advancing in one's career was a modern sin—but to abandon the ideals of romantic courting was unheard of. Of course Lily was looking for a man who'd either complement, or raise her status. Lily had joked about Victorian England, but so many of the same ideas held true in modern New York City, too. In the Cromwell Rules, they were the brick and mortar of the entire operation. Mother always said that suffering through a marriage wouldn't be worth it if there weren't perks. If the man didn't leave behind a hefty life insurance policy, then widowhood would be even more depressing. She heard her mother's voice now: "You go into it knowing you can lose it all—except your money. Be wise with who you 'lose it all' with."

Even though Logan wasn't cut from the same old money cloth, it wouldn't be difficult to convince Anne that Logan was doing fine for himself if she saw him pull up in this beautiful black—

Lily stepped forward. As she approached the car door, Logan tugged Lily's hand to hold her back. Confused, Lily looked up in time to see a woman in a silver evening gown step in front of her and sit into the passenger seat of the Maserati.

Logan pulled Lily back to where they had been standing, and raised his eyebrow. He lowered it quickly, but not before Lily saw the disappointment on his face.

"Not quite, killer," he said. And it was like he knew he had lost her right there, right then, despite her hand still resting right in his.

A shiny red Toyota pulled up behind the Maserati. Logan let go of her hand and opened the passenger side door. She didn't want to know what he was thinking seeing Lily frozen in place.

Lily sputtered. "I'm so sorry. I didn't mean to assume."

"But why wouldn't you? Listen. No worries. I promised I'd help you relax. You can't do that in that car. But here? Here, these rules of yours are silly. If I like you, I like you. I don't need to have a luxury car to keep your attention... do I?"

She made sure there was no hesitation this time so she'd appear more convincing.

"Making it through a meal with Lily Cromwell and still having access to her attention is a win already, thank you very much." She ducked into the car.

Lily straightened her skirt and ran a hand through her hair. Logan's hair had fallen out of its mold a while ago and she understood why; they didn't really know how to act around each other, did they? Logan was right. If he had been like the guys Lily usually went out with, Lily would have chalked him up to dust and left. She'd already be at home drinking wine and prepping her work for the next day. It was because Logan didn't follow a script that she was so unsure of how to proceed. She could hear Marley hissing now, "Just be yourself!" But what did that even look like? Who was she when the rules weren't telling her who to be and how to act? Logan cleared his throat and interrupted Lily's thoughts.

"Where to, princess?"

"Don't call me that." It sounded harsher than she intended.

Logan muttered to himself. "Rule number five-hundred eleven: Do not refer to her as royalty, but treat her as such. Got it."

Lily turned abruptly in her seat. "Listen, if it's such hard work to take me out for an evening, I don't want to burden you with more. Just take me home." She crossed her arms in front of her chest and held her breath. Oh, how she didn't want him to take her home.

After a pause, Logan laughed. "It's cute when you pout." Lily turned and punched his arm. He rubbed it, feigning pain, then laughed harder. He eased his hand back, shifting the car into drive. "It's not that it's such hard work to take you out. It's that I don't think you know how to have fun and let loose on a date. You're a strong river current that pushes anything in its path away. I'm making it my personal mission to help you slow down—let the current bring things to you for a change. And I think I know the place. Now no pouting. I have a rule that my car doesn't take angry girls anyway. Enjoy the city lights as they speed by instead."

Lily rolled her eyes but relented. "Fine. Let's see how fast this Corolla can go."

Don't Let Him Call the Shots

"He has to be at least five inches taller than me, in case I want to wear four inch heels at the wedding."

Lily couldn't believe she was just *telling* Logan about Anne's checklist.

"He should put on his best smile any time he's around me. If he doesn't light up when I enter the room, apparently I have to find another room."

"His shoes should be as polished as his personality. If he isn't well-mannered in small things, he certainly won't act with integrity in large ones. That's not to say he's a pushover; the man will tactfully exude perfection."

He interrupted her then. "You say these like they're lines you rehearsed for a play."

"This is all for performance, darling." She batted her eyes in his direction.

"If he mentions his mother at any time during your conversations, pay attention to how he describes her. Anything less than ultimate respect means he won't respect you when you become a mother."

"His eyes should make you melt. And if his eyebrows distract you, how can you be expected to hold a decent conversation with him?" This one had made both of them laugh.

"Just say 'no' to unibrows. Got it," Logan checked his eyebrows in the rearview mirror. He loved her giggle.

She suddenly sobered, as if something urgent came to mind, and took Logan's hand in her own, weaving her fingers between his. She smiled. "And his hand should feel like your anchor."

Logan had been driving for almost an hour.

When there weren't any more street lamps guiding their way, Lily was tempted to ask what he was going to do with her body after he was done. She wasn't sure what she had been expecting, but it certainly wasn't this pitch-black nothingness she saw outside her window and felt from the bumpy road beneath her. Dust and darkness swirled in the bright headlights. Logan let go of her hand and put the car in park at the edge of a dirt road.

Lily sat straighter. "Did we break down?"

"No," Logan laughed. "We have not broken down."

"Then why are we..."

Lily swirled her head left and right, but even when she squinted, she couldn't see past gravel roads and corn stalks. They had definitely left New York City behind.

"Hey." Logan reached for her hand and squeezed her palm. "Expect nothing. Appreciate everything." He kissed her fingertips.

Logan left the car—and didn't come around to open her car door; wow, he was really all-in for this rule-breaking thing—and walked towards a grassy path at the side of the road they had parked along. There was still some snow in piles similar to those she saw on the tops of mountain hikes in the beginning of summer: some larger, some smaller, but all relatively untouched. The ground was muddier than she liked and the trees shivered; there were no skyscrapers to shield her.

The stones crunched beneath Lily's feet as she rushed towards Logan.

"Where are we? Are you kidnapping me?"

Logan muttered something about her being so lucky, but kept walking. Lily shrugged and slowed down enough to take in the scene around her. Parked cars filled up most of the open field, like a parking lot before a baseball game. A warehouse loomed before them, and a line of people stretched around the side of it, velvet rope inviting patrons like a Williamsburg nightclub. Polka-dot skirts peeked from winter coats and women wearing either sneakers or heels leaned against men in vests on top of crisp white collared shirts.

She grabbed his arm to stop him. "Where are we? I'm not dressed for this. And why are these people here in front of a warehouse? And on a Tuesday night?"

Logan stopped, as if a lightning bolt had struck him into place. She noticed him gulp the cold, country air, like he was steadying himself, and fixed his gaze upon her. She dug her fingernails into her biceps, ready for a fight.

Lily sucked in a breath as Logan stepped so closely in front of her. His breath warmed her cheeks, his mouth centimeters away from hers.

"Lily, look at me." She looked up and, this time, his mouth crinkled at the corners and a dimple on his left cheek made a smile betray her. "Now look around." He gestured around them with one arm, wrapping the other around her back. "There is no chance your mother is here. And neither are her cronies. You are safe to let go." He unwound his arm from around her and grabbed her hand, pulling her towards the warehouse.

She relented. "How long will we have to wait in line?"

He looked over his shoulder at her and winked. "I have what you call V-I-P status."

Sure enough, as they wound through the ever-growing crowd of people making their ways to the back of the line, Logan cut straight to the man in a fedora with a bright red bow-tie. He was at least six-and-a-half feet tall and looked like his shirt was about to burst at the shoulders. When he saw Logan, though, his scowl lifted in a hearty grin.

"Logan, my man!"

"Hey, Mike!" They met with a not-quite handshake that Lily had seen bros in college do with twists of wrists and fingers. It made her wonder if Logan had been in a fraternity at NYU. *Anne might know his friends' parents; in which case, we might still be okay.* Lily almost groaned aloud at her instinct to revert to what her mother would think, and decided to trust Logan. He was right; there's no way her mother would be *here*, in a warehouse on a desolate looking corn field with hundreds of people on a Tuesday night. He was right: this wasn't her mother's world. Tonight, her mother didn't matter, and that freedom felt like a taut balloon finally deflating.

Though it wasn't her world either, she could adapt. With a reach around, she released her bun, then shrugged out of her leather jacket. The rush of freedom was the same as when she visited Marley in Spain; she didn't have to choose which action was right or wrong, full of etiquette or fully without; she could be the Lily who didn't have to watch out for whether her next action would be impressive, mediocre, or in line with the Rules. She could just *follow*.

After raising an inquiring eyebrow in Lily's direction, Mike nodded to a shorter man who opened the heavy door. He looked at Lily with wide, admiring eyes and furrowed his brow at Logan, as if he were suddenly confused by the pairing. Logan's palm gently led Lily through the doorway. If she could feel like this—safe, free, and valued—all the time, she'd follow this man anywhere.

* * *

It was like they had stepped into a balmy New Orleans' jungle where the instruments had lives of their own: dissonance and chaos met somewhere in the middle to create music. Trumpets blared like elephant trumpets until saxophones took over and drums marked a beat that warned an impending stampede. The glistening foreheads of young people and seasoned veterans made Lily grateful for the loose dress she had put on under the leather jacket and the painkillers she had popped before the date—her knee and her wrist were cooperating. For now.

Twirling women made skirts rise and land like parachutes as they were swung and thrown all around her, dance in full swing—literally. Lily patted her skirt, the material too heavy for her to repeat any of the moves occurring around her. Logan led her through the crowds, weaving through dancing couples. It looked like he could predict where the dancers would step next and avoided collisions. Lily tried to follow, but by the time she filled in the space Logan left behind, the dancers' feet moved back and their arms swung into Lily.

She began to apologize, but there wasn't time in the beat for that; the dancers hadn't noticed and Logan was already pulling her forward.

Something that felt like a raindrop hit Lily's forehead. This place really was climate controlled. She expected to see condensation dripping from overhead pipes. Lily squeezed Logan's hand to indicate she wanted to stop and tilted her head up to see from where this rain was coming. Instead of long running pipes, though, Lily was surprised to see cables from the ceiling holding rows of floating pentagonal platforms. Male partners were throwing women above their heads and dragging them between their legs as if there was no chance they'd slip between the golden railings. She suddenly knew what the raindrop had been. Lily grimaced.

"Oh, no. Is that sweat? That is so…"

Logan leaned against a pole with his arms crossed.

"…natural." She tried for a smile.

Two dancers promenaded across, flowing from one platform to another. Lily held her breath. The petite female had her legs around the strong male, ready for the turns that he controlled. Though Lily couldn't hear them over the music, she could see they were laughing. In Lily's world, the only balconies were those attached to high rises where she felt like a queen. But here, they held dancers passionate enough to drive out here on a Tuesday night and be together. The music came to a rest and a man set his little dancer down. They crossed to rest their arms on the railings and looked down. The woman waved at Logan and he grinned back with a small wave. Lily noticed his shoulders ease and felt a tinge of jealousy that this woman was able to relax Logan in a second, but Lily was the one who made them rise to begin with.

People high-fived, nodded and smiled at Logan. A man with a white fedora winked at her and saluted with a white glove before he turned back to his partner.

For a girl who was used to standing out in a crowd, this was one instance Lily would have preferred slinking into the shadows. She latched onto Logan's arm as he wove her through the crowd. She carefully guided her stilettos so as not to accidentally step on toes. An elderly woman wearing a pair of bright white and black saddle shoes tapped past them, head thrown back in glee as a white-haired grandpa pulled her out onto the dance floor. Lily couldn't hide her smile.

She pulled Logan back and pointed at the couple. "I bet those shoes carry a lot of memories."

Logan looked at her with what looked like intrigue, but he made her so nervous she had to turn away. She couldn't help but keep looking at the couple and ran into Logan's back.

"Oof, sorry," she said, but he seemed unaffected.

She looked over his shoulder to see they had arrived at a bar that appeared to be from the Wild West with its saloon doors and wood panel-ing. He turned and winked, side-stepped, and presented her in a grand bow to the bartender.

"Sloane," he shouted. "This is Lily."

Sloane finished pouring the beer on tap and served cold mugs to patrons. She wore a Rosie-the-Riveter scarf and boasted colorful tattoo sleeves. She wiped her hands on her apron before offering her right one to Lily.

"Well aren't you a pretty thing?" Sloane's voice was low and slow. "Where'd *our* Logan find a stunner like you?" She winked and Lily laughed, mixing in with the high timbre of the trumpets. She wondered how many people here referred to Logan as "theirs."

"What would you like to drink, darlin'?" Sloane asked.

Lily said, "Amaretto sour, please."

While Sloane was fixing her drink, the music changed and something about it made Logan push himself off the bar and sidle up near Lily.

Logan clasped his hands around Lily's and looked at Lily's feet, then up at her face.

"You ready?"

"Right here? By the bar?"

"People are dancing on balconies above us. There's no 'right place' to dance here. You just do it."

"I'm sorry," Lily said. "But I don't know how—"

"Nonsense. Everyone knows how. It's in our blood. Our evolution. Just follow my lead. If I kick my leg back, you kick yours forward. It's like we're mirrors for each other. I'll kick my left leg back first, so…"

Lily kicked her right leg out. It felt funny to kick air, but it was kind of cool to not feel any resistance. When she kicked, she kicked, and no one was telling her she was kicking *wrong*.

"That's it! Just keep following me!"

With a strong grip, he pulled her in one direction, then spun them both around. Logan pushed into her hand and she understood to back up. When he pulled her hand, she knew to follow. Like a yo-yo.

The thrill of being somewhere new, with people who didn't know anything about her or her mother, was vibrational. Her kicks became crisper, pointed toes looking like she had been doing this for years.

Logan wrapped his arm around Lily and swayed to the music as it slowed into a blues rhythm and the lights dimmed. Lily rested her cheek on his shoulder—perfect height—and allowed herself to feel held, not remembering the last time she didn't have to think about how she was holding her own body in order to create the most pleasure for her partner. It was enough that she was feeling it—and she could feel Logan agreeing. He whispered into her ear, his breath creating tiny wisps of air that tickled and soothed her. "Who are you when no one's looking, Lily Cromwell?"

He pushed her away, then twirled her once, twice. He pulled her back in.

"You were gorgeous before, but now you're *real*. And if it didn't feel so good to have you against me, I'd always have you in full view."

Her skirt didn't fan out like the others' did, but she could imagine swirls of fairy dust surrounding her all the same.

Physical intimacy never made Lily uncomfortable, but this emotional kind was like sprinkling water on hot wire. She didn't know what to say. "Thank you" felt too lame, though she wanted to say it a million times. She was glad when she saw Logan wasn't finished. He pulled her in closer, his right hand holding her left, a thumb gently grazing a spot her lower spine. She wanted to purr.

"You know, I've been coming here almost every Tuesday, for *years*. This is the first time I've brought a girl 'from the outside'. That's why everyone keeps staring. I'd say I'm sorry about that, but it feels really damn good to have you with me. At least for tonight." Logan bowed and kissed the back of Lily's hand.

Lily could have melted right then and there.

Logan leaned close. "This is my favorite part."

"Showering me with compliments? Smart man."

"No. This." Logan tightened his sudden clutch and Lily gasped at his all-encompassing embrace and something deep and rumbling awoke in Lily. It was like he had reassured her of many future hugs to come, and Lily wondered how many would be *too* many. She wanted that feeling of being wanted again and again, despite knowing the danger that things could erupt and cause destruction at any time. Anne warned her against emotional chaos, but this was the opposite: Logan was *healing*, but she didn't know what she had needed healing of in the first place. She let herself melt into release, resting her head against his chest.

She didn't want to break the comforting silence, but she wanted to hear his voice so close to her ear. "So what are we waiting for?"

His lips tickled her cheek. "Just wait. It's coming."

And with a trumpet blast and answers from a rush of tambourines, men in white shirts, black pants, tight suspenders and bright red bow ties flowed into the room like someone had shaken the bottle and removed the cap. They clapped along to the beat, feet moving too quickly for Lily to recall for future imitation. Were these dancers Broadway stars? It was like their warehouse was being invaded by the lot of them. More importantly, IceStorm party in mind, were they for hire?

As the clapping increased in intensity, the men split into two lines, making room for women in bright red dresses in sharp black heels. They sashayed between the men and then each woman found her partner. In white gloves, the hands of the couples flew to one side and the other, behind backs and in front, perfectly in control and yet totally at the will of the dance. The speed with which they kicked, spun, and dove up and over shoulders awed Lily. Her eyes wouldn't leave one dancer in particular: a woman who was in charge of every movement except the bounce of her tied hair.

Lily pointed in the direction of the woman and started asking, "Who is—?" but she stopped herself. Logan's face was the same up-lit and alive expression it had been when he had been dancing with her brown hat in the middle of the street—bright eyes, wide grin. He looked down and smiled at her like he had already unwrapped his most awaited gift. She wanted to ask someone to stop everything take a picture of this very moment. Or at least give her a manual on how she could make sure such tranquility would stay on his face forever. It suddenly wasn't important how much money he made or what kind of car he drove. It didn't even matter what Anne thought. All that mattered was that this man looked at her like all he wanted to do was share such beautiful moments with her for as long as they lived.

Her hand flew to her purse anyway, phone at the ready to take a selfie of them.

Logan pressed his hand against hers and shook his head.

"I don't need a photograph to remember this."

And then his lips touched hers. His lips reminded Lily of sweet mango, but not so sweet that it was too much. His kiss was soft, but strong. He wrapped his hand around the back of Lily's neck and tightened one arm around her waist with the other supporting her back. As the music trembled in brass ecstasy, he dipped her with the expertise of a seasoned dancer. He held her there as slow piano and a steady bass replaced the loud jazz, like a gentle drizzle after a powerful storm. Lily felt her heart pound as Logan's kiss deepened.

Such a public display of affection should have been too much, too soon, but Lily's desire to have more of him told her more than she had been willing to admit to herself—he satisfied a part of her that every other suitor had not been able to. She smiled behind their kiss and he mimicked with upturned lips. Logan brought her back to standing and leaned back on his heels with a sigh and a smile, reaching up to replace a stray hair behind her ear.

A woman with raven black hair approached Logan to greet him, wrapping a friendly hug around him. Lily squeezed Logan's hand, claiming him.

"Hi, y'all. I'm so sorry for interrupting." The way she said it didn't make her sound sorry at all.

Lily cleared her throat and smiled. "No worry at all. I have a drink to claim anyway."

Lily walked toward the bar. She *wasn't* worried. Not really. Not that she'd ever show it anyway. According to Anne, to show weakness was to *be* weak, and she just watched all this dancing where she was certainly no expert. There was no weak woman here tonight, no sirree. She needed to hold her own if she was going to keep convincing Logan that she was worth his time and attention.

But will he be able to convince Anne? The desire to please her mother overcame all. After all, it had only been Lily and Anne for more than two decades. Her opinion counted for *something.*

Lily felt Sloane watching her as Lily sauntered towards the bar. Usually, Lily welcomed such appraising eyes from men and women alike, but in front of Logan's friends, she didn't want to stick out so easily.

Lily accepted the mason jar Sloane offered her and lifted it in cheers before taking a sip. She sat down, grateful for the weight off her heels. What time was it anyway? There was a big meeting with the execs tomorrow morning and they were going to want to hear about the hotel she and Jeremiah had checked out the day she met Logan. It felt like a lifetime had passed since then.

"They're wonderful, aren't they?" Sloane nodded, the skin around her eyes crinkling. Lily followed her gaze back towards the dance floor, where the woman who had apologized for interrupting was now dancing with Logan. Lily put her drink down and placed a foot on the floor, ready to run and remind the raven which girl Logan *really* belonged to. Instead, she leaned across the bar to get closer to Sloane. "What does it take to be one of them, anyway?"

Sloane placed a hand on top of Lily's and patted it. This was certainly a touchy-feely community. "You havta be willing to follow, darlin'. You havta trust the people around ya to both call out when you're taking the wrong steps, but also trust that they'll catch ya when ya make 'em."

Lily considered this.

Logan had been coming here for years, he had said, and he chose *her* as the woman to bring as his partner. On their *first* date. That was special. She relaxed, hooking her heel back on the rungs of her bar stool. Lily smiled into her drink, watching Logan spin and kick and lift Raven Hair into the air. His hair had fallen out of the mold completely now. He had never looked sexier.

Somebody shoved into Lily's back and her drink sloshed over onto her skirt. Rivulets of Amaretto flowed around sequins.

"Hey." The voice with metallic strength made Lily spin, the liquor almost baptizing those around her. The owner of the inauthentic apology jumped back in time to avoid any splashes. This was the same woman who had been so in control of her movements earlier in the group dance.

Lily recognized the look on her face; it was the smirk Anne had taught *her* *to* use when it was time to show who was boss. It was all in the exaggerated tilt of the head and pursed lips. A snake about to strike. Lily held her drink tighter, but it felt like it'd slip out of her grasp at any point.

"I don't know who you are," this woman whispered loud enough for only Lily to hear. "I don't know what you want with our Logan. But that man has been through so much. He has worked too hard to…" she swallowed, as if it was difficult to share. "Well, it's not my story to tell. But this place has given him nothing but joy. Don't taint this place for him. Logan isn't someone to take advantage of. He's a good guy and—" She took a step forward and narrowed her eyes, spitting out the rest. "You're the type of girl that makes the nice guys finish last."

The girl's partner appeared at her shoulder, almost a full two heads taller. His eyebrows furrowed in apology and he wrapped his arms around her, as if his muscles could hold this jaguar back. He whispered into the wild cat's ear, urging her to calm down. Lily tightened her fist around her drink. *I know where all the strong-ass women are hanging out on Tuesday nights.* After another glare, the woman turned on her heel and charged away. Her partner looked at Lily like his partner had proclaimed everything he was thinking as well and left.

Lily looked around to see who else had witnessed this, but no one seemed to have caught the confrontation. Sloane held out a cloth towel. Lily smiled in gratitude before she grabbed it.

Logan sidled up beside her, sweat glistening against his brow. "I see you've met Maya. Really welcoming." He took the beer Sloane was already holding out for him.

She was glad she wasn't drinking, else she would have spit out the liquid. "Welcoming" is not the word she would have used.

"Oh, perfect!" He took the cloth towel from Lily and wiped his forehead. He stuck it in his back pocket and Lily couldn't help but appreciate the taut back on that man. "She's like a sister to me now. Uriel, her dance partner, actually works with me. That's how I found this place."

Lily threw her arms around Logan's neck and grinned up at him. She hoped Maya was looking. *And damn her for being 'like a sister' to him. More people she needed to convince.* "I didn't know you could dance like that!"

"C'mon, you must have said some idea. Now you know why, when a 1920s swing hat made its way towards me, I just had to rescue it and find the lady to whom it belonged."

Logan rested his hands on Lily's waist and swayed them back and forth against the rhythm. He looked so at ease, but what Maya had said kept Lily from total serenity. The Cromwell Rules said that Lily had to find out his story, quickly, before getting in too deep. One step ahead. *Never follow. Gotta get the scoop on any dirt before you find yourself stuck in mud*, Anne would say. But if she had been leading tonight, they would never have ended up here.

Lily pressed her lips gently against Logan's. Kissing him felt like coming home after a long stay away. She took his hand and squeezed it.

"Teach me some more of your moves."

Get What You Need

As much as she had tried, she hadn't been able to fall asleep. Rehearsing Logan's choreography in her mind's eye had kept her moving all night. He had invited her for the following Tuesday and Lily was determined to show Maya that she was staying, a force to contend with and accept. Though Maya's warning was a hiccup in her evening, she hadn't brought it up to Logan and was glad she hadn't: that was the only thing that may have soured the night, and if Anne had taught her anything, it's that not drawing attention to something was more powerful than doting over it.

Lily tapped her phone's alarm and withdrew her hand under the covers. The billow of the white comforters cradled her sore muscles. The cool sheets tickled her cheek and reminded her of how Logan's gentle kiss woke her when he had parked the car. He whispered something about taking her up to her room, but she'd blown him a kiss and promised to call soon. It was a relief that she had been so tired. She wouldn't have been able to resist otherwise.

She pulled herself out of bed. Her yoga mat lie at the foot of it. She stood with feet flat on the edge of the turquoise mat, the towel from Logan's back pocket hung over the bottom rung of her bed's frame. She was about to spread her arms like she was extending wings when her phone rang. She tiptoed to her night stand, grabbed her phone and, assuming it was Marley, swiped the screen right and gave a chipper "Hello!"

"Where in the world have you been?" Anne's voice was more high-pitched than normal.

Lily piqued her chin and groaned.

"Oh, don't be a brat. You haven't called since you stormed out of the shower. So inappropriate. I spent all evening apologizing—"

"It's over. I'm fine. What do you want, Mother?"

"Can't a mom call her daughter out of worry?"

"Oh, please. You knew I was fine. You called a few times on Sunday and have been silent ever since. You would have called Monday and yesterday if you'd really have been worried."

Anne was silent. A point for Lily!

She hadn't allowed Maya to ruin their night; Anne plunging into her psyche with a cold hand wasn't going to mess up Lily's morning either.

Lily eased into a stretch, pushing her palms down to hold up a plank. She sunk into it, breathing out. The stretch was almost painful, like a taut elastic band about to break.

"I'm sorry," Lily muttered.

Pressing all her weight on her left foot wasn't an option—the knee had swollen more since dancing—, so she lifted it unceremoniously in the air and let all the heaviness sink through her shoulders, down her shaky arms and around her wrists. She imagined Anne's comments sliding down her body's plane.

Anne finally spoke. Her voice was soft, her words slow. "How can you say I don't worry about you? I have worried about you your entire life. It's the whole reason we have the Rules."

"I know. I'm sorry. You're right." *Did she really meant that?* "I should have returned your calls." *She definitely didn't mean that.*

Logan probably always called his mother back.

"Yes, you should have. But. I understand why you left."

Lily rested her left leg and sat on her haunches. She lifted the phone to her ear and widened her eyes.

"You do?"

"Yes, of course I do. You've been going from man to man to man without any real prospects. Seeing all your childhood friends and hearing their stories must have been so upsetting."

Lily threw the phone over her shoulder, hoping it landed on her bed. She wasn't going to listen to this again. Lily stretched again and deepened the plank from her hips to feet. *Maya probably didn't have such a difficult time easing into a Wednesday morning,* Lily thought bitterly. Anne's voice was muffled. She'd keep it there until the beep told her the call was disconnected.

Lily stood. She cupped a hand around her coffee mug and glanced at her phone again. She'd miss Vanessa and Genny's morning visit this time, but she didn't think they'd mind too much: she had left the gladiolus on the balcony railing. Hopefully the wind wasn't going to knock it off.

Anne's voice was getting louder. "—and I'd feel that way, too, if I hadn't met your father when I did. He saved me from spinsterhood. Too bad he didn't tell me about the widowhood later." That was enough. She hated when she brought in this stuff about Dad dying—as if he had *chosen* to leave them like a divorcer would.

Lily flipped over the phone. "You're being macabre. Stop it."

"Come to dinner and spend time with your poor, widowed mother."

"You're doing it again."

"It's not like you offer your time willingly. I have to guilt you into time with me. Pick an evening this week."

She didn't know when Logan would be free next, but obviously it wouldn't be two nights in a row. Some rules *had* to be strictly followed. And it's true: she didn't know if her mom would die as suddenly as her father had. Lily *had* to see Anne while she was still alive and breathing.

"How about tonight?" Lily said.

"Perrrfect!" Anne sang the words. "I'll send Travis out for that Zinfandel you like so much. Wear the outfit that's your favorite nowadays. No yoga pants!"

* * *

"You're here early," Greg said, nodding in her direction. He lifted the messenger bag over his head, set it on the floor and walked to the shared kitchen.

"I sent a code review your way."

"Thanks for making the coffee already. The hotel visit must have lit a fire under you."

Hotel visit or a night of dancing? Memories of Logan's breath on her neck kept her from answering right away.

She swallowed the waves that flowed through her and cleared her throat. "Yeah, they were super receptive. We can totally hook up a demo for RACE by logging into their building automation system. Set off the alarm right after dinner and be back in time for dessert."

"Well, that's good," Greg said. He sat in a wheelie chair and pushed himself off the edge of one of the desks to sit at Lily's side. "We already have huge investors sending in their RSVPs for this party. There's one in particular —a Nicholas from Dove Hospitals— who is on the lookout for an investment opportunity like ours. This is huge." He looked at her and his eyes gleamed. *This* was his baby. And she wanted it as badly as he did; it felt *purposeful* to alert people of danger—both natural and man-made—not just create them in social scenarios and walk away.

"So what do you need from me, boss?"

"You have to schmooze those sharks, especially Nicholas. Work your magic. You've got that killer combination of brains and..." Lily raised her eyebrow, pursed her lips, and bit her laughter as Greg searched for the right words. She loved making him uncomfortable. He had the predictable nerd quality of saying too much, too quickly, digging himself into holes that only nice guys could get out of. He turned red and she put her hands on her hips. She couldn't hold it anymore and burst out laughing.

He hung his head. "Please don't report me for harassment."

She lay a hand on his shoulder and patted a few times. "Only if you give me a raise."

Greg raised an eyebrow. "If you can get this Nicholas guy in *our* boat, I'll give *you* enough money for *two* boats."

Lily thought of Logan. "I don't know, Greg."

"What?" Greg said. She had never told him "no" before—not really. And she had never backed down from an opportunity to "schmooze" a man, even if her mother had forced him onto her. It wasn't the poor rich man's fault, after all. She realized Maya's claim wasn't wrong: she used men to get what she wanted all the time. After a drink, some dinner, and a kiss or two, she won every time, too. How was she going to convince Nicholas that he should invest *and* keep Logan in the picture *and* tell Anne that she thought she had found the man of her dreams but, no, sorry, he's not what the Rules called for? She felt like she was getting in head over heels, but she was Lily freaking Cromwell. Of course she could do this.

Greg leaned down and raised an eyebrow at her. "Lily? Are you in this, or what? I need you."

"Yes," Lily said. "Yes, of course. You can count on me, boss."

Make Connections

The circle drive was well-lit by the heavy bronze sconces attached to poles, making Anne's driveway look like a suburban neighborhood street. Thankfully, there weren't any cars she didn't recognize. It appeared that they would finally have an evening for just the two of them. Maybe, if it were going very well, she could find a way to bring Logan into the conversation.

There was a faint light through the windows to the left of the front door boasting a lion's face larger than the bouncer's from the warehouse yesterday. Lily lifted its jaws and let it fall for a third time. The live-in housekeeper opened it before Lily could lift it for a fourth knock.

Lily stepped into the foyer. The smell of evergreen and violets reminded her of a funeral home at Christmas time. There was a faint smell of roasted duck as well, which made Lily's stomach rumble. It was already past seven and she had only eaten a salad for lunch. Coming to her mother's house for dinner had its perks, and Lily was prepared for a full meal.

Wooden arches led to three different spaces: her dad's old study, a hallway, and the drawing room. Lily slipped out of her coat, letting the housekeeper take it. She called towards the room on the right. "Mother! Where are you?"

Anne's heels clicked as she walked into the drawing room. She stopped, squinting at Lily's forehead.

"Darling, make an appointment with the dermatologist. Your face is doing that thing again." She stepped back. "The jeans are nice! This white sweater hasn't been over worn though? It looks a little tattered here at the bottom."

Lily rolled her eyes. "Hello to you, too."

Anne proceeded without missing a beat. "You won't believe who just walked in."

Anne gestured to her right and a tall man who looked to be in his 50s appeared behind her.

"This is Hugo Bartlett. Hugo, my daughter, Lily."

Lily's heart sank. This wasn't going to be a dinner with just the two of them. This was another set-up. It wasn't beyond her mother to find someone more *mature* for her, but thoughts of Logan's hands on her body made thoughts of sidling up next to Hugo repulsive. She nodded to this man in his crisply pressed navy suit. He transferred his wine glass to his left hand and reached out with his right. Lily shook it. His hair was already more white than black and there were so many wrinkles around his eyes when he smiled, but he looked more gentle than predatory, and she couldn't help but smile back. She knew Anne usually preferred younger men because of the lower chance that they'd die with such short notice, so this Hugo must be raking in the hundred dollar bills.

"Anne, she is as beautiful as you said."

Anne led them to the library. "Isn't she? She's smart, too! A software engineer at IceStorm. She's going to be promoted." Lily stopped herself from doing a double-take. Was that *pride* in her voice?

"Oh, really? I've never had the pleasure of meeting a female engineer before."

The smell of leather and old books reached into Lily's memory and reminded her of many evenings spent reading on her father's lap, wrapped in his embrace, on the big leather couch. Sometimes Anne would lean against her father's arm and they'd sit there, together, laughing at his voices. Anne led them there now. She sat on one end. Lily waited for Hugo to sit next to her mother, but Hugo waited for Lily to sit in the center. When Lily did, Hugo smiled wide and sat next to her. His knees touched Lily's and she moved her knees away so quickly that she knocked them against her mother. The pain was sharp, a reminder that the swelling really needed to go down if she were going to dance again next week.

Anne hissed, "What's the matter with you?"

Lily whispered back, "Your boyfriend is—."

She turned her attention to Hugo and said sweetly, "Hugo, do you mind if I speak with my mother privately, please?"

"My pleasure."

He walked to the bar in front of the cold fireplace and poured drinks for them, as if that was private enough. She needed him out of the house.

Anne kept her eyes on Hugo, but her whisper was for Lily. "We couldn't have talked later?"

"No. We couldn't. Who is this strange man in your house?"

"I should ask you the same thing about that man you were out with the other night."

Lily's thoughts flew to Paolo. "What man?"

"The one I had to hear about from Rose's mother. What an embarrassing moment. He wouldn't stand to acknowledge you *or* pull out your chair? Like, really. I hope you walked out on him immediately after."

Lily's eyes widened.

"Yes, of course I know, Lily Anne," Anne said. "You forget I have eyes all around this city. Especially on you."

If Anne knew the details of Logan's appearance, then it really would be over before it began.

"So, then, according to Rose, what did this man lack... other than manners?"

"She didn't give me physical details. She didn't need to. I trust you will never see him again."

"Yes, right. Of course. Now about this guy in Dad's study—"

"Just give him a chance before you walk out in anger. I heard about him from one of the women at Ashley's shower. She's on the Board at Dove and Hugo is an administrator. I thought you might appreciate it."

"What did you say?"

Anne almost looked wounded. "I know you don't like me 'doing things for you' but I swear, people network like this in the Midwest even, all the time. This was just that networking stuff. Please don't be mad."

Lily threw her arms around her mother. If Lily could talk to Hugo, then she could avoid "getting to know" that guy Greg wanted her to schmooze and Logan would be safe and Maya would be wrong.

Anne patted her shoulder. "Show me you still know how to play the game." When Lily lifted her head, she could see her mother wasn't entirely serious. She believed in Lily enough to know Lily could play the game beyond dating. There was a reason she was on the brink of a promotion. Code was her tool, but cracking social codes was her gift.

Though she had been looking forward to a quiet evening, she didn't mind working overtime. Besides, if Hugo was hoping to impress Anne, Lily already had the advantage.

"Alright. Let's go."

The women stood up and walked to Hugo. Anne grinned and slipped her hands around Lily's arm. Hugo handed each of them a glass and raised his own.

Lily lifted it, winked, and said, "To an evening of great fun."

* * *

"So how long have you been at IceStorm?" Hugo asked as he passed the russet potatoes.

"Long enough to know it's an honor to work there, sir," Lily said, as she passed the bowl on. She didn't need Anne telling her later that potatoes are for the guests—not for her hips. She did place a healthy serving of vegetables on her plate. She could feel Anne's approval.

"Why haven't other hospitals jumped all over this yet?"

"Product testing happens when disasters happen—or when simulations of disasters occur. As you can imagine, it's difficult to convince a hospital full of patients that a drill would go off without a hitch when removing patients from their rooms could be potentially fatal," Lily said. "So we needed to find a market that wouldn't be quite as tumultuous. A hotel came to mind. But to get hospitals on board, we need major players within the hospitals at the hotel demo party."

She added, in case he still wasn't satisfied, "We *will* know more once tornadoes start hitting the Midwest."

"That makes sense, but you didn't answer my question." He coughed, then gulped some water.

"It's enough to say that others aren't jumping on just yet because we *want* Dove Hospitals to be the first in on it. If you get to boast RACE first, then you present yourself as the cutting-edge leader in the business that keeps people safe, no matter what."

He nodded. "That would be nice. We haven't had something to distinguish us as leaders in the field in a good while." He cut the sirloin on his plate. "What do you love about Dove in particular?"

Lily had been ready for this question. "It's not about what *we* love about you. It's about how much *you* love your patients and how much we love *that*."

Hugo chuckled and nodded towards Anne. "You've got a bright one there, Annie."

Lily sucked in her breath. Her mother never let *anyone* speak to her in nicknames. But her mother sat there, melting like the butter on the roll Lily *was* allowing herself to enjoy. Probably the reason she'd been breaking out on her face lately.

Lily looked from her mother to Hugo and back again.

"How do you two know each other again?" Lily asked.

Her mother blushed. "That's not so important right now. What is important is that you two are getting along and I can breathe a little easier. I was so worried you wouldn't think Hugo a suitable suitor for you."

Lily dropped her fork with a clang. "What?"

Anne's laugh bounced off the walls of the dark dining room and it fell flat in front of Lily, who was still trying to steady her hand.

Her mother patted her hand and said, "Relax, darling, not everyone is for you."

Hugo chuckled as well, the twinkle in his eye such a relief to Lily.

Maybe if Anne had been so worried about Lily's opinion—and Lily accepted *Hugo*—then Anne would be more willing to meet Logan. The squeeze around her heart lessened and she bit into her bread. She thought of her mom, dad, and herself as a young girl on the leather couch. Yes. Logan would be here for a family dinner sooner than she ever could have hoped, and they could be a family, all four of them.

And she would finally feel whole again.

Saturday Mornings Are Sacred;
Protect Them

The rink must have downsized. It had appeared longer, wider, and entirely less crowded when her father would bring her here as a young girl. Now, it seemed limiting. Or maybe there were more people here than she was used to seeing on a second date. Usually, she'd have suggested a more intimate location - like box seats at the theatre. Logan was a man who embraced his inner child, however, so Lily decided that he should get to see a snippet of her childhood, too.

Looking at it now, however, made her second-guess: What if Logan preferred women who played a damsel in distress? She could pretend to have weak ankles. No. There's no way she could make herself fall on skates; she'd *actually* hurt herself by feigning incompetence. She sucked in her breath, pulled her shoulders back, and walked towards the rink.

She spotted him sitting cross legged on a wooden bench sprinkled by wet snowflakes. His head was bowed, as if he were praying. Or texting. If he were like the guys she normally dated, the text was usually a Plan B if the date with Lily didn't work out. She had never blamed them; her Plan B would already have been planned for the evening. But with Logan, she'd care if he casually dated someone else after her. She wanted to be his entree, not his appetizer.

How Logan's butt wasn't freezing was beyond Lily's imagination. Or not. Maybe those long-johns were tight enough to hug him in all the snug places. Good thing Logan couldn't read her thoughts. Yet.

She stepped directly in front of him, lifted her right hand in greeting, but forgot that it was the same hand holding the skates' laces and the hard shoes hit Lily's cheek. She cursed softly into the boots and tried to play off the lack of grace as an adorable snafu.

He hadn't noticed the klutzy move, but her groan had been enough to get Logan's attention.

His eyes snapped up and rested on hers. "Oh, wow," Logan breathed out. "You're wearing *that*?"

"Well, I—" Lily cleared her throat. She had spent close to an hour trying and re-trying on different vests and long-sleeves and jeans or just leggings… She pulled at the strings of her mini-sequined tunic. It had shimmered when it caught the light in the boutique, so Lily had purchased it right away.

Logan was looking below her chin and heat rose up, dancing along the tiny hairs of her neck. The side of his lips lifted. "You didn't think of anybody else, did you, girl? Everything will melt once you touch the ice."

"Then they should have stayed inside today." The response was quick, but it didn't reveal her true feelings. Though she wanted the attention, she didn't want skimpy clothing to be a reason why Logan thought less of her. She waited for more; then, she'd know how to respond.

"At least we won't be trampled when we fall," Logan pointed out. "Your sparkles will ensure everyone sees you."

Lily scowled and Logan threw his head back in laughter. He thrust his arm in a crooked circle towards her. Lily balanced her way to him and clasped her hand around his wrist.

"How's your wrist?" he patted her hand.

"It's okay." And it really was. "My knee is a little more worrisome, but the swelling is going down."

"What happened to your knee?"

"Ah, I fell onto a sidewalk's curb the other day. Nothing tragic. I popped some painkillers and I'll ice it later. No worries." She didn't mention that she had a hard time sleeping yesterday, what with committing Hugo's advice to her memory and trying not to move her knee too quickly one way or the other.

"Well, I'll make sure you're near me at all times." Logan patted her hand.

"And just think," Lily quipped, "you can have your very own disco ball for the day."

He grinned wider and motioned towards the space next to him on the bench. She started taking off her boots and replacing them with the ice skates.

The silence between them was loud and comfortable all at once, like when she'd sit in the library and hear the rustle of her father turning newspaper pages. The yells and laughter of children on the ice made her tie the laces faster. She couldn't ignore the rush and sudden confirmation that she had made the right choice in inviting him here today. Logan extended his hand and she clasped onto him. He led them onto the busy ice.

"This might sound random—and I don't want you to take this the wrong way—but I'm so glad you're the type of girl who can laugh at herself." Logan said it like he was trying on every word like a new suit. It sounded as if he liked how he looked in it.

Giving a guy something to laugh at was *not* listed anywhere in The Cromwell Rules, but Lily tucked that compliment in the mental folder labeled "Ways to Make Logan Smile."

She hadn't skated for years. The daily training sessions with a private figure skating coach ended when she began high school. Her mother had promised it would grant her poise, confidence, and balance. For the most part, Anne had been right.

One foot slid onto the ice and then the next. Familiar movements emboldened her leg muscles. Lily was grateful for the decade of practice as she extended her arms, creating a figure skating show for Logan. To show off, she practiced the choreography he had taught her earlier that week. She didn't need to look back to feel his eyes following her body. She wished she could blame the weakening of her knees on her injury.

She knew the deep satisfaction of being watched by the man she wanted to impress would eventually distract her, so she tried to forget he was there. This led to a keen observation of the people on the ice, especially the children. It didn't take long to spot the four year-old girl holding her father's hand. He scooped her up from behind, spun her around, and placed her back down with ease.

She skated back towards Logan and, when she was right next to him, slid her hand into Logan's pocket and squeezed his gloved hand. He squeezed back, but didn't turn towards her. He was looking in the same direction she had been. As Lily and Logan glided around the rink, Lily watched snowflakes fall into Logan's blonde tresses like travelers finding a warm bed into which they could finally melt. When her gaze fell from his hair to his jawline to his smile, Logan locked eyes with her and she could feel herself melting into his blue eyes.

Lily forced her legs to slow down as her mind raced. Their soft laughter sprinkled itself around them like embers from a pulsing fire. She suddenly couldn't resist. She gripped his hand and pulled him towards her.

"Logan," she called, though a whisper would have sufficed.

He looked around to ensure no one would be interrupted by a sudden stop and skid to a pause, clearly intrigued.

She swallowed. "Why is someone who is clearly not a *player* interested in someone like me, who could be so full of dating drama?"

Logan asked, "Well, *are* you full of 'dating drama'?"

Lily shook her head vigorously, but then stopped herself. The dating game was *built* on bluffing, but she couldn't lie to this man. She shrugged. "I guess I'm not around long enough to see the havoc I create. When it starts getting complicated, I bounce. It's kind of my M.O."

"If that's true," Logan chuckled, "then I'm jealous of all the guys who get to watch you leave."

Lily's jaw dropped and she slapped him playfully. She was used to men flirting suggestively, but because she never expected it from Logan himself, she was shocked and felt she needed to defend her honor.

If laughter threw confetti, then there was a party in his eyes.

"Let me finish. I bet these men who can't hold on to you keep wondering what it is they didn't have to make you stay." He let go of Lily's hands and pushed himself away from her, gliding backwards. "Are you always going to interrupt my silver lines?"

Lily felt her heart tug at Logan's suggestion of an "always." She tilted her head, waiting for him to go on.

"The point is - you might be used to walking away. But if the guys you keep going through don't have what it takes to keep you around, then maybe I'm different enough to keep you walking—er, skating—towards me."

His hair blew in the wind he created, but he didn't see that he was heading straight for the little girl's father, and Lily noticed it a second too late.

"Logan!" Lily cried.

Logan pummeled into the man whose daughter was waiting for another lift.

Lily sprinted, preparing herself to see broken bones and ready to yell for medical attention.

Logan was on his knees, apologizing profusely for his carelessness, and asking if there was any way he could help. The father pushed himself up using the rink's boards to standing position and wiped ice chips from his jeans.

"No, no," Lily heard the little girl's father assure Logan as she approached. "I'm just glad you ran into me instead of my kid." Then, he passed a knowing glance as he looked from Logan to Lily. "I remember being blind and in love, too. It brought me this one," the man added as he gestured to his daughter, smiling affectionately as he hoisted her on his hip.

Logan lost his balance. Lily reached out, but touched only the sleeve of his tan workman's jacket to watch Logan fall to the ice again.

"Goodness!" she said, bending over him.

"See?" Logan said in a low voice. "You're practically throwing yourself at me."

Mumbling into his shoulder, Lily said. "You're not exactly throwing me off."

They balanced to standing position together. He tightened his grip around her, and she sunk into him. It was like the release after a long work day. Tension escaped her shoulders with every extra squeeze. Lily's skates slid backwards as her knees weakened, and Logan caught her, kissing her cheek as if pressing too hard would break her. Though she had always wanted to be seen as a strong woman who could handle anything, Lily didn't mind thawing within Logan. She felt that, somehow, he would be able to catch all of her, even the parts Anne told her she had to keep together all these years.

Lily shook her head, grin spreading wider on her lips, and she blew him a kiss as she left his side and beckoned him on with curved fingers. She turned with her back to him and pumped her arms in rhythm with her legs. She didn't have to wonder if he was going to follow. She likened the feeling to magnetic connections: nothing, nothing, then an attraction all at once.

* * *

She breathed out, satisfied.

"I did it! I win!" Lily bellowed triumphantly. She had passed the most people in the quickest time—without causing anyone to fall. Her heart pounded and her eyes stung from the cold, but the rise in her chest meant more than winning the race—it meant being one step closer to what she hoped would come next.

Lily yelled, "I get to shower first!"

Logan threw his hat on the ice in faux anger. "Ah, you got lucky. You won't get my honey with that victory. Should have sabotaged the game."

Lily shrugged as she walked away from him, leading him towards the edge of Central Park where her apartment building stood, a formidable reminder of her father's wealth and the status that her mother expected Lily to maintain. Lily thought of Logan's little red Toyota. She turned her back on the building and walked backwards.

"You can soothe your ego while I make us a batch of hot cocoa," she said. She turned back around. "Do you like marshmallows?" she asked over her shoulder.

She enjoyed hearing the shuffle of his pants as he caught up to her. "Only if they're held up by whipped cream."

"I think I can make that happen. You just have to be able to hold me up later."

Logan stopped in place. At his reaction, giggles bubbled to the surface.

"Because I haven't skated in such a long time and I'll be *tired*. You really will have to hold me up if I'm expected to shave peppermint and chant some magic incantations around your cocoa, too."

Logan shook his head and passed his hand to tug in front of his pants. Lily smiled to herself.

With her mittened hand, Lily clasped Logan's palm and led them along in silence down the paths where other couples were also passing. If this were a date with anyone else, she'd be comparing her happiness to that of other women. If a woman was laughing more than Lily was at the moment, she'd judge her own date null and void; Anne had always said that Lily ought to be the happiest woman in the room. Lily could never find the logic smart enough to refute that statement, so she accepted it as truth. But now she understood that a woman could be unsmiling in quiet anticipation, looking forward to the moment when there was no one else to compare herself to. It'd be just her and Logan, and hot water.

Lots of hot water.

Never Settle

The apartment door yawned open and soft lights from the hallway eased the darkness. Lily scurried inside, peeling off her soaked-through poncho and letting it fall to the floor. She stepped over it and flipped on the lightswitch to see Logan shrugging out of his coat.

Anne would say something about moving too fast, or question how she would ever gain the respect of a decent man, but Lily didn't need more evidence that Logan was decent. He danced in the street. He teased her. He went ice skating and fell and didn't let a bruised ego sour their afternoon. He apologized when he was wrong.

She blinked her eyes against the bright lights and dimmed them. Before her courage evaporated and she changed her mind, Lily stood in front of Logan and fumbled with the buttons on his plaid long-sleeve. The heat trapped within her chest wasn't quite reaching her fingertips; her numb fingers meant the shirt was staying very much on. Giving up on the stubborn clasps, she tried to pull at Logan's sleeves, but huffed away when he didn't cooperate; even if it had been going well, Logan's raised eyebrow was enough to stop her from continuing. *Okay. So it's going well, but not that well.*

She picked up her poncho and hung it on the coat rack on her way to the living room.

Slow down, Lily warned herself, turning casually to the fireplace to switch the electric flames on. Anne always had to remind her daughter not to come on too strongly, and she was right to, seeing as it took all of Lily's energy to keep facing the electric fireplace rather than push Logan on the couch and have her way with him. The embroidery on Paolo's abandoned handkerchief rested on the mantle and winked at her. *Paolo who?* He seemed like a distant memory compared to how badly Lily wanted things to work out with Logan. Paolo had been a passing snack, a practice run, a quick pit stop in preparation for game day.

Truth be told, the "pre-emptive" intimacy would help embolden Lily when it was time to introduce Logan to her mother. She was able to dump any man for any reason, but the ones she connected with on a different level took a little longer to forget. And if Logan hugged her in a way that made her want so much more, to forget him would take the longest, and she didn't need that kind of emotion weighing her down. It'd be easier to give him what they both wanted, soon.

She was untying her boots when she heard him whisper. "Oh, wow."

Lily's heart swelled at his appraisal and turned to see where he was pointing. She moved the boots to the side and kept her hands in front of the fire. She knew he'd be able to hear the smile in her voice.

"My favorite view of the city is from that bay window. It's on the west side, so you can imagine the sunsets. Maybe you'll be here long enough to see it." *I hope so.* He tread across the white rug that wrapped around her favorite grey couch and bold red armchair.

"How high are we?" Logan asked.

"Three floors."

He nodded and kept looking out while he stripped himself of the plaid fleece. She scanned him as if she were memorizing the scene for a future sketch. Underneath he had on a deep blue sweater. It had been a good choice; his muscles were well-defined in the tight material. The sweater's color brought out the turquoise in his eyes. Or maybe it was his jaw that was his stand-out feature? It was set so confidently, yet his lips stretched with ease when Lily smiled at him. He sat on the bench, elbow resting on one knee, the other leg bent at ease.

She cleared her throat and, making her voice as light as possible, said, "So-o-o, Logan."

Logan lifted an eyebrow and smirked.

Too excited. Damn it. Why is this so hard? She tried again. Firmer this time.

"Though I won the race fair and square, I am willing to compromise. Would you like the hot cocoa now, or after I take my shower?" She tried to make it sound like she was asking if he took one lumps of sugar or two. "I'll start the water while you decide."

Logan's voice travelled down the hallway after her. "The shower might be good. There's something about the image of Lily Cromwell serving me hot chocolate after I'm wrapped up in a robe, scrubbed squeaky-clean...."

Lily stopped and spun around. "Who said anything about a robe?" she called.

She heard Logan chuckle and shift in his seat. She switched on the bathroom fan and made sure the lights were only lit in the shower stall. Did Logan prefer hot, hot water or lukewarm? Oh, the things she couldn't wait to learn. She turned the control all the way to the left, closing the door gently.

Lily tugged at her tank top to reveal a healthy bust and hoped her hair looked ruffled enough to appear naturally disheveled.

Washing her hands filled the air with peppermint and the scent awakened her. This was *right*. They might not even get to the hot chocolate if she executed this shower plan successfully—and after she'd lay wrapped up in his arms, she'd explain the intricacies of Anne Cromwell and why they had to be careful. She knew he'd understand and, after some time, she would introduce him to Anne and Anne would understand and voila! They'd live happily ever after and...

He knocked on the bathroom door. Logan stepped in and wrapped an arm around Lily's waist, whispering in her ear as he passed. "I decided I didn't want the hot chocolate if there was something sweeter hiding in here."

"I don't blame you. My soaps and lotions are—" Lily sucked in a breath as Logan's lips found hers, crashing into them like waves might push one's feet in to the shore: with grace and power, where escape feels nearly impossible. Lily straightened her back so her hips pressed into his, arms clasped around his torso. She wished he'd bury her beneath and within him. So *this* is what she had been missing all this time.

His hands were stronger than she had expected. His palm covered her hip, pulling her tighter against him. She stumbled forward, knees suddenly weak.

"Careful," he whispered into her ear. His hot breath tingled against her damp skin already matted from the rising steam.

She giggled. "I didn't do it on purpose. I promise."

He wrapped his arms tightly around her, like she'd flutter away from him if he didn't. He disconnected in time for her to steal a deep, shaky breath in. His hands lowered, wandering beneath her shirt, fingertips caressing the clasp of her bra. His nose nudged her hair out of the way, and his lips found her bare neck. The pinch of skin he bit sent shivers down Lily's spine. His thumb pressed against her spine and the moan escaped her before she could stop it.

Lily thought she heard a clasp open and shut, but attributed it to the water splashing against the wall, like Logan was pressing her into him...

Logan sighed in pleasure as Lily pressed herself closer against him. The sound of pleasing him opened a door in Lily that she hadn't realized was closed. It was as if thousands of wings had been released, relieved to fly free as though they had been fluttering against a cage all this time, ignored and wished away. Lily sunk into Logan's kiss, relieved that she didn't have to protect herself anymore. This man would not hurt her—of this she was sure. He teased her and intrigued her and made her want more, but he would never leave her because of some whim or woman that briefly caught his attention. He wasn't like anybody else. He didn't have to follow rules to be a man— he just was one. Logan pulled away, but Lily tightened her arms around his neck. She wanted this moment to last forever.

"Lily!" her mother's voice rang out. The tin was unmistakable. Lily threw her arms off Logan like he was a broken toy no longer available for play.

Logan's eyes grew wide, but sharpened as if to follow Lily's signal. Stiletto heels heralded a sharp, precise march through her apartment.

"I know you're here! Your poncho is *soaked* - what were you doing? Saturdays are your sacred days. That's why I'm here to visit! Thought we could talk about Hugo some more. Where *are* you?"

Logan made an exaggerated sign of the cross and Lily bit back a panicked giggle. This was not how Lily wanted to introduce Logan to her mother. To convince Anne that Logan was the one who was going to stay—the one who pulled her in and kept her there —Anne could not find Logan in a steamy shower with her. She'd get the wrong impression, compartmentalizing him as a one-night stand rather than a vow to love 'til death do them part.

Anne was walking down more briskly now, her cantor echoing down the halls.

"Lean over the toilet bowl," Lily hissed.

Logan took a step back. "What?"

"Pretend you're fixing something! Please!" She knew she must have looked like a little sister begging her older brother for attention: desperate and, consequently, a complete turn-off. She hadn't had enough time to explain the essence of her mother to Logan and now she feared the worst. Anne pulled open the door and steam escaped through the door as quickly as Lily's resolve. Though condensation was climbing onto the mirror, Lily felt her own temperature drop from 90 to 2.

"Well. I shouldn't be surprised that you're ignoring your mother's calls with some..."

"Mom! No, no. This isn't what you think. This is Logan West, one of our new maintenance guys. He's here checking a leaky toilet and tricky shower head." Lily shut the water off. She turned towards her mother. "But it's all fixed now! He was just on his way out."

Lily avoided eye contact with her mother. Logan was smart. He would figure out what was going on.

"In fact," Lily said to Logan, "I appreciate that my requests are taken seriously. The fact remains, however, you must never put yourself in a situation where a mother may... misinterpret... your intentions, despite the resident's ignorance to do otherwise." She hoped the more deliberate articulation would reveal her game, "Do - you - understand?" She hoped she was getting this right.

"Oh?" Logan looked at her like she had gone insane. "I am so sorry, Miss—" He hesitated. Goodness, did she even tell him her last name? His improv was awful.

"Cromwell. Miss Cromwell." Whoa, she sounded legitimate. Might as well keep going, maternal audience in mind. She directed further: "Please write that name on a new work order for someone else to complete at their earliest convenience." *Logan really can pull off the handyman look.* She'd have to tell him that later. Instead, she waited hungrily for Logan's response.

Logan's lips stayed still, but his eyes darkened. *What a hunk*, Lily mused. Oh, how they would laugh when they talked about this later, cuddled in bed with big spoons dipped in ice cream.

But any hope of him understanding her plan melted when she heard Logan's voice dripping in contempt.

"Of course, Miss Cromwell. It won't happen again." He pivoted and left the bathroom.

Anne followed him out. "Well, that's a relief. Will you be looking at her heat too, Mr. West?" she called after him.

Logan spun and his eyes reflected ice. His voice was still. "Not today, ma'am. Probably not tomorrow, either."

"I understand. Service staff needs a day off on Sundays. First thing Monday morning, then."

Logan continued down the hallway. "Ms. Cromwell will need to call someone else."

"Mom, I'll be right back," Lily panicked. "I need to talk to Lo—Mr. West."

"Very good, dear."

Lily followed after Logan. "Logan," Lily said, "please wait. I need to explain."

"I knew you were a new type of girl I was getting myself into, but this is too much, Lily. I know I'm not the type of guy you want to show off to Mommy, but a little respect surely wouldn't be beyond the realm of your ability."

"Maintenance men deserve respect! I gave that to you!"

Logan lifted an eyebrow. "Do you hear yourself right now? Let's be real. We wouldn't have worked together anyway. We're two very different kinds of people. This was fun while it lasted, but it's time for me to go."

Lily grabbed his hand. "You don't mean that." She searched his eyes. "You can't mean that. I can explain everything. Please."

"But I don't want you to." Logan leaned his forehead against hers. She wished she could freeze him here forever. He whispered, "Doing the right thing never requires an explanation." He kissed her cheek and walked away.

Lily didn't know what to say. She watched him leave. It looked so easy for him to do, like a wave that buried her deeper and then retreated. She felt frozen into place, Logan's words drilling a hole deep inside her.

Lily walked, stunned, into the living room, trying to ignore the pounding in her right lobe. Anne Cromwell was sitting with a glass of wine.

"Very good, dear. Next time, don't feel the need to say 'Please.' It lessens your demand into a suggestion. Good parents don't do it and neither should you." It was difficult to hear Anne's words over the hard beating of Lily's heart. *Where is this panic coming from?* Surely Logan understood that Lily was only playing. It's what she did - all her relationships were games, and this was basically role play. She thought Logan realized that.

She forced herself to listen to Anne. "Hugo enjoyed your company. It was nice to see you back to your charming self instead of that… angry woman at Ashley's shower. Does next Friday still work for our shopping date? We need to find you a dress to that IceStorm party you're throwing. Hugo is so excited to be your guest of honor. That was a magnificent move."

"Good. Yes. Thank you." Lily swallowed the lump in her throat.

"Wonderful." Anne stepped through Lily's doorway. "Oh, and Lily Pad?"

Lily lifted her head and hugged her arms to herself. "Yes?"

"Make sure you don't find yourself in a steamy bathroom with a maintenance man. If he's anything like the man who just walked out, it'd be hard to explain to someone that he was *just* your handyman. That would be something. You really would have lost your mind then." Anne laughed at her own joke. The sound broke Lily of her stupor.

"Why would that be a sign that I had lost my mind?" she snapped.

"Well, dear, because that would suggest that my daughter was *settling*, and that is antithetical to The Rules. The Rules put you on top so you can be with the one's at the top—*not* a common employee."

"But why not, Mother?"

Anne lifted her eyebrows so high that Lily struggled to maintain her stance. She repeated her question. "Why would it be a problem?"

"Lily Cromwell, you deserve better than someone who follows orders. You deserve someone who makes the calls, not answers them. Someone who… oh, I don't know. Someone who choreographs a dance instead of learning it in a class full of fools."

The comparison to dance landed too close to home. Though Lily nodded in faux agreement, her veins ran with steaming blood only her mother could boil. Anne needed to leave. The last thing Lily wanted was for Anne to see her crying. Few things were more demeaning than crying in front of someone who wouldn't tolerate your sadness.

Lily picked up a pillow from her couch, walked to the window and hugged the cushion to herself. She attributed the gnawing feeling to hunger pains, and not the lingering sting of Logan's leaving.

Don't Apologize for Who You Are

L ily opened and closed her blinds, a Morse code S.O.S. for those walking along the edge of Central Park. Even though it was much too cold, she wanted to throw open the window and ask how normal people handled this frustration. How was Logan not responding to her texts? She reread her latest attempt: "Hungry? We can order some Mexican. I still owe you a night." *I can be your hot tamale.* Pathetic. She held the 'delete' key and shut off the phone, throwing it onto her bed.

She didn't want to doubt her initial judgment of Logan's easy-going character, but surely he was being a little dramatic by icing her out with the silent treatment. Apologizing for her behavior was out of the question: he should have waited and understood, instead of jumping to rash conclusions. Anne was right about this one: *Don't apologize for who you are. If you tell people how it is and they don't like it, that's their problem, not yours.* But part of her did feel bad for placing him in such an awkward position. *But!* If he had played along, she wouldn't be here, alone, waiting, wondering if he'd ever call back. Anne hadn't met someone Lily was actually interested in since high school—and that didn't end well. The boy she had really fallen for had been alone at Prom, and she'd been hiding tears with a grin with the Prom King. Lily hadn't wanted her mother to meet Logan under such impromptu circumstances lest she ruin that, too. But it was only natural: where Anne went, chaos followed. If she'd had time to explain it all, Logan would still be here. The worst part was that Maya was right.

But oh, Logan would have dressed up so well at a real Cromwell House dinner. He'd have charmed her mother, had great conversation with Hugo, and even been genuinely kind to the wait staff. After all these years of dad being gone, the house would have felt complete. The void created after her father's death would have been put to rest with new relationships. She even noticed how badly she wanted Hugo there.

This ever-present avoidance—and fear—of loss was what Anne had mentioned at the inception of the Rules, wasn't it? *Live by these and you won't be heartbroken a day in your life.* Too bad Anne hadn't mentioned anything about being alone most of her life be*cause* of the Rules' restrictions.

She trudged into her bathroom. She let the make-up remover wipe away both the mask she painted and to push down the rising worry she felt. What if Mom was wrong? What if apologizing to Logan *was* the right thing to do? It couldn't be a show of weakness to do something that felt so difficult. As the wipe floated down into the wastebasket, however, so did Lily's hope for Logan's understanding. She didn't want to feel like this, as if her insides were the slime on an expired piece of fruit.

She turned from her neatly decorated bathroom and switched off the light. She sashayed to the fleece robe hanging unceremoniously from her bedroom chair and wrapped it around her, hoping the play of confidence would find its way back into her veins. When the rouse didn't stick, Lily tread to her vanity, the only lighting in the room, and sat on the rounded ottoman. She slid open the drawer that contained her small journal.

She opened to a clean page, clicked the pen, leaned against her vanity, and began to write:

Logan walked out. But that makes it sound like he had been around for a long time. He wasn't; not really… just long enough to make a difference. I understand why he left though; I would have done the same. How insulted I would be if I was asked—no, commanded—to act like a janitor just to help someone save face?

She put her pen down and rubbed her palms up and down her face, as if scrubbing off the memory. Lily sat back into her chair, crossed her legs and pulled the journal onto her lap.

In hindsight, Logan totally would have been able to finagle his way around Anne's prejudices—because that's what they are, let's be real. Maybe he would have thought of the janitor shtick himself if I had just waited an extra second.

I let Anne under my skin and I ruined the best thing that's happened to me the last couple years—besides IceStorm, of course (I'm a boss at that).

Lily reached over to write on a post-in note: *Call Hugo to set up a coffee date* and returned to her journal.

What have the Rules been good for, anyway, other than getting free meals out of unsuspecting millionaires? It's been fun, but it hasn't fulfilled me. Nothing has, really. Logan found the thing I'd been hiding without realizing I was hiding it. But I glimpsed it. I felt it. Anything after this will fall flat.

The Rules need to be retired.

Right after I get him back.

Game on.

She scratched out the last two words, then re-wrote them, then scratched them out again. The scratches looked like the jagged rocks of a high peak. It made her think that if she were a mountaintop, she'd be the eroded side, made harsh by the relentless winds of her mother's warnings. Instead of being made hard by her circumstances, however, Lily had done it to herself.

She wasn't looking for an upper hand with Logan. To be held *in* his hand would be enough. Lily had to win this man's heart, if only to find out what was hidden in her own.

Logan: Bad Dog

Heat crawled up his neck. It was only twenty degrees in the Toyota, but Logan threw off his coat and took off his flannel. He hit the steering wheel. Stupid, stupid, stupid. As much as he tried to resist it, his memory of Katie's voice rang with "told ya so" confidence: "She's out of your league, brother. You'll get one or two dates, but that's it. Sorry to say it, Logan, but a girl like that doesn't take a guy like you to see her mother." So as much as he didn't want to go home, he certainly couldn't go to Frankie's. Katie would be working, and there was nothing that would make this moment more humiliating than feeling Katie's pity, especially since she happened to be right this time.

He started the car and let his thoughts be the GPS on his way home. He hadn't thought much about meeting Lily's parents—it was still so early—but he had wondered. If that tight-lipped broad was in the running for mother-in-law, though, he'd pass. There hadn't been any pictures of her around her apartment, a stark contrast to his own photos of him with Katie and their parents, or of him with Maya and the rest of the dance community. But the way Lily made herself so submissive when Lily was so not the submitting type, well, he'd heard a mother can make her child do that.

If Lily had just been honest, Logan would have used all his charm and won Lily's mother over. But then Lily had such a rich, prissy idea, telling him to lean over to fix the toilet. She spent the whole morning holding his hand and, later, essentially throwing herself at him, just to have it all come to a screeching halt when a little adversity walks in? That was not the woman he had loved spending his time with... the one who tripped in snow and chased city buses. That woman got up and made it happen her way anyway. This one was timid. Not *Lily*.

He tried to think reasonably: Lily's mother's opinion obviously meant a lot to her if Lily had disregarded him so quickly and had so easily cast him aside. Lily had mentioned those Rules the other night at Burkette's, but she had scoffed at them—not revered them. She had held onto her own stance with conviction, like a spring leaf in a summer storm: like the idea that carbs are good, not evil. It was so refreshing to be with a woman who knew how to be a lady, but didn't let decorum run her entire personality. Her mother's rules had seemed a guideline at best, not law.

The worst part had been Lily's tone. Eyes were the window to the soul or whatever, but he hadn't wanted to look up when her tone so clearly said, "Sit. Stay. Bad dog."

And if he really was a bad dog, he certainly didn't want to stay. He wanted out, and now he had a way. His desire for escape was tempting him to hit the nearest exit out of the city, but he steered his car under the opening garage doors.

He put the car in park and rubbed his eyes. He had only spent a few days with Lily, so it bothered him that this was bothering him so much. Was it because he felt like he had been played the fool?

He really was the seasonal meal. He'd felt so specially ordered, but then sent away after only a few hesitant bites.

If Lily didn't want him, he would be fine. He had dealt with disappointment before. He just needed time, and maybe a strong drink. He opened the lid of the center console and dropped his phone into the dark. If Lily wanted to play, she'd have to find a different dog.

Logan: Fired

The hard knocks were muted by the Yellowcard blaring in his air pods. It helped him focus on his research. He clicked over to the portfolios and included his notes for tomorrow's meeting.

The pounding on the door grew louder - enough to push Logan from the desk with a diffuse of his eyes and a left-handed rearrangement of his pajama pants. Logan had barely swung the door ajar when his colleague and best friend Uriel stormed through.

"Where the hell have you been?" Uriel said.

"Well, hello, to you, too." Logan shut the door, then leaned against it. "What do you mean where the hell have I been? I've been working."

"I've been calling since nine this morning. Where's your phone?"

"In my car's console. Off."

"This isn't the early 2000s where you can get away with not answering your cell phone, dude. It's only making you look worse."

"Worse?"

Uriel paused. "You really don't know, do you?"

Now he couldn't stop the ire from entering his voice. "Know *what*?"

"The firm thinks you purposely sabotaged them and then ditched."

"Ditched? I took a sick day. That's hardly ditching."

"...after the market closed for the day on Friday. And it opened with most of your portfolio plummeting."

Logan cut him off. "Is Barbara being dramatic again?"

"Barbara is actually saving your ass. She keeps saying you wouldn't have the heart. But the fact is that the market opened on Friday with most of your portfolio plummeting. You couldn't have planned it any better. I just wish you would have told me; I had no idea you had such a vendetta against the guys."

"What? Uriel, no. I didn't plan to nosedive any of the company's investments. That would have totally screwed me in the process of screwing the company. That wouldn't make sense."

Logan sat at his desk. Uriel sat on the couch across from him.

"Well it certainly looks that way, man. And you couldn't even pick up your phone to tell anyone anything different."

Logan cursed the phone sitting in his car's console and rebuked Lily as well. The phone was in there because of her bullshit role-play. Screw the fake maintenance man idea. He was going to lose his *real job* over this? *No way.*

Uriel leaned forward, elbows on his knees. "Did they raise your risk limit a month or so ago?"

Logan nodded. Within the last few months, he had been recognized for his dedication and contribution to the firm's success by being handed control over almost an entire quarter of the firm's capital - over five million dollars in power. In fact, it was the combination of this promotion and his growing relationship with Lily that had made the last few days especially exhilarating.

He tried to keep his voice even. "Yes, they did give me greater authority over the company's portfolio. But I always research so heavily into the prospects before I make my moves, so the fact that they all plummeted this morning is actually quite the insult. Is *anyone* questioning what else would have made the stocks plunge besides my own lack of good will?" He could feel the rising growl in the back of his throat. He always gave others the benefit of the doubt, but when it was time to receive the same grace in return...

Logan watched Uriel pick up the small metallic planet that was resting on Logan's coffee table. Uriel's toss up into the air and careful catching on its way down made Logan feel the gravity of his situation. If the company doubted his loyalty after one day, how the heck was he going to explain what had gone wrong? The markets were stable today, and he was always careful to diversify his choices.

Uriel's voice interrupted Logan's thoughts. "Sorry, man. It's not looking good. Ben and Yoshi looked over your choices and noticed that, although you did diversify, there is nothing ostensible about what went wrong. You need to talk to Jenny, and fast." Jenny was the CEO of Logan's firm and one of the most no-nonsense people he'd ever met; it's what made her a great boss, but also hella intimidating if it meant his job was on the line. "Did you check your e-mail? Maybe there's some clue in there so you know what to expect on Monday."

Logan appreciated Uriel's sense of practical tranquility with Logan's own anxiety on the rise. *If only I could have Lily's cool,* Logan mused. *Or at least call her and borrow some. She would know what to do.* His mom always reminded him not to let pride get in the way of asking for help, so maybe this could be his excuse to call her. The possibility was enough to buoy his spirits.

Logan logged in to his work's email system expecting a list of urgently marked messages. Instead, he found just one still-bolded messaged entitled, "Investigation Pending." Logan's heart rate increased. He could feel Uriel's presence behind his shoulder, but didn't mind the company. Both seemed to be holding their breaths.

Mr. Logan West,

It has come to our attention that your trading account dropped 72% during after-market trading last night. As you can imagine, this is a dire circumstance that requires external investigation. You are suspended until further notice. The results of the investigation will reveal what criminal charges, if any, will be taken. Please understand the severity of this situation and cooperate with authorities.

And that was it. Twice in three days he couldn't ask questions or explain himself. Granted, even if Jenny gave him a chance to explain, he wasn't sure what he'd say: *I really messed up. I made the wrong choices. It was the girl.*

Even Logan himself was wary blaming so much on Lily. He had to man up on this one and take the heat. He had not prepared himself as well as he normally would have, and now he had to pay. But how much? And at what price?

Uriel whistled. Logan spun around in his chair to face his friend. He knew he couldn't hide the panic in his eyes. "What do I do?" Logan asked desperately.

"Man," Uriel ran his hand through his buzz-cut hair. "I would find a lawyer. Stat."

Then he added like a good friend would: "Where's your Jack?"

You Will Not Date a Drunk

S he felt like she was seventeen again, checking the phone every time it made a noise. It was terribly annoying—this man of a distraction— and it was hard work to fill the growing hole in her ego. She wasn't used to *anything* rocking her focus. She was almost embarrassed by the stink of her desperation; it was terribly unflattering, and she felt drenched in it.

Three days had passed since she had magnificently blown up the opportunity to claim Logan, fully and intimately. He was right *there*. She had had him! If he could have felt her wrapped around him, there's no way he would have been able to walk out on her so easily. Thoughts of him pining over her or thinking of her when a sad song came on the radio made her feel better—steadier. Maybe he had skipped dancing last night for the first time in years since he didn't want to be reminded of Lily's absence. Or maybe he and Maya were cuddled in a corner, Maya reminding him that Lily wasn't meant for him anyway. Or maybe his sadness made him vulnerable to a dancer's advances and he was sweating over a body that wasn't Lily's...

No wonder she couldn't fall asleep with this nonsense swirling around her mind. Surely she had captured Logan's attention enough that he wouldn't be in a corner with a different woman for a while. With time, she would find a way to wrangle him back in. She allowed the comfort to drape around her body. *Yes,* Logan would be back.

The ringing phone startled her.

She reached over her head in the dark to mute it. When the phone became silent, she sighed a breath of relief. *This is what they made voicemail and mornings for.*

The second time, the ring seemed sharper. Brassier. More jarring. She reached for the phone but, in the dark, accidentally pushed it off the edge of the night stand. She sat up, trying to push away scenarios of Anne pinned under a semi-truck or Jeremiah in the hospital for partying too hard this time. As she grabbed at darkness with one hand and tried to turn the light on with the other, the phone shrieked, like when she was four and her mother was packing a bag and Lily couldn't understand where her mother was going and why Lily couldn't come. It wasn't until later that night that Anne had come home, climbed into Lily's twin bed—which she *never* did—and cried and cried. "Promise me," she had kept muttering between gasps. "Promise you'll never love so hard." Her rocking to and fro had made Lily wonder if Anne should have stayed at the hospital for her own sake. The training for the Cromwell Rules had started twelve years and a few months later.

Lily threw her blanket aside in haste and, on hands and knees, grabbed under her bed, felt the hard case, and swiped the phone's screen without looking to see who it was.

"Hello?" she asked, voice full of panic.

"Lill-ly." Logan's voice reached into her chest and squeezed her heart.

"Logan?" She leaned against the bed frame, letting the panic run out of her so that confidence could flow back in.

"Lill-ly," Logan said again. "How ya doin'?" Since when did he have a Southern drawl?

"I'm okay. Busy days at work keep me up all night, you know." She lied. He didn't need to know she couldn't handle his silence and it was keeping her up way past her bedtime.

"Ohh yess. You're a hard workin' woman, you are."

"Are you drunk?"

"No. I mean, I had a few. But no. Maybe. Probably." *Was that a hiccup?*

"Jeez, Logan, call me back another time."

"No, Lily, p-lease. Hear me out. I need your help."

"Why? What could I possibly help you with?"

"I'm in big trouble. Maybe. Probably. I need a lawyer."

"Oh, my God. Are you in jail?"

"What? No. I might be soon, though. I don't know." This guy wasn't making any sense. What trouble could he have done while *dancing?* Her spirits rose at the thought of him getting violent because he was alone, without her. That'd be quite the story.

"Logan, what's going on?"

"I messed up, Lill-ly." He fell silent. She wanted to reach through the phone, grab his shirt and yell, *Of course you messed up! You left without listening to my explanation.* But she waited for him to continue; she wanted to hear the groveling for herself.

He reported miserably, "My trades crashed overnight. I don't know why or how. I must've missed sssomething."

Work? He's talking about *work?*

"I'm a terrible trader," he continued. "I failed. You don't deserve a guy like me. Maybe I really can be a main'nance guy in your building."

Lily winced. "You're not a bad trader, you just made a mistake." She paused. "Probably. Maybe." Lily was not in the mood for handing out compliments, but she threw him a bone. Again.

"No, like... I think my company thinks it was intentional. Do you have a good lawyer you can recommend?"

"What am I, your Rolodex?" Didn't he know this wasn't her mess? She had nothing to do with this. She wanted good-time Logan. The one that, you know, made *her* feel good. He leaves abruptly and then expects a *referral?* What was this, a business transaction? Because he had closed the account the Saturday he walked away. *If she had kept her Saturdays sacred...*

"Logan, I'm sorry, but I can't help you. Be a big boy, put on your work pants, and figure this out." It made Lily angry that Logan wasn't calling to apologize. He didn't even seem to want to get together to fix it. He just called to complain and wanted Lily's connections. What else was new?

"This'ss your fault," Logan accused.

If Logan's voice had been a hand, it would have been a slap across Lily's face.

"What the hell? It's not *my* fault that you're in hot water, Logan!" Seventeen year-old Lily was definitely alive and present—and she hated that Logan brought this vulnerability out of her. How could she still be pushed over her own edge like this? "I think you need to get some sleep and try again tomorrow. Goodbye, Logan."

She hung up and threw the phone against the crumpled blankets. She didn't know what she was angrier at—the fact that she no longer had any inclination to sleep, or that the call had the power to make her so angry.

It didn't matter that she had been all wrong about Logan. What was important was how she reacted: without him in the picture, she would rock this IceStorm party, secure her promotion, and show Anne Cromwell that Lily wasn't settling for anyone: a promise she knew she could keep.

Don't Let Him Be a Distraction

T he work week passed quickly. Following the usual balcony chats with Vanessa and Genny, Lily would taxi to work to make headway on IceStorm code. She'd work through dinner with Jeremiah, and come home to sleep and do it all over again in the morning. She started understanding more and more why she couldn't be in this puppy love business *and* be a boss in her career. Greg often reminded her that this promotion would make her one of the most revered software engineers. So she wouldn't be married, but she'd be *remembered*—and wouldn't that be fulfilling Anne's hope for her daughter more than a piece of paper naming her "Mrs."? The next feature of IceStorm was ready to deploy, which meant Lily could focus her attention on the Dove Hospital-IceStorm launch party.

And where Lily felt bogged down by details and checklists to make sure the demo went flawlessly, Jeremiah was excited for the ambiance.

"...and we'll call for an ice sculpture! Ooh! What should the figure be? What says 'hospital'? A plus sign? A snake? A stethoscope?"

Lily shook her head. "The moment a nurse walks into the party and sees we've spent hundreds of dollars on an ice sculpture instead of donating that money to St. Jude's or something, we're screwed. They'll never advocate for us."

"I doubt that's true. Nurses need fancier things than the average person because they have to deal with so much... human... every day."

"You say that as if nurses are shallow and humans are disgusting," Lily said, dipping her chip into the guacamole they ordered for lunch. "And I don't think that's true."

"That you think humans aren't disgusting animals makes you an angel," Jeremiah said. He furrowed his brow. "Girl, what's this towel doing here? It looks like it hasn't been washed in weeks."

She silently cursed herself for not throwing that stupid sweat towel away the night Logan left. She thought about updating Jeremiah on the drunk dial, but decided against it and stuffed the rag in her bag. "It's Anthony's or something. He must have accidentally left it here earlier.

By the way, I talked to Hugo again last night. Left him a voicemail message that he probably listened to this morning."

"The man who you thought your mother set you up with, but now it turns out he's doing your mother?"

"Jeremiah!"

"See? Humans *are* disgusting. Case closed."

Lily pushed Jeremiah's shoulder and laughed. He grinned. She loved how his eyes crinkled at the corners.

Being around Jeremiah was like stepping her feet into a rushing brook: an exhale would be imminent. "You're not disgusting, but what you imply certainly is. Regardless, I'm glad you'll be my date to my party. Why do you have to be gay?"

Jeremiah winked at her. "The question should be 'Why do I *get* to be gay while the rest of the world must suffer?'" He spun his chair around. "Call Hugo again. Can't hurt. He's probably eager to set up a solid rapport with you so he can keep doing your—"

"Okay! Okay! You've proved your point. Humans are gross. I'll call Hugo."

She squinted at the numbers on the post-it stuck to the corner of her monitor and punched the number pad. As it rang, she pressed the speaker phone option and leaned back into her chair. Even Jeremiah seemed to be holding his breath. They didn't want to admit it, but they needed Hugo. He had big pull with connections that IceStorm could benefit from.

Hugo picked up on the third ring, his gruff voice filling the conference room.

Lily leaned forward as if he were physically present. "Hi, Hugo! It's Lily Cromwell. I hope I'm catching you at a good time."

"No time like the present, my dear. I was hoping you'd call. Our chat at dinner was such fun. If everyone is like you at IceStorm, then we'll have the best launch party on the East Side."

"Just the East Side?" Lily exclaimed. "Why think so small?" Lily loved the surge of social adrenaline coursing through her veins. "Best launch party in New York is more my speed. We need to reach as many hospitals, businesses, and homes as possible if we're going to save lives, Hugo."

She imagined his head nodding in agreement, his shoulders relaxed, feet kicked up on the corner of his desk, bringing the phone closer to his ear. He sounded like a man who had a corner office.

"I can see why Gregory entrusted the whole party to your direction. Your passion for IceStorm is contagious. That's why we'll need you to bring that out to Salt Lake City."

This was news. She and Jeremiah made eye contact.

"Ooh!" Lily crooned. "What's in Utah? It's not enough to have *you* convinced?"

Hugo barked in laughter. "What a generous thought," he said. "There's one more person you need to get on board. Nicholas Archer." *The guy Greg mentioned.* "You get him to come to New York for the launch party and you'll essentially get the contracts of every hospital, movie theater, and commercial building in this country. People follow his every move; everything he decides upon seems to bring massive returns. We're lucky he works for our hospital;

that's probably why you became so excited when I told you I work for Dove Hospitals. There's a reason we're number one, and he's it."

Lily grinned up at Jeremiah, who was waving his hands back and forth, fanning himself to cool the excitement.

"I can do it, sir. Thank you so much for the opportunity."

"I have no doubt. What's the earliest you can fly out there?"

Lily's gaze rested on the towel sticking out from her bag. She thought of Logan, remembering how his kiss felt like flying. But this was the chance she had been waiting for: now, more than ever, Lily had to bring her best game and forget about anything else.

"I'll start packing right away."

Lily promised Hugo she would update him immediately upon her return from Utah and the call was over. The high five she shared with Jeremiah was still burning on her skin.

"Girl, you better go shopping for something nice. Nicholas Archer needs some IceStorm schoolin', and if Lily Cromwell can't do it, then nobody can."

"Do I have full permission to be myself?" Lily asked mischievously.

"If it gets me a raise, yes, baby, yes. Even better if you get this Nicholas Archer man to raise his—"

"—money for IceStorm, is what you mean, surely," Lily said.

Jeremiah took Lily's face in his hands. "Sometimes you have to... *give yourself...* to save others. Like Jesus."

Lily widened her eyes and removed Jeremiah's hands from her cheeks. "Are you pimping me out on the premise that I'd be doing what Jesus did?"

"It worked, didn't it? And my kingdom come right now would be an extra bedroom. Get packin', Cromwell."

If He Wants to Be With You, He'll Be There

L ily spotted her name written in capital letters. She put on her biggest smile and walked over to the man holding the sign, appreciating his gelled black hair, aviators, and shiny black shoes. *Men were here to serve, not to be served,* Mother said. She couldn't help but feel a rush of tenderness and gratitude for her mother's guidance. Even if everyone else left her, her mother would not abandon her—no matter how much Lily messed up.

As she powered on her phone, any fantasies of landing with unread messages and a voicemail from Logan were dashed. She shook the disappointment from her mind, but it still weighed on her heart. As if she were the woman who waited! *If he wants to be with you, he'll be there. It's as simple as that.* So who cares if Logan was a bust? She had many others to meet during this trip, especially Nicholas Archer.

She snapped the picture of the Jimmy Choos covertly so the people waiting around her wouldn't assume she was just another self-absorbed millennial. If she didn't send the picture of the pink leather pumps—which actually were pretty cute—, Anne would guilt trip Lily, reminding her that not everyone has a mother who still spoils their daughters and isn't she so lucky?

Her phone pinged.

Anne: I knew they'd fit you. They're stunning.

Anne: Now go get this Nicholas.

Lily smirked and slipped her phone into her carry on, setting it next to her on the backseat. She imagined each movement as one farther away from the emotional chaos that was Logan West and three steps closer to the man she would use to seal the deal with IceStorm. She imagined Mr. Nicholas Archer to be short and stocky with a bald spot caused by stress. When a woman like Lily took an interest in him, he'd give her his full attention—she was sure of it.

Logan's effect on her was a fluke—a lesson—and a reminder of why emotions should never get in the way. Anyone who caused emotional reactions was really a trap, not a salvation. Her man would steady her, anchor her, not make her feel like she was losing control of reality.

Lily entered the Tahoe like she and this chauffeur had done this dance for years. She might never know how to swing dance, but Lily Cromwell knew how to score. It was time to secure the future she had always dreamed of.

Logan: No Game

The sun forced its way through a sliver in the curtains. Logan groaned at the unwelcome ray and glared at the whiskey bottles winking at him from the sun's reflection. The wooden kitchen table under him was suddenly hard and cold, no longer passing for a bed like it had after the eighth shot of whiskey. Logan blinked quickly, like doing so would be enough to remind him. What happened after Uriel had come back with the beer bottles and a couple boxes of pizza? Logan did a quick survey of the room to get some hints. He was about to chalk up his resolve and allow himself to forget the fact that he couldn't remember, until he looked down and saw his phone at his feet.

Logan opened the phone and clicked to see his outgoing calls. He gaped at it in horror.

Shit, shit, shit, shit, shit. Lily. What the hell had he said?

He had *zero* memory of their conversation, but evidence of the one minute and thirty-three seconds outgoing call was undeniable. That wasn't long enough to mess it *all* up, was it? Logan knew better than most did though: if so much could change in a day - your dad is alive in the morning and dead by bed-time- how much can change in a drunken night?

He felt the shame wrap around him like a slime that would stay on his skin and keep his fingers sticky long after he tried to scrub it off.

Cold showers usually brought him creative ideas for work, so maybe it'd help in this case, too.

As he stripped his way to the bathroom, he felt weighed down—the effects of the hangover, no doubt, but also from the thought that he had let Lily down.

He stepped into the shower and turned on the water. He moved towards the cold rather than jump out like Lily was probably apt to do when the water wasn't warm enough. Logan had a feeling that his hands had been one of the only things that'd be able to melt the ice that Lily used to guard her.

He couldn't stop replaying the memory of Lily pretending not to recognize him when that woman entered her house. It certainly wasn't the first time in his life he hadn't been acknowledged. But Lily's nonchalance affected him the same way Ronnie's had in high school. Logan frowned as he remembered.

One day during his junior year in high school, Logan's best friend Ronald had walked right past him in the lunch line because Caroline was finally paying attention to his best friend after all this time. Usually, Ron would brag about his new conquests. This time, though, despite Logan's clearly audible, "Hey, man!" Ronnie had completely ignored him.

But Caroline had noticed. She'd turned around and nudged Ronnie, who had steered her farther down the buffet line. When Logan had confronted Ronnie later, Ronnie hesitantly replied, "Man, I'm sorry. You're just..."

"Just what?" Logan had demanded.

Ronnie had run his hand through his hair. "You're just not a great wing-man for me, man. You don't play the game well enough."

"What game? What are you talking about?"

Ronnie had shaken his head and muttered "Exactly" as he walked away.

For hours later that evening, Logan had grappled with this idea of "playing the game." He had ignored his mom's questions and went directly to his attic bedroom. He tried to turn up the rebellion and had started looking up half-dressed women on the internet, but the culinary arts book at the corner of his desk was more appealing. He shut off his desktop's monitor and opened to the page that he had bookmarked. Good thing Ron wasn't here; he would have gaped at him and said, "See? Told you so. No game."

Weeks before, he had been hoping to convince Ronnie that Caroline would enjoy a great date at Cafe Logan. Logan would hide in the kitchen, cooking and baking whatever Caroline's favorite foods were, Ronnie would present the food as his own and *boom!* Caroline would be Ronnie's girl. *Chicks dig a guy who can cook*, Logan's dad had always told him. Suddenly, Logan slammed the culinary book shut and threw it across the room. How dare Ronnie - his best friend - say that Logan didn't have what it took to attract a girl's attention? Food *was* Logan's game. And one day, the right woman would appreciate that.

"Dad, I don't have any game," Logan had told his father.

To his dad's credit, there had been no laughter. Since his dad wasn't saying anything, Logan kept going, talking into the black shade created by his crossed arms.

"Ronnie mentioned something about not knowing anything about the 'game.' But I don't like that "Be the player" stuff. Those games sound stupid."

"Because they *are* stupid," his dad agreed matter-of-factly. Logan looked up at this. "They *are* stupid games, Logan," he repeated. "You think your mom had time to figure out whether I meant what I told her while she was earning her medical degree? Of course not. I had to be direct and to the point. I tried to be romantic too, of course, but I didn't play games with her. She didn't have the time, and I didn't know the rules. I didn't subscribe to the 'don't call until a week later rule.' In fact, within a few hours of kissing her goodnight, I asked to see her again. She appreciated my honesty and straightforwardness. She had been 'played' too many times before, and I, frankly, didn't think she deserved to feel like a second-thought when she was the only thought on my mind."

"Dad…"

"No, let me finish. One day, you *will* find your girl who speaks the same language you do: she'll laugh at the same things you find funny, dream of a future that you can easily see yourself sharing in, and constantly challenge you to be a better man—not just for her, but for your own sake, too. So you don't know the rules of *this* particular game. That's okay. Actually, it's more than okay - it means I'm doing a good job raising a good man. Whether you realize it or not, you have your own rulebook, and you'll be able to 'win' without reading a word of it. I promise. It'll be like that time you scrambled us eggs for the first time without any practice beforehand. Mom was horrified that you had crawled up the cabinets and turned on the stove all by yourself at six years old, but the facts were obvious: you had scrambled us some damn good eggs, and we were proud of you for it. You had figured it out, just like you'll figure out this dating thing one day, too. When you were six, you didn't know that it was dangerous to be in the path of falling pots and pans, or that hot flames could burn you. Instead, you knew you wanted the eggs and went for it. You just have to find the girl who's worth scrambling the eggs for, and then forget about anything that could go wrong when you decide to make it happen."

As adult Logan lathered, his thoughts bubbled back to Lily. He felt a strange nostalgia, both for who he used to be, and for who he hadn't yet had a chance to be. He was saving a special recipe for a truly special woman and had hoped Lily would be the one.

Though there had not been enough time for Logan to invite Lily over to his home for a meal all his own, maybe it wasn't too late.

Now, Logan shut off the water and stepped out into the cold bathroom. No more moping. He was a good trader, but that's because he *had* to be. He had enough money saved that a change in career wouldn't really hurt him. Maybe it *was* time to explore other options. If Lily could be enticed with a good meal, then he would make sure she would taste his.

Know Your Target

She was usually shut up in the dark blue walls of the IceStorm office, so Lily was used to closed quarters. New York winters didn't exactly make it desirable to be outside for longer than it took to hail a cab, but Utah *wasn't* New York, so where the hell were the windows?

The sconce lights barely emitted any light and mirrors hung where windows should have been. Lily wished the walls were stone so at the very least she could pretend they were in a cool dungeon instead of a hotel conference room for eight hours or more these next three days. She was so glad the Wyndham they chose for the RACE reveal wore walls of glass. When thousands of people were tucked within the skyscrapers in front of them, it'd be easier to show who they could save *just in case* the city was thrown into chaos.

People were filing in to check in. Rectangular tables were set up in straight diagonal lines throughout the room, white tablecloths draped over each one.

Regardless of the lack of light and the number of nervous attendees, these rooms were where Lily made magic happen, and today that spell needed to charm Nicholas Archer and make IceStorm take up the entire scope of his mental flashlight.

The game always started with the same purpose: to find the mark. To a chess player, this equated to finding the piece that seemed unbeatable, but could be overtaken by a master in just a few moves. In her case, the first strategy was to scope out the room: in the center of it was a stocked bar, bottles gloomier and darker than they would have been at a nightclub on the East Side.

The 50-something bartender was bent over a crate of glasses like the weight of gravity was heavier against his back alone.

"Good afternoon, sir. Expecting a large crowd today?"

He straightened, but his slouch was still profound. "Oh, yes, Miss. They tell us three or four hundred people." His thick South American—Argentinian?— accent threatened to make her swoon, but she kept her composure.

"Wow." She made sure to keep her gaze directly on his. "And I bet you'll handle them all so well that each person gets exactly what they want—and quickly, too." She flashed a big smile. Lily noticed his muscles ease as he gave one in return.

"That's the hope!"

She snuck a peek at his name tag.

"Julien, I'm Lily. We are going to be great friends this week. Thank you in advance for all your work." He gave her a slow-motion wink and turned to the other patrons.

There were a few gentlemen with slicked back hair and older women loitering with martini glasses. Now that she introduced herself to the bartender, she was noticed by the men in suits and, judging by the heads and sideways glances usually found in a football huddle, she knew she had gotten them to talk about the tall blonde in pink heels. They would wonder about IceStorm's lead architect and they'd ask about the product. Her marketing plan was working already, but these social pariahs were not her end goal. The real target would be located through a registration table investigation, where she'd find the conference check-in sheet with Nicholas Archer's name on it. Then, the game would really begin. She hoped he wasn't the one in the white suit; she could work with a big ego, but those who chose to wear white suits outside of beach weddings had insecurities that she didn't have time for.

A young woman with jet-black hair tied back in a ponytail stepped in front of Lily with an outstretched hand.

"Welcome to the Dove Hospital Annual Conference!" Her ponytail bounced, the girl's sidekick. "How was your journey in?" The woman's name was sprawled in hurried cursive on her tag: Diana.

Lily shook the woman's hand and sidestepped her questions. "It must be early if you somehow have the energy for handshakes," she said, breaking the regular "Hi, how are you? Fine" script. She enjoyed watching Diana's eyes widen.

Diana's brows furrowed and laughed nervously, like a tittering bird that had lost its grip on a branch. "You're so right. I should reserve them for those who look particularly down—not someone like you, huh?" It sounded like she had spit out the "someone like you" part. *Pent-up anger, Diana? Maybe that guy in the white suit would help release all that tension later.*

Lily tried to soothe Diana with a smile. "Lily. Lily Cromwell. I've worked many of these tables in my time. I know how tiring it could be, working at registration for three days, where there aren't even any windows. It's nice to meet you, Diana."

Diana's eyes shone now, her shoulders dropping. "Yes! It's seriously the worst. Now let's find you here…" Diana hummed while she scanned the lists under "C." Meanwhile, Lily turned the "A" list towards her, scouring the list for "Archer." He wasn't listed. *Of course not.* He was a keynote speaker. Diana handed Lily a folder, notebook, and name tag. "Here are your conference materials! Events will begin in a couple hours. We'll see you then!"

Lily thanked Diana and looked up towards the bar. The men were looking at her. She nodded her head in Julien's direction and turned on her heel. It was time to look her best for Nicholas Archer. The list had only confirmed what she should have remembered: the guest of honor always arrives fashionably late.

Make Alliances

The vibrations of deep voices combined with high-pitched laughter nudged Lily from her nap as groups of people passed her door. After leaving Diana's registration table, Lily had supervised a group of contracted engineers to install a demo of RACE. Directing men around a system they thought they knew everything about was exhausting; they assumed she didn't know anything and she was certain they didn't. She shook it off; the system was good to go and would be demonstrated later in the conference.

The opening statements would officially kick off the conference in a few minutes, but now Lily was still under the covers after her nap with no desire to leave. Though she was strong in a group, there were moments before a social obligation that reminded her of how nervous she used to be.

She remembered how surprised her mother was when Lily said she hadn't wanted to go to homecoming her sophomore year: "How else are you going to learn how to be the Belle of the ball, Lily? Start with Homecoming, then winter dances, and finally, *prom!*"

"But, Mom, I don't even have a date!"

Lily could picture her mother's smug grin and confident nod. "It's better to arrive single. The confidence of a single woman's glow is enough to catch the attention of the Prom King who's been dating the same girl for four years."

"You're asking me to steal someone else's date?!"

"Honey, if he's got wandering eyes, he wasn't anybody's to begin with. A man like that is free for the taking, even if it's just for the fun of the evening. Lord knows you don't want a man like that forever. How you found him is how he'll leave you— remember that. Besides, you're sixteen. It's not like they were engaged to be married. Relax."

Later, Anne had asked Lily why she was flipping through the pages of the yearbook.

Lily said, "I'm finding the guys I think are the cutest. They'll be the ones I ask to dance."

Anne shut the book and sat next to Lily. "Never decide on someone specific. The cutest ones might be the worst, what with their big egos. Just let it happen."

And let it happen she would.

Lily pushed the covers away from her. Because she hadn't performed any online searches of Nicholas Archer, she didn't know what he looked like. Anyone going into a networking event like this would have scoffed at her, but Anne's ideas worked: though she might be in front of the most impressive target, Lily's confidence would never waver; instead, she'd make the best, natural impression first and *then* ask who she was talking to. The question was, had she already run into Nicholas? *Was* he the guy in the white suit?

She peeled her dress off the hanger: velvet, knee-length, and black with white cuffs. The blazer she sidled on reminded her a little bit of Cruella de Vil, but she knew a strong man like Mr. Archer wouldn't be intimidated by her. She wished she could stay in and put on her pajamas instead, but her bright red heels were waiting

Her hair was second-day, so it wasn't too frizzy. The brush tamed her frizz and made her blonde highlights gleam. She thought about how different her life had been just a week ago. Almost convincing herself that she wanted to be tied down? How else would she get to explore this wild side she let run free during nights like these? An application of bright red lipstick later, Lily was satisfied with the woman staring back at her.

Nicholas Archer would come to her. She had years of experience to prove it.

* * *

With a drink in her left hand and a quick snatch of the passing hors d'oeuvres with her right, Lily scoped the room like she imagined an undercover detective would. She ignored any wearers of scuffed shoes immediately—the man she was looking for wouldn't be caught dead with unpolished shoes. She searched instead for men with colorful pocket-squares and tight smiles that broke into grins a little too quickly.

It didn't take long to find her two bullseyes: the red-headed man leaning a little too casually against the bar with a dark-haired stallion of a man who kept glancing at his watch: eager to leave the conference already? Or maybe he was waiting for someone more important? Lily identified Watchman as her first subject. She felt her seduction switch turn on: shoulders back, chin up, a sway in her step and she was on the move.

She finished chewing the mini mushroom bite—too salty—and shone a smile at the man speaking in a Texan drawl. She greeted Julien like an old friend and asked for a glass of Pinot, ignoring Watchman. By the time Lily finished her mental to-do list for tomorrow's conference presentations, both men had found seats next to hers at the bar.

Here goes nothing. "The conference binder says the speakers will talk about 'thinking big with great vision' and you two look like you have some ideas about what it might be about. Care to share?" Lily asked. She turned her head towards Watchman, offering a soft nod complete with a sweet smile and alert eyes. She stretched her legs to demonstrate their length. Watchman glanced down and she grinned wider.

"Shouldn't you ask us our names first? Body language is important, but it shouldn't trump a polite introduction."

Lily raised her eyebrow. *Provide a hint that you noticed him before,* she heard Anne whisper.

"I didn't think you'd have the time," Lily said pointedly, glancing down at his watch and back into green eyes that seemed to look beyond her. *It will embolden him, but also make him wonder what kept you from coming up to him in the first place.* She turned away from him.

"Where are my manners?" To really capture the fish, Lily extended her hand to the man on the left. Poor guy didn't know he was bait. "I'm Lily Cromwell. And you are?"

"Jameson Vasseur," the average-built, just-tall-enough-for-her man responded. He started answering her initial question—*suck up*—, but Lily soon lost interest. For all the advice Anne Cromwell gave Lily, that of getting the man to speak about himself was most effective. She tried to catch the name tag hanging from the lanyard around Watchman's neck, but the lapel hid it from view. Somehow Jameson was having trouble finding a safe space to park his most recently acquired Audi. *I don't care,* Lily whined in her mind, and she couldn't help but think of how trapped she felt in this windowless room. At least the little red Corolla had leg room.

Lily glanced at the Watchman, who she felt watching her. He had noticed she was not really paying attention to her left-hand man and he smirked. "Oh, what a tough situation." Lily was tempted to join him. She used to, at the very least, humor the men with whom she played. Her apathetic response surprised even her.

"I hope your Audi finds a nice place to rest, Jameson," Watchman said. "I prefer to drive mine."

Watchman settled into his seat, like he wouldn't be going anywhere for a while.

She breathed out like the release on a pressure cooker. "Bold, bully. And where does your Audi take *you*?" she challenged. Who was this man who didn't care to be kind to potential investors? And why was Lily so curious to hear more? She saw the spark in Watchman's eyes, but she didn't want to stoke the fire in them just yet. Lily gave Jameson something close to a sympathetic smile.

Watchman said gruffly, "My Porsche takes me wherever I need to go, thank you."

"And where does a person like you go?" Lily asked.

"There are Dove Hospitals popping up in cities and counties all over. I have to make sure I'm there on time."

"And people don't have a problem with a man in a Porsche driving up next to a mother who can't afford her next car payment because of hospital bills? I'd think you'd want something a little more humble in the day time." *Like a trustworthy Toyota.*

"People trust social symbols that express affluence. You should understand—look at what you wore this evening."

The moment a woman chose to wear something bolder than a Puritan skirt, she was slipping on armor. "Some might argue my clothing choices would be intimidating and, subsequently, a signal for *dis*trust. The same might be true for a man who pins on cufflinks and ties on polished shoes. It's meant to draw people's eyes *to them* - not their genuine selves."

Lily's most poignant conversations occurred on the comfy couch in her best friend's bedroom in cartoon pajama bottoms and a mismatched t-shirt, so she was surprised to be having one now. She continued, "People dress to arm themselves, not reveal their deepest secrets. And deep secrets usually lead to trust."

"Those people shouldn't be the people you work with anyway. Too much life and emotion to get in the way. Besides, how can you raise money if you don't convince people *with* money that you'll be smart with their cash?"

"Agree to disagree." Lily raised her glass and Watchman clinked his against it.

She grazed her fingers against his coat and moved the lapel to the side, revealing his name. *"Nicholas Archer.* A pleasure to be in your company." The pun wasn't an accident. She extended her hand.

"You can call me Nic." Nic's fingers wrapped gingerly around hers as he kissed the back of her hand. A Victorian gentleman. "A man of second chances meets a woman who probably rarely gives one."

"An architect of IceStorm's RACE wouldn't provide one solitary chance, sir. Saving lives often takes more than one try."

"Then it seems we have the same philosophy." This time, his fingers moved her hair to the side, though she knew her name tag had been in clear sight. "I look forward to discussing your system more later, Miss Cromwell. Please do excuse me for now."

She smiled into her drink, watching him weave his way through the growing crowd of people. When others noticed Nicholas Archer was climbing the stairs to a podium, the room hushed.

As he welcomed the crowd in a cool, comfortable, strong voice on behalf of Dove Hospitals, Lily beamed. When she noticed the slightest change in Nicholas' posture at her touch, she knew she was a little closer to knowing more about the actual man in the suit - not just the label on it. The thought of knowing what made Nicholas Archer "tick" was exciting.

She'd never met anyone who understood the game as well as she did, and she already felt proud of him. Obviously a man who could steer the direction of successful hospitals by playing by similar rules was an example of why she should stay true to her training. Anne had been right the entire time: the Cromwell Rules really were meant to protect and guide her daughter.

When Nic said how much he looked forward to getting to know every-one, she knew he was bluffing. How could he get to know everybody when he was only looking at her?

Stay in Control

The alarm blared and red strobe lights flashed; everything but the sprinkler system was going off. Lily stepped into her flats, wrapped a light cardigan over her loose thin cotton shirt, and left her room, following confused guests out of the building. A steady male voice directed the panicked stream of people to doors at the north end of the building, repeating directions, assuring them that real danger was not in their proximity: it was only a precaution. She felt a little bad for the couple with a screaming toddler. She scanned the crowd, looking for those who'd normally be trusted with authority. Three bell boys and two desk managers looked confused by the booming voice coming from their computers as well as from the digital thermostats at the corners of every hallway. Then, she looked at the open laptop in her hands. All systems were working; Greg would be thrilled. He would be receiving an alert soon that a hotel in Salt Lake City was using RACE—and he'd see the same flawless design that she was seeing currently. They needed to run a few more demos before the big reveal, and if they were going to get Dove Hospitals on board, this drill going off without a hitch was exactly what needed to happen.

A tall disgruntled man with ruffled dark hair passed by her in a blue bathrobe, eager to see everyone safely outside.

Lily smirked, closed her laptop, and sidled up next to Nicholas. He looked lost in thought. She said, "So I guess I'm stuck with you, huh?" He jumped and turned to her.

"Hey, Blondie." His grin made his eyes seem brighter. Even with his unkempt hair and slightly swollen eyelids, Nic still looked like he could pitch an idea to those standing around and everyone would buy it. Lily mentally swatted her eyes away from his and gestured around her before hugging her laptop to her chest.

"So how long do you think we'll have to stand out here?" The exterior of the hotel was blocked off. People were already laying themselves down on the protruding curbs of the parking lot. "That can't be comfortable."

"I don't know. I was hoping it was a false alarm, but now…" Nic noticed her laptop. "You know exactly what's going on, don't you? Or have you only saved your dearest possession?"

She ignored his question and sat down on the sidewalk's curb. "Did you notice anything different about this alarm?"

Nic nodded and went to sit next to her. "Yes, I did. It sounded like the walls were speaking."

She opened her laptop. "They were. Based on the threats RACE assessed in the building, guests were led out quickly, safely, and without panicked leaders making rash, unsafe decisions." She pointed to the blueprints on her screen. "According to this screen, the hotel is safe to re-enter. Just say the word, boss, and we'll let everyone know it's okay to go back inside."

"We should be kind and let them return to their rooms. I'd be okay with a longer delay, but I have my own reasons for that." Nicholas winked.

"Right. Let's do it." She pretended not to understand his hint and typed a sequence of commands. The hotel's sign flashed on and off and this time a female's voice echoed through the parking lot: "The building is now safe to enter. There is no danger. You are welcome to return."

She shut her laptop, stood, and was about to wish Nicholas a good night. She didn't want to sell him anymore: it'd be more effective to leave him here to process what RACE could mean for safety in emergencies, especially for Dove Hospitals.

Nic reached for her hand. "Miss Cromwell." His touch stirred something within her.

She looked up at him, his robe darkening his green eyes, reminding her of the tall fir trees that made her feel at home when she went hiking. "Yes, Mr. Archer?"

"This is important. Let's talk about this."

"Of course. Where shall we go? Hotel bar? My room?"

He lifted an eyebrow.

"It's not what you think! I have all my equipment and manuals in 112."

He laughed. "We can walk in the direction of your room."

As she walked next to him, butterflies beat their wings against Lily's rib cage, fighting to escape. Was it the pride she felt for executing this test run of RACE so perfectly? Or the way he was looking at her, like she was the most fascinating woman in the world?

The pair discussed the details of RACE and how it could be embedded into a hospital's architecture without compromising the care and efficiency with which the hospital staff did their jobs.

"In fact, imagine an emergency scenario," Lily said. "Maybe an earthquake on the west coast compromised some elevators. The nurses need to be focusing on the care and safe evacuation of their patients rather than testing out which elevators are safe."

"True. But can RACE take action, or does it just give instructions? Can I customize it to standard operating procedures? Can my sleep-deprived staff operate this? Is it flexible enough for different hospitals? Some of our buildings were built by us, but otherwise they're old, acquired."

The way he curved the left corner of his lips in a smirk when he asked a difficult question was attractive. It made her want to please him.

"We could standardize all Dove hospital buildings using RACE as an excuse. Your donations would come flying in once people realize what you're trying to do. And I'm not going to lie to you—if one of those donors are parents, too, they'll want RACE in their children's schools, too."

He looked impressed, and she whispered a million *thank yous* to the universe that she didn't need to sleep with this man to convince him her product was worth his attention.

They entered the hotel's lobby and began walking toward 112 when Nic asked her what she did for fun when she wasn't working.

She thought about telling him that work *was* what she did for fun, but didn't want to come off as a workaholic. She wanted to tell him she loved to hike, but she didn't want him to suggest a hike during this trip—she was grossly unprepared. She wanted to admit she loved sleeping after a particularly intense yoga practice. But she figured honesty about how she spent most of her time would be the best option. After a swipe of Lily's card, the door's lock turned green. The night was over; it wasn't as if she were opening the door for an intimate relationship with Nicholas. The thought almost made her sad. She leaned against the door frame in the threshold.

"I am a professional dater." She extended her hand like she was settling down an excited dog. "Before you judge, I can't help that my standards are so high that I'll wine and dine men until they check off all my boxes."

"Seriously?"

"Absolutely," Lily said. "Unfortunately, not many are good enough to get the good night kiss. But that usually doesn't come until the second date anyway."

"Well, then." Nicholas raised his eyebrow. "It's been a while since I've set a new personal goal. We'll see if a professional Archer can capture that kiss." He took a step backwards, his grin spreading wider with each step.

Lily shut the door and leaned against the back of it, a groan escaping her lips. She didn't need want to open anything with Nicholas after already feeling it with Logan. Nic was good at the game… and it was always so fun to play, but what if she was tired of playing? And did she really have to take one for the team if it meant scoring for IceStorm?

Always Accept a Proper Invitation

J eremiah opened his arms from behind him in a flourish and thrust a bouquet of wildflowers in front of Lily's nose. "These came for you."

The flowers were beautiful—a pick-me-up after a long day of meetings and code reviews. The gladiolus caught her eye first. Pink ribbon was wrapped around the stems. It made her think of Frankie's immediately.

"Who delivered them?" She tried to ignore the sudden spike of her heart rate.

"A blonde guy, quite handsome."

"Blonde?" She cleared her throat, hoping to sound natural. "You think everyone's handsome." Meeting Logan at Frankie's seemed like it had happened so long ago, but Lily couldn't deny the hope that he would finally realize his life was better with Lily in it than without.

Lily ran her fingers across the pedal of a red lily, soft and smooth. Hugging the yellow of a sunflower were Gerber daisies of bright orange and red, like a fire about to consume the rest of the bouquet. Lily put her nose closer to the daisies and placed them on her list of favorite flowers to report to Genny.

Lily noticed Jeremiah staring at something in the bouquet, a straight-lined smile steamrolling his lips. Jeremiah pointed to the center of the flowers and wagged his finger. In the midst of the wildflowers rested a little card, and Jeremiah's fingers were already reaching for the message.

Lily grabbed it. "I'll take that!"

Lily was used to these shows of courtship more than most, and would have gladly forwarded many similar bouquets to colleagues like Harriet and Beth Anne, who Lily often caught narrowing their eyes in her direction when a delivery boy walked into the office. This bouquet, however, felt different. Her well-manicured fingers gingerly opened the small envelope. She drank in every word of the confident penmanship, hope budding in her chest.

"Miss Cromwell, please grant me the honor of your company at dinner tonight. The Silver Bullet. 8pm. - Professional Archer"

Lily drew in a sharp breath, reacting as if she had been stabbed, so clear did she feel Logan's sharp rejection. But her exhale brought tranquility. Stability.

"Well!?" Jeremiah demanded.

"I heard rumors that Nicholas was in New York, but I wanted to keep my distance. I didn't realize he'd come to New York right after the conference ended *yesterday*." She grinned at Jeremiah. "He wants to have dinner with me. Tonight." Lily playfully tossed her hair to the side. "I do believe sushi and a slammin' outfit is on the menu tonight."

Jeremiah shivered and winked, celebrating as he walked out of her office. "Two bedrooms, here I come."

If It's Too Good to be True...

The cab's sudden slow-down made Lily realize she really had returned to dreary New York after Utah's warmth. The grey streets looked like the underbelly of fast food wrappers overflowing from curbside trash. Meeting Nic in her hometown was a natural transition, creating a more trusting and less contrived relationship—maybe. If he were treating her like a conquest, then he had another thing coming.

But it *was* attractive the way he asked her questions about IceStorm and RACE and really wanted to hear the answer. Usually, Lily was the one with the power to make her target giddy, but around Nicholas, Lily had to work ten times harder to maintain her cool composure as she explained her company's function and future. Something about his engaged evergreen eyes and inquisitive body language when Lily said something he found interesting made her blood run a little quicker—the familiar adrenaline of playing the right cards, making sure she said and did the right things to keep him interested.

When he had asked to see her again the day after the final conference event, it took all of Lily's willpower to reject him and say she was tired—when she was anything but. *Lead him to the bridge, but leave him on the other side. Let him watch you walk away.*

His perfectly framed eyes showed understanding and appreciation of her choice to lengthen their time spent apart. Nothing he said was ever uncouth or racy, and she felt the familiar calm and cool of being calculating with him that being an engineer provided her. She felt smart around him. Valued.

When she had told Greg that Nicholas had agreed to host the IceStorm party on behalf of Dove Hospitals—it had taken all of Lily's willpower not to stand and yell in victory with Greg right then.

"We still have so much work to do," Lily said.

"But look at how much closer we are," Greg said. "And it's all thanks to you. Keep it coming, Cromwell. COO would look good on you."

Her hands felt clammy and she tried to shake the nerves out of her system, causing her dangling earrings to hit her cheek, knocking some sense into her. *Don't allow yourself to get the shakes now, Cromwell.*

Nic was suave enough to make a personal connection with Lily as a core member of IceStorm since he wanted to invest in it, but Lily knew she was written in his appointment book for other reasons. They had stolen pieces of conversation during that conference, covering everything from their favorite restaurants to laughing about how relieved they felt to be swans after the ugly duckling years. She almost laughed at the thought of Nic ever being a chubby-cheeked kid, a Goonies character coming to mind. The lightness of their laughter buoyed Lily now, and gave her a greater desire to spend more time with him.

This time, they weren't meeting to get to know each other to discuss IceStorm or RACE more in depth. By sending a bouquet, Nic made it clear that he wanted to spend time with *her*—not the engineer, but the woman.

Lily spotted the restaurant in the distance.

"Right here, ma'am!" She grabbed the hundred-dollar bill that she'd earmarked for the soul who had to work in these conditions - in this case, a middle-aged Latina woman.

"Tenga un buen dia," Lily rolled off her tongue. The woman turned around, pleasantly surprised.

"Igualmente! Gracias por su generosidad!"

Lily smiled back, sent wishes for the woman to drive safely, and shut the door behind her.

"Lily Cromwell!" Lily spun on her heel to see Nicholas leaning coolly against the restaurant's exterior. He was a silhouette cowboy, with one foot on the maroon bricks and the other resting solidly beneath him. He pushed himself off casually, his smile a light illuminating the blanket of night. He looked older in the city lights: approaching forty, surely, but he wore it well. In what was quickly becoming tradition, Nicholas cupped her fingers in his and kissed the back of her hand. *Chivalry isn't dead*, she heard Anne echo. *You just have to expect it, and too many women don't believe enough in men's capabilities for romance.* At first, Lily had fought her mother on this, saying it made things way more complicated than they needed to be, but Anne Cromwell hardly batted an eye when she responded, "Darling, we do complicated for a living."

Nicholas smiled as he dropped her hand, but clung onto it a second longer than he needed to. She squeezed his thumb gently to let him know she liked him there. "Despite the reservations I made, they're still getting our table ready. Sorry about the wait," Nicholas said. The confidence behind his apology suggested he wasn't sorry at all.

"It just means more time with me," Lily sang.

Nicholas took a step toward her, pressing his lips almost against her ear. He whispered, "Exactly."

Was that whiskey on his breath? She felt her scarf rearrange around her neck and looked down to feel Nicholas' fingertips graze her cheek. Heat crept up her ears. He dropped her hands and leaned back against the wall.

"Good day at work?"

Lily hugged herself, creating a shield from the wind that pinched her through her coat. "Many people took off for the extended President's Day weekend, so it was nice to have a quieter space."

"You didn't want to join them and go outside the city with all this slush and ice?"

Lily thought of the warehouse where people danced in tropical humidity. "No," she smiled. "Besides, being with you can be my vacation."

"Good answer." He looked her up and down in quiet appraisal. Lily felt like squirming outside of his gaze. She was glad she wore her white boots since they showed off her toned calf muscles. But she wished he'd stop: if he looked too long, maybe he'd find something wrong, too. insecurity wasn't a typical feeling for her, but since she was afraid that disapproval of her would lead to disapproval of her software product, she felt it.

The maître d called for "Mr. Archer and his guest." Nicholas extended his arm in a "May I?" gesture, sweeping her once more with a brilliant smile. She slipped her arm into the crook he made for her and let him lead them inside.

Usually, this was the time she'd perform a quick inventory of the restaurant's interior. As they followed the maître d and Lily stepped behind Nicholas, however, Lily's eyes searched Nicholas hungrily for any clues that would prompt a first "real" conversation. Look at his eyebrows. His shoulders. Are they taut, or relaxed? Are his hands balled up into secret fists, hiding some secret frustrations? *Pay attention to the micro-expressions. They tell you everything you need to know.*

His hair was impeccably styled. He was so freshly shaven she could almost feel the sting of the after-shave. His cufflinks were shining as much as his shoes were polished and his watch gleamed with a beautiful silver hue that complemented his eyes. His green eyes seemed brighter than when she looked into them in Utah. Although she was usually the one making a man stand taller, Nic's flawless effort lifted Lily's chin a little higher, the aura of attraction flowing easily between them. Where was Rose now?

As Nicholas walked Lily through the restaurant's labyrinth to the table in the far corner of the restaurant, his palm rested on the small of Lily's back.

She had hoped he would feel welcome there; it was a critical reason she wore one of her longest black dresses with the open back. The gold sequins reflected in the faint light of the restaurant.

Nicholas pressed a little more suggestively against Lily's back. The gesture reminded Lily of Logan's hands pressing themselves against her, pulling her closer, not away. Nicholas pulled a chair out for Lily and Lily aggressively shook the memory of Logan away, her hand shooting out to steady herself with the help of the chair's backing. *Not here, Lily. Logan is done. No more. Not with Nicholas here.*

Nicholas threw her a concerned glance. To his credit, he didn't ask what the matter was, and Lily didn't offer an explanation. He pulled out her seat and pushed her in when she sat down.

He waved down the waiter, then looked at her. "Your hair looks flawless. I love waves."

"Thank you. I'm glad it cooperated with me today." Why couldn't she think of more to say?

Unlike her date with Logan, Lily found herself memorizing every little detail of the one she was having with Nicholas. This particular restaurant was clearly well-researched and intentional. This bar was nothing like the one manned by Julien in Utah or Sloane at the warehouse. It boasted a sleek metallic silver that bordered a mirror covering the entire wall. Soft blue lights emanated from behind liquor bottles. Black stools were welded in place and red lights met the tips of shoes when bar guests rested their feet. The lighting highlighted the tops of the square tables expertly spaced around the restaurant. They were sitting on the higher level, able to see those seated around them and below them. If he wanted to make her feel like the guest of honor tonight, it was working.

"What a lovely space," Lily complimented. Oblivious to the common civilian but enough of a clue for her, Nicholas' ease into his chair told her he was relieved to hear her comment. "Really," she continued. "The lighting is always a challenge; how do you set the mood and make sure your guests avoid squinting all night?"

"I don't think we would need a light to set our own mood, do you? Those diamonds of yours are ceremonial enough to tell me I'm in significant company."

"I don't know; you were pretty disgruntled the night we had to evacuate the hotel. And from what I noticed, those red lights affected your mood substantially. Who knew Nicholas Archer valued his safety more than his styled hair?"

Nicholas squinted into the distance. "I'm not sure I know what you're talking about," he said.

"Sure you do," Lily pushed. She could see he was enjoying the banter and almost embarrassed at the thought that she had seen him in his plaid pajama pants and white undershirt under the blue robe. "You have nothing to be ashamed about." She touched his hand. "Trust me," Lily said for emphasis.

She slid her hand into his palm as she spoke, her nails tracing the rivers of his palm. He didn't react. There was no squeeze of her thumb or caress in return.

Lily needed a moment to regroup. She excused herself. As she stood and straightened her legs, she could feel Nicholas' approving gaze. She was doubly aware of her hips as they swayed her away.

When she turned the corner to enter the hallway before entering the ladies' room, Lily smiled at the beautiful display on the solid gray wall to her left. There were four rows of individual roses, one row in red, and the row beneath a blinding white balancing the stark colors with ease. Maybe roses were Lily's favorite? Individually cut like this, they didn't look too intimidating. It was only when they were bunched together that they were overbearing. The bold lily of Nic's bouquet and the strong gladiolus quickly wilting at her apartment came to mind as Lily pushed open the door and took in the refreshing space.

The dark panel wood felt like a comfortable den, contrasting sharply with the elite snobbery of Grecian sinks. But they didn't jive, this elitist countertop against homely cabin comfort.

It's going well, she tried to convince herself. *He's stoic. Chill. Comfortable.*

She already knew Anne's justification. What you need is a man with the ability to give you diamonds - not a smile.

She ran cool water over her hands. As she lathered her hands with the silky soap from the tacky seashell dispenser, she scrolled through a quick check-list in her mind - a practice Anne created when Lily was in high school, and conducted on every date since.

Did he open the door for her on the way into the restaurant? Of course. He had been waiting for her like a proper gentleman in front of the doors, hands behind his back. She couldn't help but notice his height and confidence and how he smiled and nodded at other guests walking past him as he waited for Lily to accompany him. How was he able to look like the potential owner of the establishment and not a member of the valet? It was all in how he held himself. And how he held her lower back as he gently guided her to their seat. Secure, but not demanding. She liked that.

Did he pull out her chair before she sat? Yes.

He was doing everything "right" - so why did she feel so off? She removed her hands from beneath the automatic spout and shook the doubts off with the excess water.

She hoped she would catch Nic looking around at the other women around him, doing a quick compare and contrast exercise in his mind's eye. He would, of course, flash her a big grin when he spotted her returning, like a hungry hyena trying to coerce his prey into his possession. He would stand—*if he doesn't stand, Lily Pad, you do not even think about returning to that table, you hear me? You pivot immediately and retreat. That is unacceptable behavior.* And the date would proceed, though she'd know it was over:

she would thank him for a lovely evening, decline his invitation to drive her home, and order a return taxi home for herself.

That's what *should* have happened with Logan.

She knew what it was. Nic looked perfect, but felt fake.

She pulled a bottle of lotion from her clutch and rubbed a small dollop into her hands.

Nicholas' eyes never left Lily's as she sauntered back to the table. She stuffed the conflicting emotions down: she needed this date to be successful for IceStorm, she reminded herself.

When she sat down, she looked around her place setting for her black cloth napkin. Nicholas noticed, and reached down to retrieve it from the floor. As he leaned over, Lily noticed a jarring scar beginning at the base of Nic's thumb running up around his wrist in the shape of a raised J, extending up his forearm. At Lily's gasp, Nicholas quickly transferred the napkin back towards Lily's side of the table and hid his arm.

"What happened?"

"I don't want to talk about it." Nic answered too quickly, but must have realized his rashness and sighed. "Here. We don't have to talk about it here when the food is about to be served." She had thrown him off his debonair game and she was glad.

"You think I have such a weak stomach?" Lily jested.

"No, but I do," Nic confessed. "It's in the past. You know as well as I do that one doesn't discuss these things on the first date. At least give me a chance to appear like perfection." The gleam in Nicholas' eyes sobered Lily up.

"Listen, you don't have to tell me if you don't want to." She shrugged. "I just thought you'd have rebellious tendencies." Like Logan. She ignored the pit in her stomach and blamed it on hunger.

Nic shrugged. "Hey, if the lady wants to know, she has a right to know. Just don't include this in the criteria when you're judging the date tonight." He gulped a large swig of his whiskey. "It happened because of a woman."

Lily's wall immediately rose, red flags waving in the wind. He was injured because of a woman? What kind of situations did the man put himself in? Nic must have sensed her sudden abhorrence.

"Lily, it was in defense of her. I promise." Lily could feel her eyes soften, but her shoulders were still braced. She waited for more.

"My dad hurt the woman I love most. He would come home after work and complain about all that hadn't been done for him. He claimed to have been spat on by his own bosses and wasn't about to be spit on by his own wife, who had never done such a thing in her life.

It was only me and Ma around the house most of the time: we would have fun making the living room our space station and the kitchen was our green room for the action movies I would direct. We would get so carried away that Mom wouldn't notice the time - or maybe she had and didn't let it interrupt our playtime. Dad would come home already pissed off. It wasn't too bad in the beginning; only words... hateful, unappreciative ones, but still just words. One day though, Mom must have known that day was going to be a bad one, so she made me lock myself in the bathroom. I had just spent most of the day pretending I was a chemist in my very own laboratory, so I was happy to go back and continue my experiments. When I heard Mom cry out, though, I knew something had gone wrong. The sound—" Nicholas seemed to choke on his words. Lily's hands were clutching the edge of the table for support. She wasn't trained for this. How was she supposed to react here? Who told deep, impressionable childhood stories on a first or second date? Why had she pushed him?

Nicholas recomposed himself. "The words weren't just words anymore. Instead, he was using a heavy lamp to leave bruise after bruise on Mom. I must have blacked out from the anger. All I remember next is running into the living room and ending up on my bed with tape around my wrist and too much red gauze on my arm. I guess the light bulb had broken and the break had found its way into my skin. I was bleeding everywhere."

A heavy silence stepped on the string of sentences that had rushed out just minutes before.

"Oh, my God," Lily said. Her voice sounded broken and weak—something Lily wasn't used to.

After their water glasses were refilled and dirty plates recalled to make room for clean ones, Nicholas smiled. "Mom's okay now. As soon as I was able, I made sure she could start making her own real adventures wherever she wanted. We have our own deal - wherever she wants to go, I make sure she gets there. I make sure Dove Hospitals is successful for a lot of reasons, but making sure my mom is happy is number one."

Lily's heart swelled with pride for the man who sat in front of her.

"That's amazing, Nic."

"No, it's just the right thing to do."

Lily's hands unclenched from the table and found their way to the center. She waited for Nic to bring his own hands to hers. When he did, she broke all the rules her Mom ever told her about and allowed warmth to sweep through her and into Nic as she brought the scarred wrist to her lips and kissed it. She felt him withdraw his hands and, rather than face him, she cast her eyes down. She kept them down. Too much intimacy so soon were not part of the rules.

Who was this woman who was so bold from the beginning? It was surely backfiring now.

But she felt her head lift with his fingertips. She looked over at him, down on one knee. He looked deeply into her eyes and whispered huskily. "Let's get out of here."

Lily didn't question where they would go and hardly noticed Nic's subtle payment on their way out. She held on to his hand and let him lead. She didn't mind if he could feel her fingertips graze the length of his scar. And she tried not to mind that he didn't hold her hand in return.

* * *

Lily had never walked out before the main course *with* her date. In the case of a date going well—say, like the one she had with Paolo—she prolonged the evening as long as she Paolo. Somehow he ended up at her Central Park flat and he received quite the kiss goodbye. Pablo's second date never came, since she'd met Logan soon after.

If the evening was going poorly (because Lily's date had broken too many of Anne Cromwell's Rules for Dating Her Daughter), it was easy to leave early. She would make a show of telling the rejected bachelor that she unfortunately received word of an urgent production issue at work. On some occasions, she hadn't even lied. But this was by-far the most *affective* date she had ever been on. She felt like all her emotions were alert: her senses opened like a flower trying to grasp all of the life around it before it closed again, hoping he'd just *mess up*.

But Nic's voice made her ears reach out in genuine interest, and his eyes were a sparkling pool of hot springs that she could sink into, especially after the disappointments of Logan West. She was hoping Nic would hold her hand and let the contact warm both of them, but Nic's hands were in his pockets, and Lily's were resting at her side. They walked for a while without saying a word, with only their footsteps echoing around them. She *always* knew what to say. Why wasn't anything coming to mind right now? Where was Anne Cromwell's advice when she really needed it?

The slush had turned into more formidable snowflakes and their landing on Nic's long coat made her want to cuddle up with him in a cabin deep in the woods somewhere, not walk so somberly along the city's streets. Or maybe she was just desperate for some kind of validation since she wasn't getting any from the guy she really wanted to be in a cabin with...

Suddenly, Nic turned to Lily. "Since we walked out on our dinner, we can try one of my favorite Mexican joints. It's right around the corner here. I know it's quite the downgrade from what you're used to." He looked bashful, and it made Lily want to wrap her arms around him and tell him he was doing so well. *Just keep doing what you're doing. You're* perfect. *Anne will love you.*

"Nic..." Lily started hesitantly.

"We don't have to. It was just an idea."

Lily's eyes opened in surprise. "Are you kidding?! I love hole-in-the-wall places. They have more charm than most places guys take me to. This date will find its way into the memory books." She tapped her head with her finger and tried to keep her voice light, but she could see Nic's eyebrow lift in amusement.

Lily rambled. "I can't believe I pushed you into telling me. You were just playing it cool, like we should have kept being." She would have continued, but Nicholas placed a finger on her lips.

"Shh..," he whispered.

She cast her eyes down. "I'm sorry." She had so much to apologize for—putting a downer on their dinner plans, pushing him into a conversation he had clearly wanted to avoid, for spoiling the illusion that she knew what the heck she was doing...

Nicholas lifted her face to his.

"You have no reason to be so flustered right now. If anyone should be nervous, it's me. Just look at you." He smiled at her. She swore she saw a meteor flash across the canvas of his eyes.

Lily lifted her smiling lips up towards his. He gave a small smile and leaned a little closer. Lily felt her fingertips tingle with excitement and her cheeks warm despite the growing cold of the night. But Nicholas only smiled wider and said into her waiting lips,

"Do you prefer mild, or spicy?"

At that, Lily laughed and pulled away, watching her hot exhale become the icy mist in the night air. She felt relieved to disconnect after the corporal need that had almost squeezed Lily's will into perfect submission.

"Spicy isn't a preference, guapo," Lily said. "It's a requirement."

She could see Nic's jaw set, revealing his interest only in a raised eyebrow and subtle smirk. His green eyes darkened like a dimly lit room prepared for bedtime. "Well, then let's get you some Cholula."

"Is that what you call him?" Lily teased.

Lily bit the inside of her cheek so she wouldn't erupt into giggles as she watched Nic's jaw set again. He winked, but she could sense his excitement. He wouldn't have walked away from her and fixed himself otherwise.

She loved throwing in unexpected euphemisms—nobody ever expected it out of a classy woman like her. *Logan's reaction was the best, though.* Her heart constricted again. *It doesn't make sense. I miss him.* She forced herself to look at the man in front of her. Nic's suit jacket flapped in the wind, strong hand raised to hail a taxi, but also ready to hold Lily and take her not only to a quaint Mexican restaurant, but a promotion and maybe a wedding. *Nicholas is the one right here, right now. Logan is done with you. You are done with Logan. It was never going to work out, anyway. He said so himself.* And letting those truths sink in was like the treasure chest within her closed, burying the gold that Logan had excavated. She'd find her worth elsewhere.

She approached Nic as a cab pulled up. Nic extended his hand for Lily to take, and she took it like it was the last hand she'd ever hold. The warmth was almost overwhelming.

* * *

Lily opened the door to her apartment and slid her purse down to the floor with a thud. She didn't know if she was breathless from the stairs she just run up or the cold she tried to run away from. What she did know was that Nicholas Archer was a breath of the most refreshing air.

Who she had originally pegged as the same as all the rest - with all the right style, mannerisms, and careful adherence and appreciation to the dating rules Lily grew up with - had become quite the fun companion on this cold winter's night. *He can make you feel, but can he provide for you?* Anne's question entered Lily's consciousness like an old friend. Lily was surprised she could easily answer the question. *Yes, Mother. He's a financial warlord.*

Well. Good.

Lily felt drunk, even though she had only finished half of the lime margarita. Nic kept her talking, getting her to open like a book that had been passed over for decades.

She slipped out of her coat and draped it over the couch. She wasn't really tired, but her legs didn't want to carry her any farther. She laid down on her recliner and covered herself with the dark red blanket that had been hanging over the edge. As she wrapped herself in the cool fleece, she imagined Nic's arms wrapped around her in their good-bye hug of the night. She had so badly wanted to kiss him, but rules were rules: No kisses on the first date. If Juliet hadn't let Romeo kiss her the same night he saw her, maybe things wouldn't have ended the way they did.

But maybe.

Maybe she could take a page out of Logan's book. Maybe "just going for it" was the reason he had been placed in her life, so she could learn how to grasp what was right in front of her instead of waiting for life to happen to her. She did it with code, so why not with a man?

She'd call Nic. She could rub the misfortune of his scar into quite a different memory - a "thank you" in advance for bringing the happy place to her again, and proving that the Rules had a rightful place in her life. And it was time to write one of her own.

She retrieved her phone, and found Nicholas' name. She swiped, a blank canvas full of possibility. She connected letters like connecting dots of a constellation. Sometimes fate had to be spurred on.

Come over, guapo. I'm not sure tonight was spicy enough for you.

Lily opened her darkest bottle of wine and poured a glass for herself. She allowed herself to drink a full glass as she waited for his response. It didn't take very long for him to come up with one. She smiled at the thought of him in bed already, allowing himself to alter his plans—for *her*.

I thought lilies were more of a delicate flower. Don't want more time?

His decorum frustrated her. She didn't need politeness right now. She needed to forget about any feelings, or emotions, that could prevent her from just feeling the physical pleasure that she knew Nic could provide.

Any more time and I'll settle myself. And that's no fun for anyone.

Three dots taunted her.

She shrugged and opened the Finlandia, clear liquid that would work faster than the wine. The best way to feel the most pleasure was to shut down the brain.

The memory of her mom's rocking back and forth on Lily's four-year-old bed came in full picture. Lily didn't want that life. *Too much emotion is crippling.* She took a swig from the bottle. Nic *had* to respond, or this was going to be a tough night.

Well then let's have some fun, Miss Cromwell.

The surge of victory was an electric pulse within her.

Lily took another swig.

He Should Check off Our List

The sour of last night's liquor rose to the back of Lily's mouth. She blinked her eyes, grateful for the dark shades of her bedroom. Drool puddled on top of her smallest throw pillow—laid on top of her vanity.

"Ugh, gross." She lifted her head slowly, looking around the room to see five throw pillows thrown about and her pajamas lying on untouched comforters. She looked down at herself and guffawed. Her sweatpants were thrown on backwards, but her dress was still covering her torso. What the heck?

And then the memories came.

The hot anger she felt towards Logan. Continuous swigs of burning alcohol. Deep annoyance at being affected by the drunk boy—how could she call him a "man" after spending time with Nicholas? Sadness that Logan didn't see a future with *her,* Lily Cromwell. And tipping the bottle back, holding it there until her throat felt like it was on fire. It was the best punishment she could think of. How dare she succumb to the charms of someone like Logan West when she had had *years* of practice at never having anything less than the upper hand?

Did Nic ever come over? She scolded herself, stomach in her heart. *Lily, how could you not remember!*

Her phone's ringtone sounded louder than normal, like a trumpet blaring in the early morning hours of an unsuspecting town. She tripped over her slippers on the way to a blinking screen and swallowed rising bile. Marley was calling her. Lily sighed in relief, but didn't open the call.

She sat on the carpeted floor and leaned against the edge of her bed. Every movement made her stomach turn. The spinning in her head was too strong. *Nic had agreed to come over. If he saw me like this... the Dove Hospitals-IceStorm party—and my career—are over.*

There were two messages from Nic, sent less than an hour after she had sent him the invitation texts. If they were pictures of her drunken self... She swiped and held her breath.

I'm here, but your doorman—Lafanzo?—won't let me in unless you give permission.

And ten minutes later

Poor girl. All our fun must have worn you out. See you soon, Blondie. Sleep well.

The relief flooded her. "Oh, thank *God!*"

She decided to return Marley's call. Marley picked up after a few rings.

"Good morning, Lilo!"

"Hey, Stitch," Lily moaned, trying to ignore the reflection of her hair bun flopped over the top of the mattress and heavy bags under her eyes.

"You look like you had an... interesting night," Marley pointed out.

"You're being kind. I can see myself." Lily pushed herself onto her knees and, with one hand holding the phone and the other trying to keep her balance, crawled over to the nightstand to turn her coffee maker on.

"Wanna talk about it?" Marley asked. They both knew the answer to that. Lily never revealed what was really on her mind—*inner thoughts are another's ammo*—, but Lily surprised both of them when she nodded. Marley made a show of pushing the books in front of her to the side and out of the screen.

"You've got my full attention."

"It's not a big deal," Lily said dismissively.

But just as Marley's phone was held snuggly in Lily's hands, so too did Lily feel cradled in Marley's love and acceptance. Their relationship had solidified during all the Saturday mornings training sessions on How to Catch the Eye of Every Eligible Bachelor.

Lily started. "Remember when you were over one Saturday and Anne was demonstrating how to sit most gracefully for a pulled out chair?"

Marley raised her eyebrow again. "You're changing the subject, but yes. She made me act like the man."

Lily laughed. "Yeah, but you wouldn't stop making me giggle."

Marley shrugged. "That's what a real date with your true love is supposed to be like, isn't it?"

"I guess... and remember when Mom poured me a glass of Welch's grape juice from a wine bottle to show me how to most seductively stare into someone's eyes while I drank?"

"Yeah, if anyone is watching you drink your wine and thinking about sexing you while you do it...." Marley mimed how she would slosh the wine onto the man's shirt. They erupted in giggles.

"It still surprises me that Anne, who picked up on *everything*, never mentioned your antics."

"Maybe even Anne Cromwell was smart enough to realize that you needed some normalcy in your life. A sixteen year old learning how to dine and bed a man? Come on."

Lily didn't know what to say to that. But then, like a dam that was finally broken, Lily relented.

"Okay, fine," Lily began.

Marley waited.

Lily had a choice here. Did she want to talk about Logan or Nicholas? She felt the need to talk about Logan and how different he was from any guy she had ever dated. She wanted Marley to tell her to give Logan another chance and that she really messed up that day her mother came over. But going into detail about Nicholas would be more realistic; he was the smarter, more reasonable choice anyway.

Lily said his name slowly, like a practice for the many times she'd say it to others. "Nicholas Archer…"

Marley rushed to the conclusion. "…stuck a bow through your heart and left a gaping hole in it?"

Lily rushed to Nic's defense. "No! Nothing of the sort!"

"No sense of humor today? Okay. So, what is Mr. Archer like?"

Lily stretched her arm, feeling around until her hand felt the handle of a mug full of hot caffeine. She held the mug carefully and set it on the floor. Her gaze froze at the painting on her wall of a man and woman dancing. The man's arm was wrapped around the woman, but the woman looked like she was spinning out of his grasp. Anne had bought it for her as one of her graduation gifts. But now, it was a happy distraction as she described Nicholas to her best friend.

"Mr. Archer is a dream. Marley, he's everything my mother ever wanted. He is the perfect gentleman. He literally does everything right. You know that checklist my mom wrote out for me? Just based on last night, I could check off all of those requirements." Marley's eyes narrowed suspiciously, but Lily ignored the reaction and continued on anyway.

"His eyes are beautiful. And his hands are so warm," Lily shivered. "He respects my ideas, my work, and my dreams. He understands the rules completely and plays along. He would know how to act around… you know… our people. Society. But Logan," Lily's voice trailed off. She hadn't meant to bring him up at all.

She rearranged herself, opened her phone case's kickstand, and brought the coffee back into her hands. Marley sat up straighter.

Marley wasn't much of an interrogator, and Lily loved her for it. But Lily *wanted* to be interrogated. She needed to be. She needed to know what to do with these *feelings*.

Marley asked. "Lily, what happened with Logan?"

Lily inhaled a deep breath. "Logan… doesn't know any of the rules. He doesn't even realize there's a game to be played. He never got the memo. He's like… he's like a stray piece of newspaper that I haven't been able to shake off the bottom of my shoe."

"I thought you were fond of the extra news following you around," Marley mused.

"I would be, if he *actually* followed me around. The only thing following me around is the *idea* of him. All that rule-breaking felt so rebellious at first, you know? I even thought maybe my mom was wrong about all of it. But he's ignored me since a little… misunderstanding… we had. He called me out of the blue a week or so ago, drunk, asking for help about some legal trouble. He didn't even apologize about walking out and essentially ghosting me for so long. This is exactly what Mom talked about all those years. Let's be real: Nicholas would have never behaved like Logan has."

It looked like Marley was biting her tongue.

Lily narrowed her eyes. "Say it."

"Maybe that's the problem."

"What do you mean?"

"Well, if you made fun of *everything* Anne taught you and then all of a sudden, here's this guy who would totally make fun of the same… how is that *not* a problem? Why *wouldn't* you go for the guy who makes you giggle during a date instead of being so rigid and *'perfect'*?"

"That was before I found a guy who would satisfy my mother *and* me, but here we are."

Marley nodded.

Even after Lily and Marley exchanged their pleasantries and promised to talk again soon, Lily couldn't shake the look on her best friend's face.

What was she missing here?

And why was she getting the feeling that her best friend wasn't on her side?

Logan: Turning Her On

Logan was on auto-pilot, reaching into the fridge, shuffling through cabinets, and spinning the spice-rack to find the coriander. He had prepared this meal many times since his recipe's inception, but this time felt as significant as the first.

"Yes, I lost my job," Logan repeated, bending over to speak closer to the phone.

"What!? Are they crazy?" Katie cried out. The shock and concern in his sister's voice strengthened his own resolve to make it sound okay. "When did this happen?"

He grimaced. "A few weeks ago."

Logan popped open a bottle of Malbec but it wasn't louder than his sister's yell. "A few *weeks* ago!?"

"Yes, but don't freak out. I think it's all a misunderstanding. I'm going to let them investigate and, when they find nothing, I'll either go back, or already have figured out a new path for myself."

"What can I do to help?"

"Don't you worry, little sister. I'm finding the good in it. Your brother's been workin' in a kitchen."

"In the kitchen? Really!" Katie's jubilee made Logan grin. When they were kids, Katie would tell him that he would be a world-famous chef someday. It was that belief in him that had been driving him to make these decisions now. Katie's voice grew in animation. "Why haven't you told me about this?

I always knew you should have gone the culinary road. I can't believe it. But I can believe it. Logan! Yay! So where are you working?"

"Uriel's cousin had a conference at the Wyndham and was talking up this new up-and-coming restaurant—Zuma—that has its grand opening in a week." He didn't want to tell Katie that he was planning on taking Lily to the restaurant once they reconciled. "They needed new guys who were willing to learn fast and work hard—my Milan experience ended up helping me get the job."

"It's what you should have been doing all along, Logan," Katie said. "When you came home early from Milan…"

"Hey. It's okay. No regrets."

He had studied in Milan for a few weeks in college, on his way to being accepted into a premier culinary arts program, when he had received the news that his father had passed. He knew it was over the moment he had heard his sister's cry over a crackly long-distance connection.

"Besides," Logan reminded his sister, "you wouldn't be a senior at Miami Ad right now if I hadn't gone back to school for finance."

"I know. Well, when one door closes…"

"The open door is what I'm planning on. I'll drop by the bakery to see you soon."

He hung up. Unread messages from Lily were still blinking in his inbox. It had been three weeks, but he didn't have the courage to open them. What would he find? Rejection, surely, after that drunk call. Disappointment. Or, worse, messages full of hope and hurt and *then* rejection and disappointment.

After this time, *any* message from Lily would be welcome now. He opened the messages he had been avoiding. *Three.*

Lily had reached out the night he had driven angrily from her apartment.

What the heck was that about?

The pit in Logan's stomach seemed to expand even wider. *This was a bad idea,* he knew, but he kept reading.

Logan? Is everything okay? I hope you can understand why I said what I did.

And the next message, too vague for a stranger, but clear enough for him.

...The rules?

At Lily's last message, Logan groaned. The woman in Lily's apartment had been her *mother.* Lily could not admit who Logan was without breaking a million rules. Lily hadn't been rejecting him—she had been giving him a *chance.*

Shit.

Logan wanted to turn around right then and run to Lily. He wanted to tell her that he finally understood that her intentions were *good* and could they go back to the moment right before entering the steamy shower and start over? Those daydreams had become the night dreams he didn't want to wake up from.

But first, it was time to prepare the steak with parmesan polenta. He measured every ingredient, adjusting the required amount to match what he remembered doing in Milan the last night before his return flight to Chicago. So here he was now, years later, going through the same motions he'd gone through countless times, but feeling the same defeat he had felt in Milan. In fact, Logan mused, maybe it was sadness that seared the steaks to perfection.

While the meat's spices continued to imbue it, Logan tied his silver-blue tie confidently around his light blue collared shirt, safely hidden behind his apron. He had spent an hour ironing his suit, making sure everything was in place.

In the spirit of his father, Logan was going to show up to Lily's home with the meal he had perfected in Italy. He was going to apologize, properly, for how he had acted, and ask for a do-over. He wanted to tell her how much more of himself she made him feel. He didn't have to worry about what to say, or how. Even when he had put her hat on his head and danced in the middle of the street for her, Logan had a feeling there was a laugh just waiting to erupt behind the scowl. Sure enough, when he had approached her and bowed deeply like a Jane Austen gentleman, the peak of a smile shone through and he was hooked. He wanted to be the one to beckon that smile out of her all the time.

And he wasn't going to wait one more day. When he could smell the sage drifting from the stove, Logan wrapped the meal with a rubber band over the lid, just in case, and whispered a silent prayer.

He couldn't wait to sit on her bed, a fresh pot of coffee beside them, and talk about everything from beginning to end - from saving her hat and convincing her to have dinner with him, to falling in love with the way she fit against his body, to Anne walking in, to his sudden realization that he had let his pride get the better of him. He'd promise not to do it again, and she would understand with the ever-present grace he knew he could draw out of her. She'd furrow her brow while he explained, but then she'd throw her arms around his neck and laugh about the entire story, skin pressed against his for the rest of the night.

Show Off

S prawled all over Lily's counter were rectangular pieces of embossed card stock. "I'm looking at the proofs right now, and the black invitation looks amazing. I'd make the writing on the RSVP card more metallic, but other than that, our guests will definitely get the impression that this is an event they don't want to miss. Thanks for your hard work, Loretta." How she had become the event planner for this IceStorm party was a mystery, but Lily was enjoying it. *Kind of like what planning a wedding would be like.*

The doorbell buzzed. She switched the speakerphone off, accepted her visitor through the app on her phone, and held the phone to her ear.

"I can't wait to see what the table cards and thank you notes look like. Same theme, right?"

Lily propped the door open and walked back to the kitchen. Lily continued, "Excellent. Jeremiah will love that aqua detail. I should consider a dress in that shade. How many guests are on the invite list, anyway?"

As Anne approached, Lily pointed to her phone, miming her apologies. Anne smiled approvingly and unwrapped the scarf from her neck. Lily held a cup of freshly-brewed coffee like an offering.

"Five hundred, huh? Let's find a way to get that up to 750 by next Friday. Make calls, follow-up on those calls, and then run into their assistants at Starbucks if you have to. I have to go, Lore—, but thanks for doing this. You're a gem."

She set her phone down, trading it for the Chloe wool coat hanging in the closet. A glass rolled out of the closet. "Happy Sunday!"

Anne raised her eyebrow at the glass but ignored it. She sipped from the bright purple mug. "Nice delegation, dear."

"It's been fun. Loretta's sweet. She makes silly mistakes, but she's learning."

"So, how many days until this party?" Anne asked.

"Six weeks. The demo went perfectly in Utah, and we're currently receiving our final signatures from the police and fire departments for permission to have a one-thousand person drill at a Wyndham in Manhattan."

"Sounds scary."

"It would be, if RACE weren't at play and something tragic really did happen."

"We must find an outfit that expresses your authority, charm, grace *and* intelligence."

"Shouldn't be too hard. They're innate characteristics. But turquoise would be good."

Anne squealed at her response and placed the mug on the bar. "Ooh, you're 'fun Lily' today! Your eyes will be stunning in that color. I was thinking we could get ourselves fresh furs, a stronger coat of pink on our nails, and a later lunch at this posh Upper East restaurant Claire told me about."

"That sounds like a great day." Lily pulled on her sparkly-silver Marc Jacobs Camilla ankle booties. The highest level of bold fashion was encouraged wherever Anne accompanied.

"Those look stunning, dear," Anne complimented as she checked her hair and makeup in the hallway mirror. "You'll catch the eye of everyone. Maybe there will even be a—" she paused and shook her head. "Never mind. Nicholas will be there, won't he? And those booties are new this season, aren't they? How wonderful." She didn't wait for an answer, turning to Lily with a grin. "A software engineer who doesn't need to wear plaid and cut her hair like a man. *My* daughter is a head-turner, both in cashmere *and* code."

Anne was clearly proud of herself for the compliment, but it made Lily sad. She wasn't about to admit that she bought the coat and shoes for a night of swing dancing she hadn't been invited to. Maybe it was better this way; Maya would have scoffed at Lily's choice of shoe. It's not like they were practical.

Nicholas would appreciate the shoes more anyway. He'd laugh at the brilliance and say something about how it matched her eyes. He was always saying something perfect.

* * *

Lily and her mother waited for the short redhead in a blazer to return.

"After this party, you are absolutely not allowed to run off to Spain to visit Marley. She can wait— your ovaries cannot."

"Mother!"

"Marley will understand. She's a family-type girl." Lily tried to ignore the distaste in Anne's voice. Anne never truly understood Marley's relationship with her mom; she pegged the relationship an unfortunate circumstance: *how will Marley learn to be her own person if she's always relying on her mother?*

"I won't be going to Spain this year, although last year was a really great time." She had been able to spend the week in yoga pants, drinking countless cups of coffee with her best friend, snuggled together under heavy blankets, watching trash TV and forgetting about the adult responsibilities that had snuck up on them.

Anne pointed to a Burberry coat. The redhead passed it to the tall gentleman next to her who carried it to their dressing rooms. "That Juan sounded so promising."

Lily tried not to choke on her laughter as Anne continued. "Juan" was the funniest-looking character that she and Marley could find as they had clicked through different channels—an overweight man in his 60s who had a perpetually stained t-shirt and tried to catch his next door neighbor changing every time she came home from work. "It's a shame he was never granted a Visa. Our government must have known there'd be no way he'd be leaving once you had him wrapped around your finger." Anne laughed as the redhead held another coat up for trial.

"Maybe wait for your assistant to come back and hold it, dear," Anne said. "No need to struggle."

Lily nodded in approval of her mother's choice of faux fur. Say what she would, but Anne Cromwell's sense of style was unparalleled. Lily could only hope that she would look as impressive when she was in her 50s.

"Yeah, it's a real shame. I was really rooting for Juan." Lily almost felt bad lying to her mother.

"Oh well," Anne conceded. "There have been others since then."

Lily grinned. "But not as wonderful as Nicholas."

Anne turned on her heel. "What? Lily. Don't tease."

"Mother, I think he's *the* guy."

Anne narrowed her eyes. Lily was befuddled by the lack of response. Why was she being so hesitant? Anne searched her daughter's eyes. "You mean—he checks off our list? And you *like* him? He's not just the business connection Hugo alluded to?"

Lily didn't know whether she should shake her head or nod.

"How do you know?" Anne asked.

"How do I know *what* exactly?" Lily could feel frustration quickly mounting, like trying to slip a tight-fit glove on already chilled fingers.

"How do you know that you've 'caught' him?" Anne looked like she needed to sit.

"Well. He wants more of Lily Cromwell, and I don't mind letting him get to know me." The words felt strange in her mouth, but they sounded like the truth.

"That's not enough. Men always want more in the beginning; how do you know he *needs* you?"

"Well, I suppose I'm the next step in ensuring his Dove Hospitals are the most respected, most helpful hospitals in the country. With RACE, he's struck marketing *gold*."

"So you *need* his connections, too."

"Well, yes. For now. But he'd still be relying on IceStorm, whereas once we hit the hospitals *and* the hotels, it'll be a matter of time before condo buildings and commercial spaces are required to have RACE installed just like sprinklers and smoke detectors. We'd be quite the team."

"Oh, this is wonderful!" Anne said, wrapping Lily in a real hug. Her mother's palm on the back of her head placed Lily back into her pre-school self, when Anne congratulated her for a job well done reciting a Christmas poem for the school's pageant. "*That's my girl*," Lily remembered Anne whispering. "*That's* my *girl*."

Anne detached from their hug, and linked her arm through her daughter's. "Do you..." Anne swallowed. "*love*... him?"

Lily laughed out loud as the taller associate held up Anne's coat. "Mother. Please."

Anne's relief was palpable as she wrapped Lily's hands in her own.

"Thank heavens. Because I've told you all these years, it is *not* worth it if he suddenly dies of a heart attack after years of promises and—and leaves you with a four year old daughter... as cute as she is..." Anne swept a stray piece of hair from Lily's face and tucked it behind her ear. "A little bit of puppy love isn't worth the pain."

Lily clapped her hands to her mother's. "I know, Mom. You don't have to worry."

"Well. In that case." Anne slid into the coat and grinned at Lily standing behind her. "I want to know everything about him. I want to know how you met and what he looks like. Do you have a picture? When do you see him next?"

Lily didn't mind all the questions. She didn't feel like a defendant this time. This time, she was an open book, Logan was just a rude maintenance man, and Nicholas was the key to her mother's love.

* * *

It had been dark many hours by the time Lily walked through the revolving doors of her apartment building. After such a unique day with her mother, she couldn't imagine spending this evening without Nicholas. He didn't even realize how life-changing the kiss they'd share tonight would be. And maybe they'd share a little something more.

She stopped at the doorman's desk. "Hi, Loranzo! How's my favorite doorman?"

He pressed the pause button on his device. "Good evening, little lady." The tall man with a smile bigger than his waistline grinned at Lily. The crisp white collar of his shirt gleamed brighter against the tan of his skin.

"Now, Loranzo. I wouldn't call you 'big man.'"

He chuckled like there were bubbles tickling him from the inside. "You've got that right. But *you* could, Miss Cromwell. But just you." He winked.

She rearranged the bags on her arm, setting some down on the quartz counter. He tilted his phone towards her. She'd recognize the white uniforms with orange lettering anywhere. Looking up at her with wide eyes, he asked, "Can you believe they've won five games in a row?"

"It's like hell really has frozen over." Lily wasn't surprised she hadn't kept up with the Knicks since meeting Logan or going on the Utah trip to meet Nic. It was too bad: handling the emotions that came from mind-juggling two men was much less enjoyable than watching ten of them wrestle a ball. "Listen, I'd love to talk about the game, but I've got someone real handsome to get real pretty for."

"That won't take you very long at all, little lady." He said it like a grand-father would, and it made her beam.

"I bet you say that to all the ladies."

"Just the ones who call me 'Big Man.'" They laughed. He pointed at the off-white ceramic china with its glass lid. "Would you like me to carry this up for you?"

"Ooo, what's this?" She approached to inspect it. A rubber band held the lid in place. *So sweet.* She didn't remember the last time she saw one of those—at Marley's house, maybe, when Peggy invited her over for a home-cooked meal.

"Before I started my shift just a little while ago, Jeremy wrote a note here saying a man who was 'impeccably' dressed and 'very handsome' was here to see you and left it."

Lily's grin widened. "I'll find a way to carry it," she said.

With the dish laid across her arms and bags full of new dresses and furs and shoes strapped across both of her palms, Lily decided she couldn't wait for the elevator and ran up the stairs to the third floor.

Lily resisted the urge to text him right away. She wanted to thank him for not being cowardly, or waiting for her to reach out first. Finally, a man who wasn't all talk and no action. A man who showed effort.

She placed the bags within the large walk-in closet—Marcia would hang her dresses when she came to clean on Monday—and chose the Michael Buble playlist on her phone. Trumpets blared and Lily's heart soared. *"Well it's a marvelous night for a moon dance..."*

Lily slid the dish to stay warm in the oven until this "impeccably dressed" and "very handsome" man knocked on her door. Lily smiled to herself, imagining Nic busying himself, frantically looking up recipes to resemble the meal they didn't get to eat the other day.

What should she text him? It had to be the perfect follow-up after a successful Mexican date and a failed, drunken night-cap.

"Can I just have one more moon dance with you, my love?"

She jumped into her bed, sat cross-legged, and could barely keep her phone from shaking. The earlier approval she had felt radiating from her mother was an adrenaline rush that needed a way out, and fast.

She found Nicholas' name in her messages, opening their ongoing chat conversation.

So... are you gonna come over and help me eat, or is this all for me? ;)

Lily waited anxiously for the three dots to appear, staring at the painting of the dancers. She forced her shoulders to relax and pushed lingering thoughts of Marley and Logan aside. Finally, his reply.

Ah, sinner at your place tonight?
*Dinner

Lily answered.

I'll tell the doorman to let you in this time. You have 20 minutes; otherwise, this'll be gone.

And Lily meant it. The aroma wafting from the food wrapped around her like a familiar memory - warm, welcoming, and altogether comforting. The instrumental of Buble's "Moon Dance" took her back to when she was three, knocking on her dad's office door. Her mother would play it as she prepared dinner for them—a historical fact now. Each time, her father would open the door, wrap his hand around hers, making her feel safe and secure. He'd pick her up, spin them around, and cuddle her on his lap as he continued working at his desk. How wonderful that thinking about Nic made her think of her father. Her dad was a good man with tender spots—so, too, must Nicholas Archer be.

Buble's "Fever" was next, and thoughts of her dad disappeared. It was time to officially welcome Nicholas Archer into the love that Lily Cromwell had to offer. There wouldn't be a disastrous shower attempt this time, but she'd still bring the heat.

How to Say No

The table was set with her silver China, the turquoise candles of various heights, and two wine glasses resting next to the Merlot and Chianti sitting on ice. Michael Buble was crooning and Lily's excitement was rising. This was her chance to be the Lily that Logan didn't let her be.

And all because of such a stupid choice rooted in fear. Maybe if she had told the truth, Anne would have gotten over it by now and she wouldn't be ready to entertain someone so different than the fun-loving, free-spirited Logan she missed so much.

A dull throbbing had been at her eyes since she ran up the stairs, and rising excitement of Nicholas' arrival wasn't helping it go away.

Holding on to the semi-ironed curtains at her window, she observed the street below. She loved this apartment because of the contrast she was able to see from one side of the building compared to the other. From her bedroom balcony, she saw the trees, paths, and reminders that nature could still rule supreme in one of the largest cities in the world. On this side, though, she could look down and see the hustle of people running out of taxi cabs into their homes, only to return back to another cab to take them to dinner. She often laughed at the differences in lifestyle she observed depending on where she was in her home. It was like choosing which yoga position she wanted in order to receive different benefits. Did she want to feel inspired by those tourists who wanted a slow stroll to see everything in the park? Or did she need to feel the rush of productivity and progress—that American *busyness*?

Today, Lily she looked for the street to prepare her for quick conversation and witty discussions with Nicholas. She opened the window for the breeze to enter.

She opened the window to hear the world around her. There was a thaw in the air that made it seem like spring could almost be around the corner, but everyone knew warm weather would be ever-elusive until May. The warm wind kissed Lily's cheek in brief affection. Then, she heard a young boy's laughter and saw a boy and girl jumping from one dirty snow mound to another.

The high schoolers didn't quite belong. Lily resisted the urge to yell at them to get out of the street and watched them instead.

A brightly colored shawl was loosely wrapped around the girl's neck so it draped down her arms. The colors of the scarf were mesmerizing and, for reasons Lily didn't understand, they made her feel nauseous the more she watched. At first the bright orange waved, and then it was the deep red that dominated Lily's attention when the girl spun in dizzying circles. The pure white seemed to meld the girl's hands to the boy's arms as he pulled her closer to him. She playfully resisted, but then allowed him to pull her closely behind him, like he was a magnet pulling her forward. The connection between the two was undeniable, and Lily wondered how two young people could be so connected. A closer look revealed the girl's grin, her slightly crooked teeth not getting in the way of her brilliant smile. The sight warmed Lily's heart, which felt like it was beating faster and faster. They seemed otherworldly, these two, like they were dancing to an entirely different beat than the rest of the world. They were alive - dancing flames shooting out floating embers. One playfully shoved another, until it seemed that they became one. The boy wrapped his arms around the girl and lifted her up onto his back. Lily shut the window. She realized she had been holding her breath.

Her excitement at the prospect of Nicholas coming over suddenly turned to a quiet dread. Between her head throbbing and her heart beating faster than she could take a breath, she wondered if it was too late to cancel her plans with Nicholas. It wasn't right. She was just playing with Nicholas—a ruse to secure a promotion at work. *He* didn't make her excited; it was the idea of him being the reason behind Anne's approval that was exciting. She knew who she wanted to dance with.

She couldn't understand the disequilibrium she felt, but she suddenly had the urge to lock her doors and tell Nic to stay home. Didn't Greg see that canoodling with an investor would actually backfire?

"Lily Cromwell," she said out loud. "Stop it. You're being ridiculous." She grabbed the edge of the bar hard enough that a half-empty bottle fell onto its side and cracked.

The buzzer rang. He was downstairs.

Lily took big gulps of air, but it felt like she couldn't get quite enough of it. She heard the knock at her door. *How did he get up here so fast?*

He knocked again.

"Lily?" Nic's voice bellowed.

In desperation, Lily wrapped the red blanket around her, like the orange shawl that had been wrapped around the kids outside.

She walked over to the door and opened it.

"Hi," Lily said weakly. She wrapped the blanket tighter around her.

Nic looked over her, eyes sweeping over her blanket-wrapped self like she was a 4-year old playing dress-up. He looked agitated. He was probably wondering why she wasn't dressed up in a pink negligee by now, with all the eager messages she had sent him earlier. "Everything okay in there?" he asked, craning his neck.

"Oh, yes," Lily stepped aside to let him in. Her voice felt heavy.

Rather than walk past her, however, he wrapped his arm beneath the protection of Lily's blanket, around her waist, and rested his forehead on hers.

"I've been looking forward to you all day. You know how to drive a man insane, Lily Cromwell."

His hands were icicles resting on the warm surface of her body. Lily wanted to pull away, but she felt frozen in place.

"Thanks for making dinner," Lily whispered.

Nic cocked his head. "Sure. I wouldn't miss it."

Lily took Nicholas's hand and led him to the dining room. She gestured towards the table. "Have a seat! I'll grab your food from the oven. It's so cute that you put it in CorningWare. Like the old days."

She walked into the kitchen and leaned against the wall. Her knees were weak; her lungs seemed to be forgetting how to keep up with her breathing.

"It smells so good," Lily called.

"You deserve the best," Nic called back. She could hear him uncorking the wine.

It felt like it took every ounce of her energy to say anything witty or flirtatious, but the instinct was deeply ingrained in her. She came out of the kitchen and entered the dining room with the dish in her hands feeling like a 1950s wife. Nicholas stood at attention. It felt like he was drinking her in. *Always a perfect gentleman.* Maybe he was imagining what a life with her would be like, too. They were playing house right now, weren't they?

She set the food on the table and lifted the cover. Rich juice and garlic scented steak wafted into the air. As she sat, Nic poured their glasses three-quarters full. Then, he served them each a piece of steak.

This wine was stronger than I thought. The usual Cromwell clarity was undoubtedly dimmed.

She could hear, distantly, Anne's warning, "*Never lose control of your faculties because of alcohol, Lily Cromwell. It doesn't matter how screwed up your life may seem; alcohol will never be the thing that screws it back into place.*"

As good as it normally felt to defy Anne, what with a man in her home and her thoughts clearly muddled, it also made her a little nervous. She could hear Nicholas talking about something, and she wanted to tell him to just stop and wait a second until she could steady her anchor. Her boat was far away from shore and she needed a steady presence to steady *her*. She thought of Logan at the ice rink and wished for him earnestly. She didn't have the energy to shush him out of her mind this time.

"...so I told them that IceStorm would be the consultant for all things emergency—not the medical emergencies, of course, but in terms of natural disaster response," Nic said. "Since we discussed that in Utah, I'm assuming that was okay to say?"

"Yes, yes, of course." *What was she agreeing to?* "Tell me more," Lily said.

She didn't care about the answer, but Anne said that a rich man will always talk about his work more than his hobbies, and she needed the time to think about what she really wanted in this moment. Why had she actually invited him over? She wanted the parts after dinner, and sharing this meal with him had seemed so heart-warming and exciting, but as he told her about his newest ideas and proposals, she felt anything but. Even though the wine had made her cheeks hot, she felt cold. Very, very cold.

"I'm so sorry, Nic. Can you excuse me?"

Nic's eyes filled with concern. "Sure, of course." He stood when she did. This really was Anne Cromwell's perfect guy.

But not hers.

As she walked to her master bathroom, she held onto the walls of her hallway. When she arrived to the washroom, she leaned onto the counter with shaking hands. She looked into the mirror and hung her head. The pink of her cheeks had turned into a gaunt yellow.

Turning the cold water spout felt heavy and laborious, but she needed to remind herself that cold was okay. Winter in New York? She was used to it.

The desire to be alone enraptured her then. She wished she could be spending her Saturday evening lathering her hair with foamy bubbles like she was now trying to lather her hands. She would release her hair, currently in a tight knot holding loose strands of hair, and watch it fall to just above the middle of her back. She would turn sideways and run her fingers through, relishing the fact that she didn't have to go anywhere or see anyone. But no, she was here, and instead of retreating to her bedroom, she had to entertain this guy.

How had Nic so quickly lost his luster?

She walked back to the dining room and sat down, patting her skirt. Where did that blanket go?

Nic offered her the wine glass and a grin. He was always grinning, but she knew it wasn't always genuine. Not like Logan's.

Lily knew she didn't want more wine. She wasn't interested in any more of this fog, but she also didn't want to be on her A-game right now. She wanted to be simple Lily: small and hidden in her bed covers, or barefoot in the street with the one who'd hold her in a magnetic embrace.

But instead, just as she always did, she smiled as wide as she could and asked, "Now who would I be if I said 'No'?"

* * *

The breathing next to her startled her awake. Next to her was a sleeping Nicholas, hair still strangely in place, though Lily suspected her own had been tossed about, a probable consequence of their night together.

She didn't remember much from the night before; she drank that last drip of wine greedily, hoping it'd mask the rising migraine. But now that she didn't remember much at all, she found that, in addition to the fog, she also had a sick feeling in her chest, like all the scarves she owned were suddenly tangled in her intestines, pulling tighter each time she breathed.

The covers weren't as warm as they usually were, and the air around her felt dry and suffocating. She slid herself out of bed as gently as she could. She shut the window that Nic must have opened. She looked around her room, but could only see the room in pieces: clothes strewn over her ottoman, vanity, bedpost, and floor. She wanted to re-dress and assess herself, but reached instead for the bathrobe hanging on the back of the chair next to her coffee pot. She didn't care if the sputtering would bother Nic's sleep. She didn't know what she'd say to him, and she found that she didn't really care.

She had apparently already slept with the man Greg asked her to get close with, so as far as she was concerned, she was one step closer to that promotion. Now that she was *that* woman, she couldn't wait for Vanessa and Genevieve to visit. She yearned to recreate some innocence and normalcy— and wishing Nic would stay in her bed wasn't part of that agenda. She just wished Nic would have the wisdom to stay inside; she didn't want to have to explain this scene to Genny.

She wrapped the robe around herself and heard in the strangled gurgle of the coffee pot that it was struggling. It sounded like it was choking on itself, unable to handle what it had been asked to filter. As Lily waited for her filled mug, she tried to find her voice.

"Ni—," Lily started. It felt like an anchor was weighing down her tongue, twisting it down. And her heart was pumping too hard. Her hangovers never felt like this. She took her cup and couldn't wait for the warmth to run through her fingers and down into the deepest parts of her.

She stepped onto her balcony, shutting the door behind her so she could forget Nicholas and their night together and focus instead on Vanessa and Genevieve.

She needed to sit.

But instead of resting on the chair, she stumbled forward. She couldn't stop herself in time and felt the cold bar of the balcony's railing slam into her jaw. Sharp pain made her see stars. Concrete kissed her hands and her cheek rested on the cold rock, throbbing like someone was holding a burning knife to her face. Somewhere, far away it seemed, her mug broke with a crash. She blinked her eyes once, then twice, enough to watch the cold liquid spill over.

Cold coffee isn't good anyway, Lily thought, before early morning New York became the darkest night.

Logan: Served

L ogan rearranged the scarf around his neck. It was getting colder by the minute, and it was quite the distance from Zuma to her flat, but he needed time to think. He had spent the entire night *and* walk to Lily's apartment thinking about what he'd say to her when she opened her apartment door. *If* she opened the door.

He expected to be more riled up before this reunion. His mind felt separated into two roads: to throw himself into his new career opportunity at Zuma wholeheartedly and wonder if Lily would accept a chef for a partner or put all his energy into making sure he wasn't fired from Travis Investments.

After his successful interview, he was told that he'd begin as a sous chef, learn from prize-winning chefs, and then move on up the ladle. He had done a pretty good job ignoring his phone during his shift to see if Lily said *anything* about the food he left for her. Before Logan fell asleep, he changed Lily's phone number to play a different ringtone than the default option and increased the volume to the max setting. He didn't want to miss any chance to make things right.

You're being pathetic. According to all those games you always saw Ronnie play, you should be playing it cool.

But this time the stakes are too high, he argued with the voice in his head. He was taking his dad's advice all the way. No games. Just the truth. And the truth was that he needed to see Lily. He needed to see whether he still had a chance with the beautiful girl whose disarming, flustering smile made him feel whole. And, selfishly, he wanted to see if she genuinely enjoyed the meal he prepared for her. Maybe she'd even have leftovers that they could share and chat over. The anticipation was the string pulling him closer to the spool.

The sun shone brightly, but it still felt cold. The crispness bit at his nose and he nuzzled closer into his scarf, regretting that he had left his gloves on his kitchen counter. The grass, frozen in time, didn't budge when the breeze picked up the back of Logan's coat. He walked faster. As he turned the corner, the majesty of Central Park revealed itself to him. He scanned the area around him, birds flying from one tree to another. They were much too loud for a peaceful day, squawking instead of singly sweetly. The shriek of an ambulance joined the noise. Logan suddenly wished he was back in Summit. If he tried really hard, he could imagine the smell of the lemon tea his mother always made sure to have ready for them growing up.

The trail seemed to lead straight to Lily's building, but there were piles of snow to climb through. He was so nervous that each step felt like his heart couldn't possibly keep up. A tall woman and her daughter laughed and pointed at two squirrels chasing each other. Logan chuckled as he followed them.

Suddenly, he heard the little voice gasp and cry. "Miss Lily!"

He spun around to see the girl pointing towards the direction in which he was headed. Surely it was just coincidence. The woman scooped the girl in her arms and sprinted towards the noise. In case it *wasn't* coincidence that they knew a different Miss Lily, he followed.

He urged his heart to stay within his chest.

The tall woman arrived to the street first and went straight to the nearest EMT. Logan couldn't see who was on the gurney. But surely it couldn't be Lily: she was in her late twenties, fit, healthy, and active.

The little girl was crying and about to scream louder. The woman with the thick black braid kept turning back and saying things like, "She'll be okay, baby. Don't worry. It'll be okay." The last time she turned around, she caught Logan's eye. He pointed, expressing what he hoped was an earnest offer to help comfort the girl. The woman hesitated, but nodded.

He walked towards the little girl and squatted down. Her bright eyes were sparkling with dew, and long eyelashes accented her bronze skin. He swallowed his own panic and offered his biggest smile. "Hi, honey. I'm Logan. Your mommy is doing an important job right now, huh?"

The little girl barely registered him; she kept trying to look over his head to catch what was going on.

"I'm not supposed to talk to strangers," the girl snapped. But her hardened face transformed to a melting waterfall once she looked up to see the ambulances again.

"She's... dead?" the girl whimpered. "How will I know her favorite flower?" She heaved to release a loud, scared cry. The noise coming from such a little body threatened to push Logan off-balance. He figured it wouldn't be effective to ignore what the girl could very clearly see.

"I don't think she's dead, sweetheart. She's sick, but she has many people trying to help her right now. She'll be okay."

Logan knew he might be lying; he didn't know what was going on or who was on the gurney, but he knew from experience it was helpful to hear empty promises in the most hopeless situations. It was all he could do to keep himself from throwing arms around this little girl to comfort her, so instead he unwrapped his orange scarf from around his neck and wrapped it around her. Wind bit at his exposed neck, but she needed it more. She snuggled into it.

"What's your name?" Logan asked her.

"Genny. And that's my mommy, Vanessa."

The sudden silence made the woman who was with the EMTs look over at her daughter. Logan tried to motion, somehow, that he wasn't doing any harm. The woman gave a reassuring smile and stepped aside. In that moment, Logan saw Lily Cromwell's long blonde hair hanging over the railing of the gurney.

"Lily!" Logan cried, sprinting towards the ambulance.

He barely registered Genny's renewed cries climbing higher and higher.

He arrived to the ambulance in time for the technicians to shut the door in Logan's face. He ran over to the driver's side and yelled. "No! I need to see her!"

"Are you family?" The driver turned the ambulance's lights back on.

"No, but her family isn't here right now," Logan said over the loud sirens.

"They'll be contacted on the way to the hospital, sir. Her phone was found right next to her."

"Where was she found?" Logan knew he was pushing it. If Lily was in trouble, he was keeping her from the help she needed. If he shouted loud enough, maybe Lily would hear him and tell them to let him in.

"Sir, we have to go."

Logan nodded, letting go of the vehicle and urging it on with fervent desire for Lily's safety.

He turned around to see Genny and her mother staring at him. Genny was wiping her eyes, and her mother was standing stoically, shocked.

Before Logan turned to run, the movement of someone standing at Lily's balcony window caught his attention. When he squinted to get a closer look, the face was gone.

He didn't have time to investigate.

The woman lifted her daughter into her arms and they ran their own way without another word.

Stay Awake

Lily's eyes were too heavy. She wanted so badly to open them, but that was like asking her to lift fifty pounds and then some over her head. She tried wiggling her fingers, but the heaviness of something covering her right hand made her flinch in pain.

Since her eyes were not going to reveal her current location, she tried to focus her hearing to pick up on any clues. She heard the flipped page of something that sounded like a magazine. She heard a beep in the distance and another right next to her left ear. Feet shuffled outside the room she was in, and hurried voices weaved in and out of conversation. Her heart beat faster, and she felt pressure gather around her left bicep. What was happening?

And where was Nicholas? Surely he was the one who had called for help. Since he checked all the boxes of being the perfect gentleman, he would surely check all the boxes of being a perfect caregiver, too. Someone so impeccable during the "for health" part of a marriage vow would also undoubtedly succeed in the "through sickness" part. He had probably driven behind her full-speed to the hospital and was now getting coffee and a Danish pastry to start his morning while he waited for more information. He probably canceled all his meetings for the next day, too. She couldn't ignore the hope growing in her that he was the type of guy to sit right next to her, flipping through a newspaper waiting for her to wake.

She tried to say Nicholas' name, but only a groan vibrated through her lips.

The page-turning stopped. A voice she recognized called, "She's awake! Nurses! Lily Cromwell is awake!"

Vanessa!

Lily had not shared as many conversations with Vanessa as she had with Genny, but the smooth and secure voice was unmistakable. Although they were mere acquaintances who adored the same little girl, what was she doing in Lily's hospital room, presuming that's where they were right now?

Hands began moving around her again, bright lights blinding her sensitive eyes. The confusion made her head heavy again, and she surrendered herself to the darkness. This was too much to try and figure out right now.

Anne's Mercy

Anne Cromwell rushed through the hospital doors like a gust of hurricane wind.

"Where's my daughter?" she demanded. Blank stares and scowls of those sitting in the waiting room looked back at her with indifference. She stomped over to the counter to a nurse with thickly braided hair. She was speaking over the phone, reciting numbers from a chart.

"I want to know—," Anne demanded. The woman held up a finger, but maintained her professional lilt for whoever was on the other side of the phone.

Anne looked around incredulously, wondering who else found it comical that this woman thought she had a right to silence *Anne Cromwell*. She hoped it hid the fear gathering within the depths of her being. It felt too much like when Richard was in the hospital, nurses and doctors avoiding her, careful not to be the ones who finally told her he didn't make it. When a broad-chested security guard stepped forward, Anne stood down for a moment. But the moment the nurse took her sweet time placing the phone back in its cradle, Anne burst.

"Lily Cromwell was brought to this hospital and I demand to know where she is."

"One moment, please."

This woman's lack of urgency was infuriating. It took all of Anne's willpower to step foot into this building after she'd spent at least ten minutes hyperventilating outside. Trevor had to hold her hair back as she retched over the side of the Rolls Royce. Just the smell of those Lysol cleaners on those deceptively clean floors made her breath catch like acid in her shrinking esophagus. As if people could forget that hidden beneath that thick wax underfoot had been blood and contaminated liquids and waste. But she could not behave with hesitancy now. Her daughter needed her.

Finally, the nurse spoke. "Lily Cromwell is in room 405 of the Intensive Care Unit. Only one visitor at a time, please. There is already a woman in there, so we'll let her know that Lily's mother is here and we'll make sure you're with your daughter as soon as possible."

Anne didn't wonder who the woman was, although it was odd that the friend was female. Had Lily forgotten to mention that Marley had flown in? Lily didn't *have* female friends; women were typically intimidated by her daughter—as it should be. *Like mother, like daughter,* she mused. It was easier this way. Less *time* to focus on her feelings meant *less focus* on them, too. But it was also possible that Lily mentioned this new friend and Anne simply did not remember the information. She regretted not paying more attention now. As the elevator bell announced she had reached the fourth floor, Anne promised herself she'd hang onto every word Lily said, as long as she lived. She didn't believe in a god that would make a child fatherless as life was just beginning, but she found herself praying to one now.

When she entered the fourth floor waiting room, she scanned the groups of people huddled in concern, whispering prayers, or those sitting alone who were lying back with earbuds blocking out anything that could remind them of where they were. She sat down between a pouty-looking teenager with headphones in and an elderly man whose head was back, a snore waking him up every few minutes. Anne made a mental note to have Trevor bring up her iPad if Lily had to stay here longer. Judging by the others waiting in the room, she'd have to call him soon. Too bad such technology hadn't been popular when she was waiting for news about Richard.

A young man who had been pacing back and forth with a little girl twisting through his long legs stopped to face Anne. Anne scrunched her brow. She recognized the man's face. His blonde hair was a little more tousled than it had been when she first saw him, but he was quite dressed up for being a -

Maintenance man? Judging by the little girl weaving through his legs, he must be waiting for somebody else. His wife? His mother? It was convenient for them to be in the same place. Anne could ask him—Mr. West, was it?—to check up on Lily's unit and turn off any running water, lights, or heat while Lily had to be in the hospital. She was sure he could use a distraction from the hospital as well. She would be happy to provide the preoccupation.

But Anne would ensure he wouldn't have to check up on her unit for too long. They would have Lily up and seeing Nicholas again in no time.

Anne nodded in Mr. West's direction to show that she was not one for disrespecting handymen, but he seemed to take it as an invitation to chat. *Oh dear.* Anne walked to the nurse's station again.

"How much longer until I can see my daughter?" she asked.

"Just a few minutes, ma'am. We are checking on her now. Lily showed physical movement, which is a great sign. Someone will come for you when it is possible for you to see her."

"She hadn't been showing *any* movement?" Anne felt whatever color had been on her face draining from it. She needed to sit down, but turned to see the tall, blond man standing in front of her, his hand wrapped around the little girl's.

"Oh, hello, Mr. West." The look on his face made it seem like he was surprised that she remembered his name. He shifted his weight from one leg to the other, but then stood straighter. He cleared his throat.

"You're Lily's mother, aren't you?" He offered his hand and she shook it loosely.

"Well, can't you see the resemblance?" Anne smiled and blinked her eyes rapidly. She was a pro at masking her fear and insecurities with humor and flirtation. Thankfully, she had taught her daughter the same. She looked around the room. "So you're also waiting for someone, I assume?" She crouched down to smile at the girl with the short pigtails. "Is this little one's mother okay?"

The confusion on Logan's face was endearing. He must have been having a difficult day. "Oh, yes. Genevieve's mother is just fine."

In a voice that sounded like she had just sucked in helium, the little girl responded. "You can call me Genny!"

Logan grinned down at Genevieve, who returned the smile. Anne felt her face harden. It was like she was watching Richard and Lily. Lily had looked at her father with those same trusting eyes, like he could do no wrong. Like he'd always be there for her.

"Mommy!" Genevieve let go of Logan's hand. A woman walked towards them with a gait like she had walked this earth for hundreds of years.

"She just moved her fingers," Vanessa told Logan.

Logan looked up towards the ceiling in gratitude. "Oh, thank God. Did the doctors say anything else?"

"Unfortunately, no. Since we're not family, we can't know more details."

Logan nodded with quiet understanding and looked at Anne, as if he were waiting for her to react. Anne just squeezed her hands tighter, nails digging into her palms.

"Ms. Cromwell, you can come see your daughter now," a nurse called.

Anne nodded curtly, excused herself from the little family and turned to follow the nurse.

* * *

Lily's face was paler than Anne had ever seen it. Even when Lily was seven and had come down with the chicken pox, Lily's bright red cheeks had defied the fatigue that illness usually wrought. But this time, Lily wasn't jumping from couch to couch, telling Anne that she *could* go to school, she could! This time, there were bandages tightly wrapped around Lily's head, blood staining the cloth where it was pressed against her cheek.

She set herself in the chair adjacent to Lily's bed and took her daughter's hand into both of her own. They were so *cold* and felt fragile. She rested her forehead on the back of Lily's hand, hoping it would cool the hot worry that pulsed through Anne's veins. After losing Richard, she couldn't lose Lily, too. It would kill any remaining hope for joy - and Anne had been running on close to empty for decades.

Before she had a chance to close her eyes and rest, however, there was a knock at the door.

A doctor with square glasses that looked stolen from the 70s walked in.

"Hello, Ms. Cromwell. My name is Dr. Jedura and I will be the doctor diagnosing and, eventually, rehabilitating Lily."

"Rehabilitating? What needs to be rehabilitated?"

"It appears that Lily lost consciousness due to dehydration. That would have been a fairly easy fix, but as she lost consciousness, her jaw made impact with a hard surface. The woman who was here—Vanessa—mentioned the top of Lily's balcony railing being the thing Lily hit on the way down. This impact caused parts of her jaw to shatter. Thankfully, she's starting to come to. We will see how much she can breathe and speak on her own. If she's stable and is able to communicate, we'll prep her for surgery to realign the fractured pieces of bone."

Anne steadied herself against Lily's bed. *Dehydration. That's not major. That's not cancer. Broken bones are inconvenient. Painful. But she'll live. She'll live!*

"Yes. Okay. What can I do?"

Dr. Jendura smiled. "Just be here for her when she wakes up. She'll be confused. I imagine she'll be quite distraught when she realizes she can't speak. The nurses will keep the painkillers and IV goin' to bypass the pain she'd otherwise feel."

Anne nodded and sat down. Her daughter's jaw? That girl's beautiful face… there'd surely be a scar. But it was nothing compared to the life and spirit and spunk within her daughter that she had been so afraid to lose. Anne wrung the edge of her skirt, ignoring the call that was probably Trevor telling her the iPad was on its way. How long would Lily struggle to speak? How long would she need breathing assistance while her jaw healed? Why didn't she drink more water and less wine?

As the doctor asked questions of the nurses that were poking and prodding her daughter, Anne stood and walked out of the room to the waiting room and back again. It was like walking from a dark forest into the driest desert—one gave way too much weight to carry and the other made her feel too alone.

Logan approached her. "Ms. Cromwell, how is she?"

Lily must have joined quite the condominium association if part of the staff's responsibilities was to visit sick clients. Quite Christian of them, really.

"I am very sorry, but I do not understand what my daughter's wellness has anything to do with you, Mr. West." Anne saw he was going to explain himself, so she moved to get over this tirade quickly. "Thank you for your role in getting Lily here in such a short amount of time. Lily and I appreciate your building's concern for one of your tenants, but please do take your family home. I will make sure Lily is taken care of now."

"But Ms. Cromwell, I am not—"

Anne felt her body shiver like she imagined a porcupine would, needles at the ready. She snapped. "You are not leaving, that's right. I can see that." She stepped forward to face Vanessa instead, who was standing close behind him. "Please, do take your husband and child away from my daughter's room. I appreciate your help, but I can take it from here. My daughter needs quiet to rest and heal."

Vanessa spoke firmly. "I appreciate your concern, but Lily is a very good friend of mine. Logan is not my husband, although he has become quite the fast friend." Vanessa smiled sideways at Logan. He returned a grim smile.

She looked Vanessa up and down. Nothing like the girls Lily grew up with, but very much along the lines of whatever Lily had with Marley. It took all the fight out of Anne. Lily would need friends when she awoke. "Very well. I can probably do fine with the company. It gets lonely in a place like this sometimes. But Mr. West, please go. If your intentions go beyond the maintenance of her home, you will be disappointed to know that Lily will already have a male visitor. They seem seriously involved with each other. We don't have to make it more awkward than it needs to be."

The Cromwell Rules protected them from caring about broken hearts, especially since that was ultimately the best thing to do for everyone involved. Her daughter would have one less thing to worry about when she woke up. Anne couldn't think of a more kind and merciful act than doing what she knew Lily would have done herself: tell Logan West that he had zero chance with Lily Cromwell. Nicholas Archer would be here soon.

Logan's Fool-Proof Plan

L ogan pushed the door as hard as he could. His relief of hearing that Lily had awakened quickly transformed into anger - at himself? At Lily? At Lily's mother? How were they so blind to how much he cared for Lily? He didn't understand it much himself, but it was undeniable.

He paced for a few moments and then sat on the curb away from the main doors. He ripped apart the velcro of his inner pocket and took out the single Marlboro. As he twirled the cigarette between his fingers, he mentally laid out before him what he knew.

Anne Cromwell cared about her daughter - that much was very clear - even though she looked like she would rather be anywhere else than the hospital. Though she was Lily's mother, he hoped she'd leave soon because Logan was not going to go anywhere else until he found a way to see Lily.

Why hadn't you just told the truth, Lily?

A van drove up to the hospital entrance, flowers painted on its sides like a mandala. Logan recognized it as the van that was usually parked in front of Janie's shop. Two men jumped out and rushed to the rear. Logan stood, holding the cigarette between his lips, anxious for a light. They reappeared with large flower bouquets, one basket on each arm. In them were tucked radiant sunflower heads, big ribbons, and a stuffed puppy.

"Whoa, someone in there is really loved, huh?" Logan said.

"Yeah, man," the delivery man with a Yankees cap answered. "There's four more baskets in the back of the truck, all with a different stuffed animal, all for the same person."

Logan hid the cigarette in his jacket pocket. "Can I help? I haven't had the best morning, and it would be cool to see someone else having a better one."

The shorter of the two answered. "We do have tons of deliveries to get through today. Can he help out, Joe?" Joe held a basket against his rounded belly, finger brushing his bushy mustache. He shrugged.

"I don't see why not. Just gotta be careful."

"Awesome. I'll take two from you," Logan said. "So you can save yourself the trip and bring the others from your van faster."

The man nodded and handed the baskets to Logan. They were heavier than he thought.

Logan turned his head to face Joe as they walked through the hospital doors. "So where are we headed?"

"We are on a mission to find the room of a..." Joe squinted at a small piece of paper tucked next to the stuffed puppy dog's ear. "...Lily Cromwell."

Logan's eyes brightened. "Flowers are allowed in intensive care?"

"She's in intensive care? Darn. I hate it when this happens. We'll have to find a nurse to help us find a storage space until she's moved. Hopefully she'll move from there soon. If not, the doctors usually appreciate them in their lounge."

Logan resisted the urge to throw the baskets at Joe and clutched them tighter to his chest.

"Ah, here we go," Joe set the flowers on the counter. "These flowers gotta be from out-of-towners since it wasn't enough for them to send one; overcompensating shite. Take care, kid. Thanks for the help."

Logan raised his hand in a small wave and turned to the flowers, searching for an envelope that'd reveal the sender's identity. He couldn't find one.

If Anne believed Logan really was a staff member from Lily's building, then she could be easily convinced that Lily's condo association would send baskets and baskets of get-well flowers—immediately? Unfortunately, he would be pegged a liar if Anne found notes that said otherwise. That was not an option. Lily had already fibbed enough for the both of them.

No. He would do his best to avoid Anne. He'd use the flowers to gain access to the room, make sure she knew he was there, and then leave. He *needed* her to know that he was there, that he cared for her, and that he wouldn't be going anywhere—even if her mother said otherwise.

Anne's Hurt

After a lifted hand, blinking eyes, and waving toes, Lily had been released from the Intensive Care Unit. Anne was relieved to feel the heavy weight of stones pressed against her chest and shoulders dissipate into dust.

As Lily slept, Anne meandered into the waiting room to watch Vanessa and Genny tell secrets, giggle, and make faces at one another. Thankfully, with Vanessa and Genevieve near her, she had motivation to keep her shaking hands still. *I will look under control.* Just like she did when Richard died.

Anne and Lily didn't have such a relationship when Lily was little; that was Richard's *forte*.

Anne turned to Vanessa. "It's such a breath of fresh air to see a mother actually interact with her daughter. Not just with her nose in the phone like everybody else."

Vanessa cocked her head to the side as if this were a foreign concept to her.

Anne continued, "If you were to walk outside this room and look around the hospital, you would see families sitting in a circle, each person on their own phone. They're all posting how sad it is that they can't see their sick family member at the moment, but they're doing this while they're surrounded by family members they could be talking to *right then*. It's a waste of life."

Genny made a face. "That sounds silly."

Anne smiled. "It is a little silly, isn't it?"

Genny said, "Mommy always says we have to pay attention to what is around us because it could be gone one day, and we'll be sad it is gone. But if we pay attention to what we have while we have it, we'll be more happy that we had it and less sad that it's gone."

Genny's words were a hot iron pressing against a drenched piece of cloth. Anne felt hot tears rise from deep within her.

"You look like you need a hug. Would you like one? Mommy says I should always ask first."

Anne nodded. Genny wrapped her little arms around Anne's neck, the hug pushing the tears out like putting a block in a vase full of water. It had nowhere else to go.

Anne sniffed. She took a deep breath. The iron gate that she had built around herself when Richard left her was now tall, rusty, and long overgrown with tight ivy. The urge to share a piece of that long-abandoned place with a little girl and a woman she had never met before was so strong. Every tear that dribbled down her cheek was like acid burning the kudzu vines around her.

"I used to have somebody that I loved very much. He made me very happy, and I was very sad when he wasn't here anymore."

To Anne's consternation, Genny bounced excitedly and looked from Anne to her mother. "That's like us, Mommy! That's just like us!"

Vanessa sent her saddest smile to Anne, a string of apologies for her daughter's unfiltered honesty, and her own understanding of Anne's pain. "Yes, baby. Just like us," Vanessa said.

Suddenly, she realized why she had recognized the look on Vanessa's face when Anne had first seen her earlier: she knew the eyes of a widow. She had seen them every day in the mirror since Richard passed away. Like all the candy in the world was gone. Like a true laugh was no longer an option for her. Like having hope was more expensive and required more effort than ever before.

"You don't have to talk about it," Anne whispered.

"Don't I, though? With this little one, I feel like I have no choice but to remind her how much her daddy loved us as much as I can. It would dishonor his life *not* to. How else will she remember him and the life he lived?"

Anne had never considered that. She waited for Vanessa to continue.

"If *I* had been the one to leave this world sooner than expected, I have no doubt that my husband would have kept my memory alive for her." Vanessa swept Genny's bangs to the side and tucked the stray hairs behind her daughter's ear. "She deserves to know her father. How else will she grow up to be like him?" Genny grinned at her mother.

Anne interrupted, "But the hurt -"

"Yes, it does hurt," Vanessa admitted. "But it hurts a little less each time I tell her a story or include her in one of our inside jokes. There are certainly plenty of them to share. She'll hear the majority of them when she's older, of course." Vanessa laughed, and Anne found it easy to laugh along with her.

Anne's words flowed easily, the iron gate pushing wide open. "Richard, my late husband, was a joker, too. He would say things that made my mother turn beet-red, and I thought he was wonderful for it. She was always so uptight and Richard found a way to make her love life again after she had been taking it too seriously for too long. I fell even more in love with him because of that. And the way he played with Lily? There could be no better father for a little girl who wants to explore the world." Anne would have kept going, but Dr. Jedura entered the waiting area. She was glad. She didn't need Vanessa to confirm Anne's growing doubt of her training. Grandchildren *would* be nice. A subject change was necessary.

"Great news, Ms. Cromwell. We have reviewed Lily's scans, and they are very promising. Though the jaw is fractured, it was a fairly clean cut at the left side. We will continue to monitor Lily's progress, but she should be well enough to wake up soon. Patients who have suffered this kind of injury are generally not able to speak articulately, if at all, but Lily will be able to understand you. She will probably also move sooner than she'll speak, so hopefully she isn't too much of a talker." The doctor winked. Anne was not sure the doctor's jovial jibe was appropriate right now, as she had yet to see Lily move at all, but Vanessa had reassured her that Lily's fingers had moved when she had been here a few hours prior.

"Thank you, Doctor," Anne said. "Is there a way to get my daughter a window room?"

"I will make sure a hospital staff member knows. Before we set up that arrangement, however, we do need more of Lily's information. If it is possible for you to come to the nurse's station -"

"Oh, yes, absolutely."

Anne turned to Vanessa. "If you wouldn't mind staying with Lily… She should have someone she knows by her side when she wakes up."

Vanessa waved her arm as if to push all worries aside. "We love Miss Lily. We'll be here."

Genny gave Anne two thumbs up.

Richard would have loved her. Maybe there *was* room in the Rules for some feelings—but only every now and then. Not too much. It's not like a jaw could be realigned because someone *hoped* it would be; it was a science: cold, hard, and calculating. No; living without hope was the only way to be certain of anything.

Logan's Showing Up

From behind two baskets of flowers, Logan watched Anne Cromwell exit the waiting room with a doctor who looked like a much older Mark Greene from that E.R. show his mom had watched all the time. He buried his face into the azaleas and pretended to be searching for something. *My dignity*, Logan mentally guffawed. As he absent-mindedly pawed around the baby's breath and white lilies, he found a small envelope that, if opened, would reveal the sender's name. He wanted to resist the temptation to read the name, but Anne was still nearby and his curiosity was growing.

He balanced the flowers using his hip and the wall and his fingers trembled. His nail slipped under the seal. He had never opened someone else's mail before, but if he was already being investigated for corporate sabotage, opening a little envelope on behalf of a woman laid out on a gurney seemed benign. The top of the card was adorned with baby blue embossing, and the message was printed in a gentle verdana,

Hey blondie,
Now's the time to be bold.
I know you'll be getting better soon, so
I'll keep our reservation.
-Nic

As Logan read, the words squeezed around him like a fishing line, the compression making it difficult to keep standing straight. Who the hell was this Nic guy? He let out a shaky breath, letting the flowers hide his face completely, trying to calm himself down enough to let the red pass from his cheeks and his hands ease at his sides. He tried to reason: Okay, so some guy was sending Lily a bunch of flowers. Baskets-full, full-time. So what? This Nic guy was only a threat from a distance. *Logan* was the one who was here. He was the one who showed up.

He checked over his shoulder. When he saw Anne nowhere near, he lifted the flowers higher so his face would remain hidden. He was using flowers from somebody else to carry him to the woman he loved. Maybe he did have game.

Finding Lily's room would have been a labyrinth, but the usually scrutinizing nurses assumed he was only dropping off the flowers in the room and not visiting with the patient herself. In fact, one particularly hard-faced nurse pointed him directly outside the doorway of Lily's room, no longer in the Intensive Care Unit.

He took another deep breath to steady himself and walked confidently into the room, breathing a sigh of relief when he set the flowers down on an open seat. He grinned at Vanessa and Genny who seemed surprised to see him.

"Logan!" Genny bounced up to him and wrapped her arms around his waist. Logan chuckled and patted the little head that barely passed his hip. He looked at Vanessa with what he hoped were the most pleading eyes he had in his arsenal.

Vanessa nodded in that nurturing way of hers. "Come on, Genny. Let's go get a snack."

Logan's shoulders released from their muscled hold. He knew he should have asked them to stay outside Lily's door to act as lookouts.

When he turned towards Lily, however, his knees buckled and he caught himself on the edge of the sink. Lily lie still in her bed, as if she had passed the entire winter in slumber. The dampness of her forehead darkened the blonde strands of hair surrounding her face—or at least the parts of it he could see. Her left eye and jaw were covered by bandages that wrapped around her. Logan wanted to cradle her head in his arms and sing her the lullabies his mother used to sing him when he was sick, just to see if he could make the sides of her lips turn up into a smile.

He slid off his jacket and placed in on the unoccupied bed next to hers. He sat down, pulling his knees almost up to his chin and waited. He found himself looking up at the ceiling, as if turned-up eyes would be enough for some deity to know what was deepest in his heart. He was willing to wait all day if it meant seeing Lily open her eyes to see that he was hers.

He reached for the cigarette again and twirled it in his fingers. He laid on the bed. He tossed the cigarette up and down. When he glanced at the clock, only a minute had passed. He closed his eyes. It would be a long wait, but he was a patient man.

As Lily began to stir, so too did Logan's heart. Logan sat up straighter and watched her eyes open with what seemed like much effort, eyelashes lifting invisible weights. When her eyes finally opened, he saw a million emotions pass through her in a matter of seconds: confusion, fear, pain.

When she turned her head, she winced. He wanted to reach out to help her sit up, but something held him back. She must know it was him, Logan, sitting next to her. He waved weakly, offering a smile he hoped was reassuring and would mask the fear that had been building since he had seen the ambulance drive away farther and farther away from him.

This was more difficult for him than he had originally thought. He didn't know where to start. He wanted to tell her that he was so sorry for how he had acted on the phone, and that he hoped she had enjoyed his favorite dish. He wanted to tell her she was safe now, and that she didn't have to worry about work even though he knew she would, because he could take care of any details. He also wanted to start figuring out how to change Anne Cromwell's mind about him being *just* a guy who was the Mr. Fix-it of her daughter's home, but he supposed that part could wait.

Instead, he leaned closer and rested his palms on the side of Lily's bed. He leaned over her, a bigger smile taking over his face as he realized how relieved she looked to see him.

"Hi, sweetheart," Logan said. Lily was trying to say something in return, but only hot air caressed Logan's cheek.

"It's alright. I'm here. You've had a little bit of an accident, huh? Don't think you were a little too dramatic? I would have brought you breakfast in bed if you had just asked."

More breaths, disjointed.

"I'll assume that was a laugh."

It looked like she kept looking behind his shoulder and he was trying not to feel nervous about it. Maybe she *was* looking for this Nic dude. He prepared for the humiliation, but kept his hands on her bed. He let his right hand wrap around her ankle. How small she looked, laying here.

He Needs to Go

Lily hesitated, casting a glance at the door. Logan needed to leave. He couldn't see her like this—not when she couldn't understand what was going on or what had happened. She needed time to know how she would react. If she were weak, she needed time to convince herself that she was capable and strong. She did know it was impossible to speak, let alone inhale fully. The effort was too great, lips and eyelids too weak. She wanted more than anything for him to come back later so he didn't see her in such an undoubtedly unattractive state.

But seeing him standing there in front of her was a nice surprise. His hair slightly disheveled, cheeks red from the cold, and the look in his eyes—a mix of desire and hurt and relief and anger—made her heart flutter. She wanted to sit up for him, but all she could manage was a spread out hand. She tried to ignore the pain shooting up and down her face.

If she could have spoken, she'd have reassured him that she was as captive as was possible. She pointed at the remote to the side of her bed. He caught on and lifted her bed into a sitting position.

Logan opened his arms and whispered hoarsely. "Come here."

The pain in his own voice caused her eyes to close as he wrapped his arms gently around her, bringing her cheek against his chest. Despite her own heavy weariness, she could feel herself melt in comfort as she felt his arms hold her, his palm resting against the back of her head. He was her sweater that she had denied needing all these years. She wanted to play it cool, play off like she didn't need to feel the comfort of somebody else's love on and around her, but now that she'd felt it, she knew she wanted it all the time. Looking back, part of her had known it from the minute he had taken her hat and danced with it on.

They sat there, unmoving. Lily's heartbeat was like that of a fantastic dirge; she was elated with the confirmation that he also yearned for things to be different, for this moment to be the beginning of hundreds of such connection. But she also felt intense sadness that, as perfect as this was, it was a fleeting perfection—and she was already missing it.

He gently pulled her head back and gazed into her eyes, palms hovering over her face like she was about to break in his grasp. It looked like he was trying to memorize every feature, and the despair in his eyes prevented any breath of hers from either entering or exiting—or maybe breathing was what was causing her pain in the first place. *What* happened?

"Your eyes are like a polar bear," Logan whispered, his voice cutting through the silence as easily as scissors through wrapping paper. "They bring you in, then attack you," It was the weirdest compliment Lily had ever received. One would think he'd compare her to a wild cat, or a snake, something with ferocity that explains its inability to be tamed—not an endangered animal that walks and hunts and lives in solitude. But maybe that's exactly why he said it. In her hospital bed, unable to speak, she realized she had never had the chance to tell him that knowing him was kind of like that—he caused an irresistible pull towards something she couldn't explain and then, what? How could anything they'd create survive? The best they could do is fantasize about a life where they could coexist. The reality would be too incompatible with her lifestyle. He'd distract her too much. It wasn't sustainable. He couldn't be in her life. Not for the long term.

He disconnected and returned Lily to a comfortable position. She knew he was studying her, but she couldn't keep her eyes open long enough to watch him.

She had spent her entire life following what Anne wanted for her in a man. The rules were her Ten Commandments, and anything less than following them meant separation from her mother, like Moses would have been smitten by God. Anne Cromwell's rules had taught her to be wary of anyone who seemed too eager or too forward. Anyone too emotionally forward, like Logan, was not "right" for Lily.

But if Nicholas Archer fulfilled all the requirements of Anne Cromwell's checklist, then why didn't Lily feel as connected to Nic as she did right in this moment with Logan?

She had never asked her mother *why*. *Why* was Anne always so resistant to men who showed women how they felt right away? What was wrong with wearing your heart on your sleeve? What did Lily not know?

Anne's voice entered Lily's room before she did. Logan's arms suddenly went slack and withdrew from Lily. She wanted to cry from the immediate cold left in his wake and felt tears spring to her eyes. She searched Logan hungrily, wanting him to see how this separation was like an extraction of her own self, like he had just reached into her body, ripped a piece of her heart like a piece of bread, and removed it without any warning - the daily prayer ignored and broken.

They watched Anne as she balanced one basket of flowers on one arm and her coffee in another. Her back was still facing them.

"Lily, did you know all of these beautiful flowers are from Nicholas? He sent them all - eight baskets in total, and each a different flower combination and different stuffed animal! What a sweetheart. He really is as perfect as you said he was!"

Lily wished she could cover Logan's ears, or tell him that what her mother was saying wasn't true. And she wished more than anything that she could speak at all. But then, what would she say?

Anne turned to face her. When she saw Logan, the coffee tumbled, spilling all over the shiny hospital floor. The outrage on Anne's face made

Lily want to cower, but also jump in front of Logan in fierce protection, a bear protecting her mate. But she was hopeless, the fatigue and pain making her queasy and ultimately unable to do anything more than lift her arms.

"How dare you!" Anne shook her finger in Logan's direction. "You get away from my daughter *right now.*" The danger in Anne's voice was something Lily had never heard; it was the tremor before the eruption, and Logan didn't need another warning.

Logan stood up, his hands up. "Ms. Cromwell, there's been a terrible misunderstanding."

"You think you can just walk in here and take advantage of my daughter while she is unable to say no!"

"Now wait a minute, Ms. Cromw—"

Anne's palm struck Logan's cheek. "What are you still doing here?!" she yelled. "Lily is not interested in you. She would have told me all about you if she were. You have no right to be here. If you don't leave right now, I swear to whatever higher power exists, you will regret it."

Logan cast one more furtive, desperate glance at Lily. They had so much more to say to each other. She dug her fingernails into her palm and balled her fists as tightly as she could.

With Logan gone, Anne's shoulders slumped and so, too, did Lily's spirit. There was no way that Logan could exist in Lily's life with Anne Cromwell around. Anne reigned supreme in Lily's life. She had always made the decisions and it afforded Lily more security—financial, emotional, and otherwise—than most humans ever received. They always had been a team, especially after Lily's dad died.

Logan *needed* to leave. If she kept saying it, maybe she'd finally convince herself of it. There was no other choice. If Lily really was the polar bear, then he deserved a chance to escape anyway.

She was sure Nicholas would be arriving in a matter of time and, though Lily wished she could have introduced Nic to Anne over dinner instead of

Anne's least favorite place on the planet, Anne would soon meet the world's best son-in-law and they could get on with their lives.

Anne walked over to Lily. It wasn't until Anne held her that Lily realized she was shaking. Lily rested her head there—as if she had any other choice—and cried. Not for what she'd lost, but for who she'd never get to have.

Recover

The poking and prodding, monitoring and waiting weren't the worst parts of Lily's rehabilitation. The worst part was trying to convince her doctors that she could work with a fractured jaw—and being denied over and over again.

She didn't need to talk, she pointed out, *but she did have code to write and perfect. Did they know how incredible that could be for* their *own hospital?*

She spent much of her time in front of the large windows, alone, wishing she could be part of the hustle outside, returning back to normal. But the scar along her jaw was much too profound. She didn't want to deal with all the staring. She was used to being the intimidating one—not the one being pitied.

Greg had called to assure her that Steven had everything under control. He probably hadn't realized that saying those words had the opposite effect he'd intended. It was a cruel joke of the universe that she'd do all the work and Steven would get all the credit. She *had* to be the face of the IceStorm party now, and with Nic by her side, no one would be able to ignore her. She was putting up with these damn baskets for that reason, wasn't she? *He's just busy,* Anne kept saying.

Ridiculous.

The morning after she was finally released, while Lily sipped her coffee, Lily called Marley. She was finally able to talk for longer, her mouth less sore every day. They talked about the IceStorm RACE release that'd be the

238

following Saturday night, and Marley asked all the right questions so that Lily could be prepared for an ego assault from Steven and crush it with her own.

Lily wanted to tell Marley how much she was trying to forget about the boy from the bus stop, but she couldn't bring herself to say it out loud. She had never missed anyone besides her father. To put another man in that category seemed blasphemous, so she didn't say anything. But Logan West was not making it easy to forget him. Or rather, the memory of him was like a guest that wouldn't leave her home. She tried to imagine pushing him away, out of her thoughts, out of that space within her that'd squeeze so hard she'd have to wait until it passed for her to catch her breath. When she had been in the hospital, she'd catch herself looking for him whenever one of the nurse's phones played jazz saxophone. Even the cars in the parking lot had made her wonder if everyone drove a Toyota now, and if Logan's red was one of them. Each time something happened that'd remind her of Logan, she'd do her best to bring memories of Nicholas to the forefront, but they just weren't as seared in her memory as much as being pressed against her bathroom door by Logan was...

So she hoped talking to Marley about Nicholas instead of Logan would help convince her more.

"The one who sent you all the baskets?" Marley asked. "You mentioned him briefly as your anesthesia was wearing off after surgery one day."

"I told Mom to hide my phone!"

Marley laughed. "It worked out in my favor. You were hilarious. Like when we drank way too much Orange Crush one night. Apparently it has similar effects."

"Hardy har har. Very funny. I hate not being in control." Lily rearranged some characters on her screen and hit "Test." Even though she wasn't officially cleared to work, she could still be ready for when she was. "So what did I tell you?"

"Well, you mentioned that Nic—though you had called him 'Dick' at the time— had yet to show up, but '*Thank God for the stuffed animals. Forgot I was four.*' Your sarcasm was golden. What else did you say? Oh yeah." Marley laughed harder. "'*I'm gonna pin all this plush to my railing so I never bust my jaw ever again. You know, for owning hospitals, he does not have the best patient etiquette. But at least my scar face will be safe.*' Speaking of, you can hardly see it."

Lily tried to hide her wince. "You're being kind. It is so obvious." Lily tried out the lie on her lips. "And he's busy, Mar. I wouldn't want to visit me either. We're not married. He's sending gifts; *that's* how he's being present. Anyway, it's better not to expect anything and appreciate everything. He's running Dove Hospitals. That's a huge responsibility." The words felt wrong— dirty—like something Rose would say to defend her cheating husband.

"He banged you, watched you *fall*, never visited you at the hospital, and now you're making excuses for him? You've got to be kidding me." Marley rolled her eyes. "These meds are making you sound like your mother. You need seventeen year old Lily to knock some sense into you."

Lily laughed. "Unless you're sending a time traveling contraption… besides, that Lily had no idea what was going on. Way too many feelings. Thank goodness I'm done with that phase."

"And what about Logan? What's he been doing?"

Lily hesitated.

"Ha! I knew it! You *are* still interested!"

Lily pressed her forehead into her palms. "Of course I am," she mumbled. "He makes it impossible not to be."

"How so?"

Lily spread out her arms like a cat stretching after a long nap. Marley always asked the right questions and it did feel good to be able to talk about Logan.

"He tried to visit a lot in the beginning. I told him that'd be the stupidest thing he could do. We don't need Anne finding him in the hospital. Bad news for everybody."

Marley nodded sympathetically. How Lily wished they could be sitting together on her couches instead of staring at each other through screens. She had wished the same with Logan for weeks. For being such a technologically advanced world, she sure was lacking others' presence.

"So what happened instead of the hospital visits?"

"At first, he sent messages as if Anne had never chased him out of the room like a priest exorcising a demon. Then, when he saw that wasn't garnering any attention, he started asking what doctors were saying about my improvement. Right around 5:00 p.m., Logan texted me. Every. Single. Day."

Since she had appreciated his relentlessness and wanted to compliment his creativity in gathering intel, she would succumb and reply: "Getting better every day." "Doctor says I'm healing quickly." "Need to drink more water." "Breathing is still kind of a bitch, but do or die."

When she pressed the "Send" button, Lily would smile as she imagined Logan's enthusiasm at reading her message. She'd never respond more frequently than a couple hours or days at a time. It was definitely a game.

"Apparently he's enjoying his new position at a new restaurant in town." She admired his career-change from financier to chef-in-the-making. She often daydreamed walking into his restaurant one day, surprising him with a note sent to the chefs thanking the prep cook named Logan for the finely chopped vegetables. Just thinking about the idea made her laugh. He'd walk out with that big stupid grin of his and start dancing right there, like music had been playing all along. But then the urge went away because she was not *supposed* to find Logan in her daydreams. She had already told her mother about Nicholas Archer, and he was the clear winner.

Lily closed her eyes and bent her head. "He hasn't responded in a few days."

Ten days. And a few odd hours. Lily yearned for the pure fun and companionship she had felt with Logan. His messages would leave her feeling full—satisfied—, and helped convince her that, maybe with time, she could have both Logan's love and also Nicholas' prestige and connections. She was Lily Cromwell. Surely she could handle both.

But the last time Lily waited four days to respond, Logan hadn't responded. She didn't blame him. How could she expect anything of him? He didn't owe her a thing. Expect nothing and appreciate everything, right?

"But Nic reached out," Lily continued. "I think we'll be meeting about the launch party soon. As soon as this doctor clears me."

Marley was silent for a while. Then, she said, "Your choice is so skewed, Lil. Surely you see that."

She would never admit to Marley that she was right. But Marley *was* right. On the other hand, IceStorm was relying on her to seal the deal with Dove Hospitals. Her mother had expectations for her. It didn't matter what Lily wanted. Logan was a feeling, not a fact; he would wash off over time, like a temporary tattoo.

"I can't judge him, Mar. Nic's dating just like I would have. No strings. No commitment. We're not in a committed relationship, so he doesn't need to fulfill any caretaking responsibilities. I understand."

Lily was cut from the same cloth. Or, at least, she had been sewn onto the same cloth and made to look like she had been part of it the entire time.

Marley made herself look busy putting dishes away.

Nicholas was literally buying her every woman's fantasy, but the arrival of these *things* were not enough to fill the gap left by Anne's obvious disapproval of Logan. With no chance to show her mother who Logan really was, Lily realized that Anne's impression of Nicholas only grew stronger. After re-reading Logan's messages every day he didn't reach out, Lily would immediately swipe into Nicholas' chat window and see if *he* had left a message. Usually, he wouldn't have.

"Listen, Mar. I have to go. This test isn't passing and I won't be satisfied if it's not running smoothly by this afternoon."

"You do you, girlfriend. Let me know when Nic is old news and Logan is proposing."

Lily laughed. "Now that's the funniest thing you've said all year."

But after Marley hung up, Lily swiped to check one more time if Logan had messaged her.

He hadn't.

"Come on," Lily yelled into her phone as it lie on its back. It looked like she was attempting to revive the electronic like she might an unconscious person. Lily had called Logan at least ten times and texted over and over. She didn't care if she was breaking all the rules, shattering them into a million pieces with a hammer. She could hear each one losing power over her as she consciously chose to fracture it.

Make him *chase* you, *Lily.* No.

Message sent. Read.

He *did* chase me, Mom, and now he thinks it was useless. And it wasn't.

Call. Voicemail.

If you appear easy, you lose your worth.

Message sent. Read.

Three dots, a sucked-in breath. Then, nothing.

Logan knew what I was worth before I made *him* feel worthless.

If you do not assert control over your own heart, then you risk it being broken by another.

Control over one's heart is a myth, Mother. Logan had it before I realized it.

And now he wouldn't answer his phone. She really messed up this time. The pain was similar to what she felt after Roger ignored her through the rest of high school. But this time, it felt more final. She knew she'd never meet another guy like Logan. She felt it as surely as she knew she needed hot coffee in the morning and a cool cover to keep her warm at bedtime. She knew she desired the laughter and carefree spirits of Vanessa and Genevieve in her life - and that to feel such joy, she could no longer worry about protecting her ego and reputation. She yearned to dance with Logan, knowing that such an intimate relationship could both burn and heal her, and choosing it anyway.

But he couldn't dance with her if he didn't know that she wanted to. And she so desperately wanted to. She hid under the bed sheets as they floated down to cover her head and fell back into her pillows. She lifted a throw pillow over her face and yelled into it. She should be thinking about RACE and that was it. But here she was, drowning in sadness she had not felt for a long time.

"Logan," Lily projected into her empty apartment. She hugged the pillow into herself and whispered huskily, "My Logan. Come back."

She picked up her phone again and, despite every fiber of her being fighting against it, swiped past Logan's name and found a different one instead.

Anne Knows

She always had a feeling her expectations for Lily were a little ridiculous, but she figured that if Richard wasn't around to arm Lily with practical advice, then Anne would have to. Lily didn't want to put away her toys? *If you want to ensure they're there again when you want to play with them, Lily, you have to put things where YOU want them. Otherwise, something you care about can be gone in a second.* To Lily, the advice was about her toys. But to Anne, the advice was something she should have heeded herself many years ago. Richard had been all she had cared about before Lily arrived. And even after Lily's birth, Anne and Richard were inseparable.

If she had only paid closer attention to Richard's condition, she could have alerted the nurses sooner. She could have run through the halls of the hospital, composure and pride be damned. Instead, she had been asleep, since she only allowed herself to rest when Richard finally shut his eyes.

Anne felt her muscles clench in tension as she remembered wakening to the sound of loud beeping and running feet. She had been too dazed to realize what was going on, but was startled to find a team of nurses surrounding her husband's bed. When Anne had finally stood and tried to ask someone what was going on, nobody would answer her. Did they not hear her? Did they not care that she was standing right here? No, of course not. Richard needed all the attention he could get. But he usually didn't like being the center of attention - that's why he gave her all of his.

Anne's heart squeezed.

Richard.

The guitar strums of "Oceanside" came through the back-seat speakers and she asked Trevor to increase the volume. As the melody wrapped itself around her, she leaned her head back and allowed herself to remember when she saw him all those years ago performing solo on stage in a Brooklyn bar. *"If only I could only get you oceanside, to lay your muscles wide..."* Anne smiled, recalling how stunned she had been by his forwardness. She had tried to be sly, like she always had, but he cut straight through her scripted conversation and found the heart of how she wanted to be loved.

She smiled small at Trevor now, who looked at her with deep concern. She told him to go home.

"Are you sure, Ms. Cromwell? I don't mind waiting here for you."

"I'm sure, Trevor. I'll be spending the night with Lily."

He tilted his hat toward her as she passed him.

She was about to knock on Lily's door and stopped herself. She tried the doorknob and wasn't surprised to find it unlocked. She let herself in and dropped her purse to the floor, locking the door behind her.

"Lily?" Anne called out. She walked into the dining area and saw the room in disarray. Clothes strewn over the chairs and dishes still left on the table reminded Anne of the days following Richard's funeral.

Anne froze when she entered her daughter's bedroom. Pillows rested at the foot of the balcony doors, and crumpled paper lie in little papers around the bed. Lily herself was in a circle, raising her head slightly to show puffy red eyes and unkempt hair. Anne's heart filled to the point of bursting. She rushed quickly onto Lily's bed.

"Oh, Lily Pad," she whispered, wrapping her arms around her daughter. "What's happened?"

"I lost him," Lily burst, crying into Anne's shoulder.

"Nicholas?"

"No," Lily cried harder. "Logan. My Logan."

Anne's eyes darkened, "That hospital stalker? He's not somebody to lose. You didn't lose anyone, love. He's the one who lost you."

Lily pushed herself off her mother. "I can't believe you just said that! I am so sick of trying to live according to what you approve of. It's not working for me, Mother."

"What do you mean *approve of*?" Anne's response seemed to frustrate Lily even further.

"There was always a list of things I could say and of those I could not, and you know it. It didn't matter if I was in Kindergarten trying to figure out how to get my toy back, or in high school trying to catch the eye of whatever boy we had found in the previous year's yearbook. In fact, it got even worse when James got involved. We talked more about what I would talk about more than how I actually *felt*, Mother. Doesn't that seem a little messed up to you?"

Anne knew Lily as a teenager; there was no stopping her now. So Anne decided to wait out the tantrum.

"It's like I've been on stage all my life, on display for all to see. I've had to worry about how my hair was styled, whether my makeup was always on-point or whether I should even have any on, how tight-fit my clothes were (and whether they needed to be a little looser, just because of who was there watching). It didn't matter that there were days I didn't want to perform. You never asked your only daughter if she needed a break, or whether she even wanted to *be* an actress! Instead, you assumed the role of the director who stormed backstage and threw props at me and waited until I hobbled on stage, where you'd feed me every single line. You told me how to inflect my voice and which audience member to focus on so I'd be 'most remembered' - as if that's the most important part of a play anyway! The actor only helps deliver the story, Mom. I have been so busy playing another character, I don't even remember what my own voice sounds like. It has always been yours. I knew it when it started to get out of control in high school, and I regret not saying anything then. But I'm telling you now. I'm done being a one-woman show. If you still want your story performed for the masses, you go ahead and do you." Lily stopped, shoulders drooping. She stared at the floor and massaged her forehead with her fingertips. "I am done pretending that nothing ever hurts me. It hurts really bad right now, Mom. He makes me so happy," Lily added, breathing back up a big sniffle. "You know, when I'm not crying about it."

Anne lifted herself from the bed. "Lily, I just wanted to protect you. I didn't want you to feel the hurt of losing someone you love."

"So you wanted to prevent me from feeling any love at all?" Lily asked incredulously. She gestured around her. "News flash. I *am* feeling the hurt of losing someone I love. Because of *you*."

"Oh, honey, no. I just didn't want you to put all your faith in one love because..." Anne's voice grew shaky. "Because once it's gone, baby, it's gone."

Lily sat on the blue ottoman chair. "Just because Daddy died." Her eyes rose to meet Anne's. "Daddy wouldn't have wanted me to miss out on the love of my life."

As badly as Anne wanted to break away from Lily's stare, she forced herself to stay. "Yes. He had been my everything since I met him. And he took my every joy when he left. Not that I don't feel joy with you, Lily," Anne interjected quickly. "That's not what I mean."

Lily stood. "I know what you mean. But Dad wouldn't want this for me. Or you. It's the exact opposite of what he would have wanted, Mom."

Anne walked over to Lily and clasped her arms around her, tears rolling down her own cheeks. "I know it, love. I know it. I am so sorry."

"It's a little too late now."

"You'll be okay. You're going to be okay."

Lily wiped any remaining tears from her eyes. "I am okay. The Rules weren't a complete failure. I know I can survive without him. It just sucks that I have to."

Anne hugged Lily tighter. "I know exactly what you mean."

Listen to Me

T he buzzer nudged Lily from her sleep. Her arm searched behind her, lethargic fingers finding the button of the P.A. system. Her voice still groggy, she croaked. "I'm awake!"

"Well, good, Miss Lily, because there is a fancy looking envelope here for you that has 'urgent' written on it."

Lily threw on an oversized sweater, enjoying the feel of heavy wool hugging her skin but letting it breathe, too. Like a good man, Lily thought. How come Anne never said anything like *that*?

She bounced down the stairs, feeling so much more energy than she had in a month. Perfect timing, too. With the RACE release just six days away, she was grateful that she had recovered in time. A large manila envelope from Spain had Marley's round, cursive handwriting scrawled all over it. She thanked James, tore open the paper, and walked upstairs slowly, drinking in every word.

Dear You (Me? Us?):

If you're reading this letter, you either frantically searched for it because you need reassurance, or everything is fine and you just found it in between a ton of your old essays, or Marley sent you an authentically-signed copy because you're about to fall for Mom's antics.

You know those rules that have dominated most of your senior year? Hopefully you've shaken them off.

Whatever the reason, you deserve to hear your own voice in this, especially because it feels like, more and more, Anne is trying to take your voice away and replace it with a dating robot who says all the right things, does all the right things, but never really makes you *feel* the right way. And isn't that what life is all about? *Feeling* all of it?

If you're in danger of getting close to giving yourself completely to the wrong guy, Marley is in charge of sending you this letter, where YOUR rules rule supreme. So here we go - your list of rules for what it takes to date and love Lily Cromwell.

1. He pays attention to who you really are - not just what you look like on the outside. He wants to know what you have to say. Bonus points if he still likes you after you've been make-up free and eating messy finger food - at the same time.
2. He lights up when you walk into the room. He tries to get your attention, not the other way around. You shouldn't have to fight for someone to notice you. He'll *look* for you.
3. He should be able to cook. You love food, but don't really want to cook it all the time. And eating out all the time sounds exhausting. Maybe he can cook while you're taking a bubble bath or something.
4. He shows up when the going gets tough.

And, most importantly - the rule of all rules:

1. He makes you feel like you don't have to try to win him over. Odds are, you'll know, in your heart of hearts, that you'll already know you've won.

You'll figure this out. I/we believe in you. You'll be alright.

Love,

Lily

Lily took a big shaky breath in. She had completely forgotten about this letter, but now the memory of writing it came back in vibrant memories. She let herself be seventeen again.

* * *

James had ignored her for the hundredth time, and she was sick of it. Lily stormed into the brick colonial, slammed the door, and passed her mother in hot tears.

"Who's the boy?" Anne asked.

Lily threw herself onto her dad's couch and hugged her arms around herself. Anne stood in front of her, leaning in the doorway. She was surprised Anne was listening at all. "I don't know. He's gorgeous and every girl would just die to be asked to go to prom with him."

"And apparently you would too, considering how messy he's made you," Anne said. Lily glared at the opposite end of the library. The frost was reaching towards the center of the window. "Seriously. Who is this guy?"

"James hasn't noticed me at all this year. Like, at all. I answer any question he asks. Any time he wonders whether we have homework or not, I send a note with everything written out nicely for him. It's so messed up. It's like the more I try, the less he cares."

Anne sat down next to her. "I can explain all of this to you, but I don't think that would help right now. I can make sure you never feel ignored ever again, though. You know that, don't you?"

Lily leaned against her mom and sniffed. "You can?"

Anne chuckled. "Yes, baby. Of course I can."

* * *

The next morning, when Lily arrived to school in a mini skirt and a hot pink streak in her hair, she was the one doing the ignoring. It had been the first day of her practical training, her mother had said. Her main goal was to keep her eyes far away from any potential connection with James and talk to other guys.

And that's when she'd started talking to Roger.

Anne had been right; James noticed the sudden drop in attention. A week later, he was waiting for her in the hallway after school, asking if she would consider tutoring him.

"Isn't that what NHS is for?" Lily quipped before walking away, just as Anne had told her to do. Somehow, Anne had known James would start changing his mind.

The very next day, James had complimented how nice her hair was, and she'd given him her biggest smile in thanks. Finally, one day, with something close to desperation in his eyes, he asked Lily if she would consider cheering him on at his final track meet of the year.

"I want to PR in the 400 for my final race - and I think you could be my lucky charm. That much is obvious with my Pre-Calc grade…"

It was the explicit invitation that Lily had been waiting for.

While Anne flipped through the pages of Victoria's Secret, Lily opened her laptop, signed onto her AOL Instant Messenger and was delighted to find Roger online.

LiLyPad: Roger! I have an idea!

RogillioPrime: What's your idea?

She loved how quickly he responded.

LiLyPad: I wanna go to the track meet to cheer on the seniors, but I don't want to be bored sitting there all by myself.

Come with me?

RogillioPrime: Idk.

Do I want to watch a bunch of sweaty dudes for hours on a Saturday morning when I could be sleeping in after a crazy Friday night?

LiLyPad: Ha. From all those video games?

C'mon. If it means sitting next to a sweaty blonde, would you?

RogillioPrime: If you're suggesting sitting next to Bruce, I'm definitely out, I'm telling you right now.

LiLyPad: Hahaha, Roger, no! Bruce is nice. I don't think he can help his B.O.

RogillioPrime: His being nice doesn't keep him from stealing the clean air around me.

LiLyPad: Roger!

LiLyPad: ...So are you coming?

RogillioPrime: You know I wouldn't miss it.

Sweaty guys are my spirit animal.

LiLyPad: Lol. You're a goof. See you Saturday.

As Lily signed out of the chat messenger, Anne called to confirm her choice of a hot pink racer-back tank top and lime green shorts with bright white stripes running down the side. When the clothes were ordered, Lily thought about telling her mother that Roger was also in the running for prom date options. But would Anne approve, since it did not take as much work to "catch" Roger as it had taken for James? They'd have less to talk about if it all came easy, she decided, so Lily kept Roger to herself.

Saturday arrived quickly.

In the couple of minutes it took to ride to school, Anne gave Lily last minute tips: "Try to stay out of his direct line of sight. You want him to wonder whether you actually decided to come or not."

"But I told him I would be there, Mom. I don't want to look like a jerk."

"You won't look like a jerk, I promise. You will look like a girl who has her own priorities that she wants to take care of first, before she shares her time with a guy. You didn't *make* room for him; you *found* time for him. Guys do it all the time, Lily, so he'll recognize his need to respect you if you begin acting like he does."

"It is kind of messed up that James didn't start paying attention to me until I started ignoring him, huh?" Lily said.

Anne raised her eyebrow in a loud "I told you so."

Lily pulled her shorts down instinctively, an attempt to preserve whatever claim to modesty she still possessed. When she straightened up, she grinned. Roger was leaning against the wall of the concession stand, throwing popcorn above his head, easily caught it with a snap of the mouth, and finished with a grin at Lily. It's like he knew she would step out of her carriage just in time to catch his jester performance.

"Nice catch!" Lily called, waving her hand enthusiastically.

"Like the one on your necklace," Roger called back. "Speaking of, nice necklace."

"Well, thank you. It's to catch my sweat beads and transfer them over to the ocean." Lily was pleased that he noticed. The small seashell was the only part of her outfit that Lily had chosen for herself.

"Sounds cheaper than a flight," Roger smiled. It was like this smile - the one that reflected the sun's rays simply because Lily was there - that made his eyes come alive and awaken for the first time.

"Let's go find a seat for this incredible show of human strength and determination." Roger led them along the black tarmac path.

Heat rushed through her body, and it had nothing to do with the sun. As she watched Roger's easy gait, she wondered. Had she asked Roger out during a day that she should have been focused solely on James? Was this part of the game her mom taught her, or was this because she felt more with Roger than she ever had with James? James made her work harder, but Roger did not make it feel like work at all.

Roger and Lily spent the afternoon in the highest corner of the bleachers, able to see the entire track, but with the feeling that, besides the announcer box, they were in a penthouse suite all their own. They would take turns going down to the concession stand, bringing back outrageous combinations of snacks and sodas, a competition of who could bring back the weirdest -and surprisingly delicious- tastes. They laughed so much that people who had sat in front of them would leave after only a few minutes, either tired of teenage humor, or -as Roger put it -agitated that they weren't in on the inside joke themselves. Lily's comfort was at an all-time high, snorting at Roger's jokes, only sobering when his arm slid around her waist. He looked down at her with those sweet brown eyes and grinned.

"Aw, well isn't this picture perfect?" one of James' teammates called. Lily wiggled out of Roger's embrace.

Lily forced as much cheer into her voice as possible. "Hi Mark! If you want a picture for yourself, I'm sure there's a camera somewhere you can use."

She felt Roger pretend like he was leaning for something behind her - trash from the snacks, perhaps - when he whispered in her ear, "I don't need a picture to remember this, Lily Cromwell."

The comment made Lily feel like she had just finished pumping up the bleacher stairs, two levels at a time. She wished Mark would disappear as quickly as he had come. She wanted more than anything to turn to Roger and listen to him say more. Instead, she raised an eyebrow at Mark. "Well? How can I help you?"

Mark looked genuinely confused. "Aren't you here to cheer James on?"

Lily felt the blood rush from her face and refused to look at Roger, afraid that the glance would reveal too much. She felt his body stiffen and her mind cried out to Mark to just *stop it, stop it right there.* Lily had to respond with something - the silence was becoming more awkward the longer she didn't.

"I mean, yeah." Lily responded as casually as she could, even though her voice was cracking, and she hated that Roger probably knew her well enough that he could tell. "I came on to cheer everybody." Lily raised her hands in feeble celebration. "Go, Mustangs."

"Well, I certainly hope so, otherwise James planned quite the show for a different girl named Lily."

"A show?"

Roger couldn't resist jumping in. "James spends all his time ignoring people, just to make up for it in the end with a fireworks display, huh?"

Mark shrugged. "Have fun being the center of attention, Crommy."

Lily rolled her eyes and turned to Roger. She didn't know what to say. Roger did. Or at least it seemed like he was figuring it out. "You do like being the center of attention, don't you?"

"What? No," Lily said too quickly.

Roger narrowed his eyes, as if she had just lied about whether climate change was real.

"Maybe," Lily flustered. "A little. But I swear I was genuine when I said I wanted to hang out with you."

"Yeah, only so you wouldn't be bored while you waited for your new boyfriend to be done." Roger practically spit the words out.

"When you put it like that, I can see why you might be a little upset."

"A little upset?" Roger stood and lasered his eyes into Lily's own. "If it's only a 'little' to you, then we're clearly not on the same page."

Lily didn't get to respond because the band began to play.

A band at a high school track meet?

Oh, no.

Lily watched in horror as cheerleaders in maroon and gold began to jump and shout, bodies forming into "L" "I" "L" "Y".

And then the worst. A booming voice, James' own, projecting over the entire field.

"Lily Cromwell is the flower of our school, and I would be more than honored to take her to our senior prom. Lily, will you go to the prom with me?"

The crowd scanned the bleachers confused, until one girl pointed in Lily's direction. Lily cowered and wished she could hide. Then, as if the wind caused each head to turn, hundreds of eyes were on her. And, at the bottom of the bleachers, to Lily's added horror, was Anne Cromwell.

This was it. This was what Anne and Lily had been working on since she came home crying that day. All the "training" and intelligence-gathering and deliberation they had done together was showing itself off, right here, right now.

And here was James, standing right next to her, a bouquet of lilies in his arm, one step shy of getting down on one knee. She turned to where Roger should have been, but Roger was already in the parking lot, walking far away from her.

It was Anne's wide grin that finally did her in. She hadn't seen her mother smile like that in *years*. So what other option did she have? She turned to James and nodded slowly. The crowd cheered and James scooped her in a hug.

She had won Prom Queen, and James had been her King.

But Roger had never spoken another word to her again.

Convince Them

The bracelet clasped around Lily's left wrist, diamond pendants shimmering against the white silk glove.

"There! Now you're ready. Changing the world with how people see female engineers *and* saving future lives from fatal emergencies." Jeremiah grabbed her shoulders and looked into her eyes. "I'm so lucky to work with you. You know that, right?"

Lily nodded and accepted the admiration in Jeremiah's eyes. They both worked so hard on RACE together that it wasn't fair that Lily was the one experiencing the glory. Before she could second guess herself, she wrapped her arms around Jeremiah's neck and hugged him close. She didn't expect the rush of tenderness that rose to the surface.

"I am so grateful for you, J. You've stood by my side since our day one. We should be walking in together instead of me and Nic."

"Are you kidding? You're getting sentimental *now*? Our work isn't done, girl. You bring up that bottom lip and strut your stuff. People buy into people with confidence, right? You've got more than what would be considered a fair share for a human being and now you have to *work* it. People's lives depend on it."

Greg poked his head into the hallway. "Lily! You ready? We're about to announce you and Nicholas."

Of course she was. Lily knew the demo would go off without a hitch. It had been tested once by Steven and three more times by her and Jeremiah the last week. She fixed the microphone so it wouldn't graze her cheek as closely, repositioning it around her ear.

Jeremiah gave Lily one last encouraging pat. "Go get 'em, beautiful. Convince them they need RACE and that Nic needs *you*."

Lily blew him a kiss and laughed when Jeremiah mimed to catch it and place it on his cheek. She turned on her heel, feeling the thick material of her turquoise dress trailing behind her, the weight a welcome distraction from the tension building in her shoulders and climbing up the back of her neck.

Lily stretched her arms back, forward and back again, like a swimmer getting loose and ready to dive in. She spotted Nicholas from the corner of her eye and reached instinctively to cover her scar. But before Nic could see, she grasped her right hand in her left, clenched them behind her back, and let her chin rise, eyes closing, composing even breaths.

"Hey, Blondie." His voice sounded like granite grating against concrete. But his face looked like it had been perfectly chiseled by a master sculptor.

"Good evening, Mr. Archer." She knew her voice sounded cold, like a window shutting against the harsh wind. How could he watch her fall and then never visit her, not once, while she was down? She could feel his sideways glance of surprise, but he straightened and gestured towards the tall maple doors.

They walked shoulder to shoulder. He chuckled. "You dress up fancy and act the part well."

"I'm sorry," she turned to him. "What are you referring to? I don't believe anyone is acting."

"No? You wouldn't rather be with *anybody* else right now? Yet here you are having to be the collected Lily Cromwell everyone expects you to be. You're one of the best actresses I know, getting me to come over to your apartment making me think you wanted more than a business partnership. I would be upset if I weren't impressed that I fell for it."

She dug her nails through the silk and into her palm. She *was* glad she was making it obvious that she didn't want to be right next to him, but such a demeanor wouldn't work in front of the investors waiting at the foot of the stairs for the long-awaited, much-hyped partnership of IceStorm's RACE and Dove Hospitals. She had read the socialite forums, undoubtedly fueled by Anne and her circle, commenting on Lily and Nic's feasibility as a power couple.

Lily didn't comment and Nic continued.

"You're making the decision of whether to keep you onboard after we acquire IceStorm much easier. I liked witnessing the venom working on others, but it's different when it's directed at me. You'd better hope the investors don't catch onto your *feelings*. That wouldn't be the best press for a stunning female engineer such as yourself."

Lily spun on her heel and faced Nic's smug face. "You've got some nerve, Archer."

She stopped short as the doors opened. Thunderous applause, loud music, and the emcee on the other side of the doors announced them. Lily pasted an artificial grin onto her face, like she would insert a command into her code. The stretching caused a faint pain along her jaw, but she maintained it. She slid her arm through the window Nic made with his own.

The ballroom was magnificent and more beautiful than she had imagined it when she had walked through it with Jeremiah so many weeks ago. The floor to wall windows surrounding the perimeter of the room revealed the lit up majesty of Manhattan. Chandeliers of various heights and widths hung in each quadrant of the ceiling. When the lights reflected off the Swarovski crystal, she thought of The Cosmopolitan in Vegas, everything bright and weightless, rainbow spectrums dancing across the walls. She suddenly felt lighter herself, and pressed against Nic's hand, grinning at the crowds of people clapping or raising their glasses in their direction. She scanned the faces of women in evening gowns and gentlemen in tuxedos, pausing when she saw Janie beaming at the flower arrangements custom ordered by IceStorm for this event. She knew Janie was excited to be in attendance, but Lily was most grateful to have signed the largest check Janie had ever received. Lily grinned wider when she saw Hugo with his arm around her mother's waist. It occurred to Lily that, if somebody had walked into the room at that moment, they would have assumed Nic and Lily were being applauded by their wedding guests, introduced for the first time as husband and wife.

The applause continued as Lily caught Jeremiah and Steven giving each other high fives. She wanted to tell them that they were celebrating much too early, but maybe it was she who wasn't in a celebratory mood. The smile on her mother's face was more radiant than Lily had seen it since her father died and it made her breath catch. How would she be able to tell Anne that she knew she would not be Nicholas Archer's wife? But it had to be done. All she had to do was make it through the evening convincing everybody else otherwise, and she'd be free to pursue Logan—not minding that she'd break all the rules to do so.

Nicholas lifted her hand and gestured towards her. She curtsied and bowed her head, gesturing towards her business partner, the cue for Greg to turn her microphone on.

"Good evening, everyone! We are so honored by your presence tonight. I'm Lily Cromwell, head architect of IceStorm's RACE software. Standing strongly in arms with me is Nicholas Archer, arguably the most loyal advocate of all health practice, particularly that executed by Dove Hospitals. As we gather to *show* you the benefits of RACE, we want to do more than seek your alliance in ensuring that New York City—nay, the world—will be led to safety regardless of the threat at hand. We want to welcome you to the future of *saving lives*."

The resounding applause was crisp, like dropping marbles against stone. She took a step back as Nic took a step forward. For not having done a run-through of this before, it certainly felt well-rehearsed. Maybe that was the result of following the rules; the outcomes became predictable. She would always have an idea of what Nic would do before he did it, and that's what made Logan so exciting. Her heart warmed thinking about him and the message he'd sent her earlier that evening: "Let your light be the smile in somebody's day. It already is over here." It was the only message and he didn't respond to any other message, but it gave her hope. And that was something.

It made the scar taut, but she was able to ignore the pain when she imagined herself smiling for Logan. She forced her attention back onto what Nicholas was saying.

"When I first met Lily Cromwell, I knew that RACE was in exceptional hands. The way she talks about RACE, you'd think she was a proud mother who raised a child about to graduate from college." He chuckled, eyes sparkling like the crystals surrounding them. The guests laughed with him.

"It's true!" Lily interjected, stepping forward. "My team at IceStorm has been working tirelessly, going through numerous versions of this product to ensure that if you—yes, you." She pointed at a particularly round man in the crowd. "And you." Her gloved finger moved to point to a woman wearing clothes that didn't quite match the formal dress code requirement written in the invitation. She looked so familiar. Lily moved on. "Or your mother, sister, or husband, were ever in a threatening situation one afternoon, you'd get to see them again for dinner time, just a little after your evening commute, like normal. We're in the business of taking every day we're safe and sound for granted, aren't we? Let's keep it that way. Tonight, you'll get to have a first-hand experience of a drill with RACE in charge. Though we're in a hotel, Mr. Archer is going to explain how RACE can be applied to hospital evacuations. We want everyone to be protected, especially when they're already in the process of healing." She made herself lean into Nic, laying her cheek on his shoulder. More applause surrounded them, music with a strong beat interjecting, dismissing the hosts, emcee announcing that dinner will be served soon. Lily moved to the left staircase, eager to be out of the spotlight so that she could observe that woman who didn't quite fit more closely. She squinted.

Lipstick the same vibrant orange color as her shirt, much too tanned to have spent the winter in New York... The woman's gaze followed Lily's, waiting. Lily tilted her head. The woman made a motion of throwing imaginary wine from her empty wine glass onto the man in front of her, and Lily suddenly realized who she was. *Marley!*

Nic's arm wrapped around her waist, his hand resting on her hip. She was much too elated to see Marley in the crowd, scar most noticeably pained now, and pushed down the reaction to shiver away from him. Marley was *here!* The music played once more and Lily took off, dress in one hand, other hand on the bannister, and—finally—both arms around her best friend.

Logan's Last Look

West!" The sous chef called from the jungle of hanging pots and pans. "Go to the dining room. Chef needs a final head-count."

"Yes, sir." Logan finished washing his hands and pat dry his hands on the black apron tied around his waist. What a perfect opportunity. He was hoping it'd come; he just didn't think it would come so soon in the evening. He pushed the door that separated the bustling kitchen with the dining room boasting a different kind of noise and began to count.

Everyone was beautiful. Each guest looked like they had their own photography studio soft box light: vibrant, alive, and dressed like GQ models in tuxedos and ball gowns. He was so proud of Lily. He knew she was in the crowd—this was her event, after all. She talked about the Zuma Wyndham event all week, going from hardly speaking to him to messaging him about every detail. The last message from her was just a few hours ago, asking if he could come over later to help her celebrate. He was surprised that she wasn't staying at the hotel for the night. He hadn't responded to her invitation, and he hoped Nicholas Archer had zero chance of captivating Lily while they were dressed up and beautiful and he was in a black apron. When she told him it'd be her and her only waiting for him in the same place he had said goodbye, he knew his prayers had been answered. *It was the food, Dad. Had to have been the food.*

He still wasn't sure how he felt about Lily seeing him in his kitchen staff outfit. Would she accept him as a budding chef rather than a workaholic financier? He had to try. He couldn't stop thinking about their last hug in the hospital.

It was one of the most difficult things he'd ever done, but Logan had stopped responding to Lily over a week ago. He needed to know she was serious. His dad may not have approved of such a move, but she really was trying. He couldn't wait to hold her like he had at the hospital, again and again. And this time, tonight, she'd be able to hug him back with more strength. More conviction. And he'd kiss that scar, careful to touch it with gentle lips, leaving soft breaths on her neck...

He counted ten people at each table, sitting at silver tablecloths accented by white branch centerpieces. Each table seemed at capacity, so seventeen tables meant that over one hundred fifty people were in attendance to experience Lily's work. At table seventeen, however, Logan inhaled sharply.

He took his time drinking her in, otherwise a sight too strong to swallow right away. Though he had spent most of the day imagining her in glasses and comfortable pajamas, she was in a turquoise floor-length dress that shone brightly whenever the chandeliers' shadows retreated. He noticed how her ankle made small rotations around an invisible center, a sign that she was a little nervous. She had done the same at Frankie's when she had sat on the couch nobody ever sat on. She lifted her left hand to fix the napkin across her lap and Logan made a sound somewhere between a wounded puppy and an old man taking his last breath. He zeroed in on Nic's fingers grazing the back of Lily's neck.

Logan could feel his elation deflate like an air balloon quickly losing its ability to stay in the sky, and his cheeks grow hot, like an iron was being pressed against his skin from the inside.

He should have known Lily wouldn't have been interested in him for long. Maybe she had texted him the invitation earlier to let him know it was over. He was glad he saw her now, shining in animated conversation with her mother, friends, colleagues and Nicholas Archer. A woman sitting next to her pointed in his direction. He ducked, as if she were about to throw something at him.

Before he could see her turn around, he took one last look at Lily's long hair as it cascaded down her back and rushed back towards the swinging kitchen door.

It would never be. He was too unlike what she was created for: fancy things, beautiful people, and a man who would be steady and predictable. And those two things he was certainly not. He liked to dance too much; everyone knew good dancers kept their partners on their toes.

He wished he could have felt Lily's regretful gaze on his back, urging him to return. But when he turned around once more before returning to the kitchen, she was still shining like the bright light he'd gotten used to feeling.

It was only he who was extinguished.

Lily's Drill

"What else would you suspect getting in the way of RACE's success in your hospitals?" Hugo asked Nic, the twentieth of all the questions she had begged Hugo to ask Nic. She had practically begged Hugo to keep Nic occupied, hoping that'd draw his attention far away from her. She didn't need him getting in the way of her launch.

Her phone vibrated.

She checked it under the table. It still wasn't Logan. She pushed down the disappointment again.

She felt Nic's hand creep around her neck and she glanced at Marley. Marley nudged her before she could read the incoming message and the nudge was enough to make Nic drop his hand.

"Isn't that your dancing man?" Marley whispered.

"What?" Lily looked up to where Marley was pointing. Blonde curls gelled back and a tall figure she'd recognize anywhere—mostly because she'd spent so many days looking for him. Her breath caught in her throat. "Logan!" Lily resisted the urge to stand and follow him. "How would you know...?" Lily turned to Marley and giggled. "You looked him up, didn't you?"

"I sure did. It wasn't difficult. He's quite the trader, you know?"

"Yeah, I know. I mean, he mentioned he trades. And that he was in trouble. That's probably why he's in the kitchen now."

Marley thanked the waiter for taking their entree plates. Then, she scowled at Lily. "Lily! Don't be so elitist."

"What? I wasn't trying to be. I'm happy for him." She lifted her cup for the coffee to be poured, though she knew she wouldn't get a chance to finish it. "He should be doing what he loves doing. I'm lucky enough to be able to say I am. He left trading for the kitchen. That's pretty awesome."

Marley shook her head and smiled. "I'm so glad I sent you that letter."

Lily wrapped her arm around Marley's shoulder and squeezed. How wonderful it was to have her best friend *here* with her. Someone who made the trip all the way from Spain to celebrate with her. Marley could have sent fifty baskets, but it wouldn't have been as wonderful as the present sitting right in front of her: real, affectionate, silly, spunky Marley.

The chandeliers began to blink on and off like S.O.S. messages. Some people gasped in surprise, but most gave cries of excitement. Chairs shifted and the sound of conversations increased in volume. An Australian woman's voice announced that there was an emergency in the building and people should evacuate towards the north end immediately.

Lily took a sip of coffee. She turned to Nic. "I thought I was the one who was supposed to start the drill? Or did you make that decision without me at the meeting?"

"Don't look at me like that. I didn't call it. I thought it was you calling the shots tonight the whole time, Blondie."

The next phase of the drill would begin soon, making it difficult to hear the person right in front of you. Lily spoke quickly. "Greg must have gotten click-happy. Now if you'll *please* stop calling me that and excuse me, I have an emergency drill to monitor."

Lily leaned over to scoop up the laptop hidden under her seat. She picked up the skirts of her dress to reveal high heels and perfectly painted toenails and ran to the kitchen doors, leaving all etiquette behind her. It was time to work.

She stumbled as her heel caught onto the floor changing from carpet to marble and cursed her lack of grace. There's no way she'd let the laptop crash; she'd break both knees and re-open the wound on her jaw before she let that happen.

The wood of the kitchen doors felt cold. She pushed them open, revealing cooks at every station. She frantically searched for Logan's blonde tresses. She walked over to one aisle, and the next, until a man a head shorter than she stopped her.

"Excuse me, ma'am, but you shouldn't be back here."

Lily wanted to push him aside and tell him all the reasons he shouldn't tell a woman what to do, but she took a deep breath instead.

"I'll be setting up the launch for RACE in here tonight, sir. It's a great location. Surprisingly strong Wi-Fi, too."

The man raised an eyebrow. "Wouldn't emergencies ruin the WiFi connection? And then everyone would just die anyway?"

"Man, aren't you a ball of sunshine," Lily muttered under her breath. "But it is a good question. If you really want to know, the 3G will kick in if the WiFi crashes. Kind of like a generator for a home that's lost its power."

He shrugged. "If you say so. I'll just leave the building. Don't need no robot telling me to exit the premises." An alarm blared outside the kitchen doors and staff started leaving in pairs.

"Sir? Is there a chance Logan West is here?"

"You'll probably be able to find him outside. He looked like he needed a smoke." He gestured to the noise outside. "Good timing, too, since there's an alarm…"

Lily shrugged. "It's just a drill. If you want to stay inside, you'll be fine."

"It's your skin, lady." He pushed the door with his shoulder and left.

Opening her laptop, Lily found an empty seat at a high gloss table at the corner of the kitchen, presumably set up for the supervisor or chef or however kitchen staff hierarchies worked.

She was glad to be in a prominent area. This way, Logan wouldn't be able to miss her.

Logan's Love

The amount of people streaming out of the hotel was more than he expected for a software release party. Guests who had dressed to impress still had wine glasses in their hands and hors d'oeuvres being served by waiters in red caps. It wasn't a very realistic scene that'd resemble the events following a real emergency, but to keep investors engaged, Logan had to admit it had been a smart choice by Lily and her team.

What seemed more out of place than the service staff, however, was the hundreds of people who were not dressed in formal attire. They seemed confused, lost, and nervous. Someone bumped into his back, forcing his shoulder into another man's back, which spilled a drink.

"Hey! Watch it, man!"

"So sorry," Logan mumbled, turning to glare at the person who bumped into him. His face softened. It was Janie.

"Janie! Hi!"

"Logan, thank Gah I found ye. There's been a terrible accident. We were tryin' t'light the candles woven throughout the centerpieces like Lily wanted for after the drill, but the centerpiece fell over before I could catch it and oh Gah—" Janie sucked in a shaky breath.

"What do you mean? There's a real fire in there right now?"

"Ay!" Janie cried.

Logan's head snapped up. He had to find Lily and tell her that RACE really did have to work *especially* if it was overriding the usual fire response system.

"Where were you setting up the flowers?"

"The room to th' left of the kitchen. We tried t'get it under control, but it was too late. The smoke must have sparked something in the—"

"I'm sorry, but I have to go find Lily and tell her what's happened."

"Yes, boy, yes. Go. God speed."

Logan passed children rubbing their eyes and wove between people laughing as if this *were* just another party. In desperation, he was about to ask Lily's mother, but found someone more useful in this situation.

"Nicholas Archer!" Nicholas spun around at his name, grin pasted on like a magazine model's. His face fell when he saw a man in an apron was calling him.

"Yes, sir, can I help you?"

"Where's Lily?"

"Lily is set up inside the hotel making sure the drill is successful."

Nic wasn't moving. Logan pressed again. "Can I speak to you, please? Alone?"

Though he seemed reluctant, Nic followed. At the same time, there was a crash, the sound of glass breaking into thousands of shards, and screaming. His heart tightened in panic. Lily was in there.

"It is not a drill. Lily is in there. We have to go get her."

Nic straightened his cuffs. "This is probably part of the theatrics that she and the Jeremiah kid put together. She said people would be so surprised to see the room transformed."

"By centerpieces, not an actual *fire!*" Logan grabbed Nicholas' collar. "You've got some nerve." Suddenly, Logan realized this wasn't the first time he was seeing Nicholas' face. "Son of a… You saw her fall, didn't you? On her balcony. That face I saw. That was yours."

"Hey, man. I called the ambulance. I made sure she got help."

Logan shoved Nicholas against the light pole. "You're lucky I don't carve your face in and then call the ambulance. At least I'll know you got help."

Logan pushed Nicholas away from him, not caring that Nicholas Archer, board trustee of Dove Hospitals, was being tossed around by the Zuma staff of Wyndham Hotels.

He needed to get to Lily before it was too late. He had already seen her weak before. This time, he was going to make sure he was strong for both of them.

* * *

He could hear the sirens behind him. He ran through the crowds and stopped in his tracks when he saw the five hotel personnel standing in a line, blocking the main entrance. Logan wasn't going to be stopped by anyone this time. They didn't look particularly intimidating, but he didn't want to attract any attention to himself.

He turned the corner to see the window had burst from the ballroom.

Best case scenario meant Lily was on her way out and would be helped by the medics and the ambulance—again. But, worst case scenario... No, he couldn't let himself think of it.

The usually crisp air was tainted with ash. Logan took off his apron, dipped an end into the stale standing water of a brass fountain and wrapped it around his face, covering his nose and mouth. When it was secure, he sprinted to the side closest to the explosion. Glass reflected the lights of the bright street lamps, and pieces lie scattered. With the glass windowed walls, it wasn't difficult to see where the fire had spread; smoke billowed out of the ballroom like clouds that were now much too large to remain there.

Logan pressed the back of his hand against the service door. It was warm, but not enough to deter him. He braced himself for the heat and, with one more gulp of fresh air, opened it. Pressure pulled the door closed, but he pulled with as much strength as he could and slid himself inside. Clouds of smoke billowed out. The heat made him hit his hands and knees. It took a moment for his eyes to readjust to the darkness. He didn't see any flames yet, but he also couldn't see his hands in front of him either. How would he find Lily? The emergency lights lit the corners of the room every few seconds, but otherwise, it was much too dark to make out any shadows. Good thing he had spent enough time in the kitchen to know his way around.

"Lily!" he yelled. His voice was hoarse. There was no way she'd be able to hear him over the noise of the alarms, and the fire itself that sounded like a freight train.

"Where are you?!"

Breathing in made him feel like a hand was closing around on his throat. He pulled the apron tighter against his mouth. He heard only the whirl of rushing wind.

"Lily!" Where could she be?

Tables crashed onto floors in the other room and another glass window burst. Logan protected his head and body out of instinct, but nothing other than the smoke drifted over his head.

Then, he heard coughing to his right and noticed the screen of a laptop glowing in the same corner.

He matted the floor in front of him, as if he had dropped the flash drive of his parents' final photos, so desperate was he for a clue to find Lily.

Finally, he felt Lily's finger tips.

"Oh, please, be okay," he whispered. His hands crawled up her arm and torso as he wrapped her into him. Lily coughed and rolled her head to the side.

He put his mouth as close to her ear as he could. "It's me. It's Logan. I'm here now, baby. I'm here now. Let's get you out of here." He sat into a squat and lifted her into his arms, standing against the gravity that felt so much heavier because of the smoke.

"Logan?" Lily whispered. Her head pressed hard under his chin. "It wasn't a drill." Her voice was thick with ash. Fire roared again. They needed to leave before something else exploded.

"Shh," he said. "Let's get out of here."

Lily smiled and dug her face into his shoulder. He pressed his hand against the back of her head, encouraging her to stay there. "I've got you."

He pivoted and held onto Lily tighter than he'd ever held onto anything before, tread as quickly as he could down the hallways, and pushed them out of the building.

Once out, the fresh air felt like opening a freezer door, New York City air almost too fresh to breathe in. Logan took a knee, pulling the apron away from his face and throwing it to the ground. He let Lily's back rest against him. He coughed, nervous that he wasn't going to stay conscious long enough for Lily to get the attention *she* needed.

Anne ran to them. He was too tired and beat up for a fight.

"Oh, my God. Lily." Anne pressed her palms against Lily's face and kissed her daughter's forehead covered in soot.

Anne lifted her hand and cupped Logan's cheek with her fingertips. "Thank you so much, Mr. West, for saving my daughter's life." Tears welled up in her eyes. "You truly care for her." Her hand dropped to his wrist. "Thank you."

He reached out to bring Anne into an embrace, Lily lying between them. He only disengaged when he saw the EMTs approaching from the corner of his eye.

"She'll need to be checked out." He picked Lily up, as if she weighed as much as a feather, and laid her on the gurney. He moved the hair out of her face and stared into it, as if he needed to memorize every beauty mark, fine line, and the way her lips parted. This was the woman he loved and wanted safe, all her days. Her eyes opened slightly.

He grinned.

"If you wanted my attention," Logan said, "you didn't need to set a building on fire. I was going to come over later."

Lily smiled weakly. "You're magnificent, Logan West." She coughed to the side.

He crouched down so his lips would be even with her ear. "It's all part of my elaborate kidnapping plan. Don't tell anyone that you know that I know that you know, okay?"

Lily laughed. "As long as you don't let them take me back to the hospital. Please. I'll be fine." She tried to sit up, but looked like she hit a wall and lay back down.

"I'll see what I can do, but I'm pretty sure your mom would be better at that than I would."

"She's got a knack for intimidation, alright," Lily said.

Logan caressed her cheek and pressed his thumb against her lips. "You've got me so whipped, girl. You can't tell me to leave, or that you're going with this Nic fool."

Lily looked confused. "I am definitely not going anywhere with that man. Besides. Fire would have messed up his hairdo." Lily lifted her arm and ran her hand through his hair. "And you look much sexier having been through hell and back. That does something to a girl, you know?"

"Doesn't need to be every girl, Lily Cromwell. It just has to do something to *you*."

Game Over

Logan texted her the next morning after she'd been sent home so she wasn't expecting the knock on the door.

Anne bowed her head, but lifted it with eagle eyes ablaze. She turned on her heel and hurried towards the door.

Lily followed her. "Please, no. Don't say a word," Lily begged her mother. "I -"

"No. If you say anything, I will feel conflicted again. And I don't want that anymore. I almost died last night. Life is too short to not feel love. I want to feel love. Even if it eventually breaks my heart. Mother! Stop!"

Before Lily could stop Anne from opening the door, Anne swung it open and stepped back. Logan stepped in, clad in dark blue jeans, and a black shirt that fit tightly around his muscles. His eyes looked clouded, but focused on Lily.

Anne reached up and wrapped her arms around Logan. He gently embraced her. Anne let go and gestured towards Lily, but Logan was already on his way.

"Lily, I know you'd be fine on your own. Shoot, you'd probably be more than fine. You'd be more successful at work without any man holding you back. You would have more free meals with all the men who still want to wine and dine you.

But they won't notice the moment your guard falls and your eyes light up when you're really enjoying a conversation. They won't see your back straighten when you feel like you have to be on the defensive with your mother." He turned around to face Anne, equipped with a small smile. "No offense."

Anne grinned, eyes blinking with tears. She motioned for him to continue.

"Nobody else would be able to tell a difference between your decision to have your hair up, or down, during dinner. But I can. I know that your joy is your most powerful gift, but it's been hidden under all the acting." Logan strode closer to Lily and wrapped his hand around the back of Lily's neck.

"Yes, you put on a great act. You know the power behind a low-cut top or a shimmery dress, or a gentle touch on an unsuspecting man's arm. Trust me, I've fallen victim to all your spells. But you don't have to act with me, Lily. You know it, I know it, and your mother does, too. That's what's scaring her so much. She can see in your eyes the same thing I can—total, resolute, unrestricted *feeling*.

And we can sense the fire that burns when we're together—and your wish to dance around it—any accidental scalding from the embers be damned. But you don't have to be scared around me, Lily. I can be the one you've been looking for - the warmth when the world is cold. And, in turn, I'll do my best to light your world just like your eyes have brightened mine." Lily's hands clasped around Logan's neck and he leaned his forehead onto hers. "Be mine, Lily. Only mine. No more rules. No more games."

Lily suddenly stepped back. "My, my. Aren't we suddenly talkative? Why don't you have a seat."

Logan's eyes widened, but he obeyed.

Lily wished with all her heart that he'd find his place there night after night.

"Now you listen," Lily began. "If somebody custom-ordered confidence, it shipped here instead. My mother made sure I would be strong, no matter what. I'm pretty good at figuring out how to spend my time and how to accept myself and love myself. You're right. I would probably be better on my own. You present a plethora of problems.

But there's something about having *your* time and acceptance and love that just absolutely captivates me. It's bizarre. I've never experienced it before. Your effect on me is undeniable. It makes me vulnerable. It doesn't matter how many times I tell myself to get it together or scold myself for being ridiculous.

If you leave, Logan West, you will leave the spaces in my heart wide open. I'm not sure anyone else can fill them. I didn't find you by playing a game, or following the rules, and I won't know how to fill them up by doing the same ol' after you. In other words, there cannot be an 'after you.' There can only be a 'with you.' Please. Be mine."

Logan stood and wrapped his arms around Lily, lifting her in the air. Lily wrapped her legs around his waist and looked down at his crystal blue eyes. She swore she could see them dancing.

"No more games. Just you and me and dancing and food and fun and arguing and... And love."

Logan nuzzled his nose into Lily's neck.

He mumbled into her, squeezing her tight. "All of my love, my Lily."

Acknowledgements

T hank God for words. I don't know how else I'd be able to express my gratitude for the people and experiences that helped me write this particular novel at this particular time in my life.

Thank God for heartbreak and yearning. Every month that I received a "not yet" was one more month's effort toward my book baby. It has truly been a labor of love: overcoming self-doubt, practicing discipline, and celebrating the little wins even if it felt like I'd never make this dream come true. Friends like Jalyna, Macie, and Stefana, Ceni, Kallie, and so many others remind me how precious the journey is. I love you all so much.

NaNoWriMo gave me an opportunity to write the first 50,000 words of what was initially *Do Not Iron* (ha ha) and my beta readers got to experience the raw writing. You were honest, but ever-supportive. Maureen, for that first binder print-out and dinner around your table; Abby, who wanted Lily to meet Logan much sooner in the story (good call); Caroline, who loves words as much as I do; Ali, a talented and driven woman. Caroline and Ali, you will be published authors before long. I am already so proud of you. Nana, thank you for your prayers and for the advice to make the story break my readers' hearts. I think it worked.

My TLE bishers, who convinced me that my words hold weight. Mollie, Tifiny, Kendra, and so many others, I thank you so much for being so excited with me. Kelly, for grabbing me by the shoulders; Holloway, who told me I sound like a published author already; Jessica Terrell, whose "Eat the Frog" poster still motivates me. Lindsay and Sloane, I'll never forget how much your eyes sparkled by the fire when I read you the first chapter. That enthusiasm helped me get to the finish line. Michelle Bishop, you light a fire under a woman. Thank you for your relentless reminders that we have more to give and hold us to the highest standard.

How grateful I am for kind authors who aren't selfish with their wisdom: April White (read the *Immortal Descendants* series, guys!) and Amy Nathan gave me more hope and practical advice than I was sometimes ready to hear, but I'm thankful for the wisdom all the same.

Daniel Pujol, I always imagined what my first book would look like in my hands. Your beautiful cover design blew away any and all expectations. Thank you so much.

My Meteors. Wow. Where do I begin? How lucky am I to have humans in my life who make me excited to live life with every day. My choir, my students… I'd name you all, but that'd be like trying to count all the stars.

I have the best colleagues/friends in the world: Tim, Sam, Chris, Marisa, Mary, Jackie, Jessica, Dr. Brown… you have all encouraged me as an educator and as a writer. I am so lucky to teach alongside you.

My family taught me discipline and convinced me that I can do what-ever I set my mind to. This is a super power fueled by great love. Mama and Tata, thank you for giving us *everything*. Tato, your "I can fix it" attitude encourages me to never give up. Mama, this book is ultimately for you. It's your turn to write one now. My brothers, you know how I feel about you, your wives, and your kids. I don't make it a secret that you keep my world spinning. My Arkansas family, thank you for being so welcoming from the very beginning. I can't believe it's been a decade. I'll never forget calling you to share my "finish."

Cody, your love drives my dreams. "So are you actually going to write a book this year or just keep talking about it?" I hope I'm half the supporter for you that you are for me. Thanks for dancing with me, anytime, anywhere. I love you.